DWELLING PLACES

DWELLING PLACES

Burke Davis III ———————

CHARLES SCRIBNER'S SONS
New York

Copyright © 1980 Burke Davis III

Library of Congress Cataloging in Publication Data
Davis, Burke, III
Dwelling places.

I. Title.
PZ4.D2594Dw   [PS3554.A93275]   813'.54   80-11283
ISBN 0-684-16598-8

1 3 5 7 9 11 13 15 17 19 F/C 20 18 16 14 12 10 8 6 4 2

Printed in the United States of America

Chapter 1 appeared in slightly different form
in the *Virginia Quarterly Review*,
Summer 1973. Reprinted with permission.

For Sarah and Kate

. . . it is because our memories of former dwelling places are relived as daydreams that these dwelling places of the past remain in us for all time.

GASTON BACHELARD, *The Poetics of Space*

DWELLING PLACES

Chapter 1 _____

PICTURE SULLY ON THE BACK PORCH, draped over the red lounge chair like a piece of worn-out silk.

"Honey," she said, "I've got so much silver I don't know what to do with it. I've got one spoon worth six hundred dollars."

She spoke in a flat toneless drawl, her voice like a clatter in an empty room. Her words fused together despite her slow care in speaking. The morning sun lit her tired face.

"I couldn't care less about it, for myself," she said. "Except for my brooch. Let them cart away the whole damn house, foundation and roof and all. I couldn't care less. What I'm worried about is Tiny."

Tiny had been my grandmother's maid; she had taken the morning off to grieve in peace.

"I know exactly what's going to happen," Sully droned. "She'll stick up for me and won't get anything for herself. Can't you see them trying to keep her house, even after Mother promised it to her? She's been more of a daughter to her than either of those in there." She tilted her head towards the wall of the house. I could see through the window into the kitchen and through the far door into the dining room.

Sully struggled upright, pulling with thin brittle-looking arms to sit up so she could reach the ashtray. She leaned over it and scrubbed out her cigarette, and she looked as though she were balancing her whole weight on its tip. She sank back into the chair, exhausted with her effort. The end of the cigarette smoldered.

"God, I wonder what those vultures are doing in there now, Little Harlan," she said. Helen and Young Irene, her sisters, my other two aunts, were limbering up their acquisitive dispositions.

"Oops," Sully said. "I bet you don't want to be called *Little*

1

Harlan anymore. Like George won't let me call him Peanut. A grown man, now, aren't you?" Her eyes roved up and down, as though she were checking to make sure. "But how are we going to tell if we're talking to you or your father?"

"It's all right, I'm used to it by now."

"God, you kids, you're all so smart, I can't believe it. College, degrees, who would believe it. What the hell are they doing in there?"

Through the window and open door I could see Helen, hovering over the invisibly squatting Young Irene. Helen looked like a quivering pot of flesh, spilling out of herself. Young Irene was fifty-eight, named for her mother, and they called her Junior. They were dividing china and silver and other goods and heirlooms piled on the table, in chairs, on the buffet, on the floor, piled everywhere; the material debris and chattel of a life spanning eighty-six years, now ended.

"Not that I'll miss any of it," Sully said. The sun made her orange lipstick glow. "One more stick of furniture or another piece of silver and my house would sink right through the ground from the weight. You wouldn't believe all the gobs of yummy stuff I've got. It's worth an *ab*solute fortune."

They sent Sully the means to come to the funeral. For days— for weeks—they knew my grandmother was dying; Sully wrote and wired and called and begged for money to come home on, to see her mother one last time, to make peace or at least be present at the final irrevocable rupture. The day Irene died they sent Sully a plane ticket, no cash; the ticket even prepaid and by special arrangement nonrefundable.

Junior came away from the cluster of goods every now and again, away from the Spode and Wedgwood and the crystal and the several patterns of sterling, bearing to Sully offerings like little sacrifices. Here she came with an ashtray. First we heard her heavy steps thumping through the kitchen, and then there she stood in the doorway, holding out a white ceramic ashtray that read WHO BURNT THE TABLECLOTH? in big red letters in the middle. Poppy—my grandfather—brought it back from a sales convention twenty years before. It looked like it would glow in the dark. It was chipped. The family belongings were all a confusion; fine, expensive, elegant wares mixed with the hopelessly gauche, the absurdly cheap. Junior looked like she had just recovered from a long illness.

"Sully," she said, "would you like to have this ashtray?"

Sully looked at the ashtray and at her portly sister through half-closed eyes, leaned forward and tried to peer at the table laden with sets of china and silver, but she could not see into the dining room from the lounge chair and she flopped back against the cushion. "I've got more ashtrays than I know what to do with. I've got ashtrays worth fifty, a hundred dollars." She sucked slowly on her cigarette, her cheeks drawn tightly in, and blew the smoke in slow rolling curls toward her sister. "Besides, I'm going to quit smoking."

Junior passed back through the kitchen. We could hear her mutter to Helen as she went into the dining room. "Well, if she doesn't want anything, I don't see why she's being so impossible about that . . ." Her voice faded behind the wall and we could hear only a vague low rumbling of indistinguishable words.

"Jesus Christ," Sully said. Her eyelids fell closed and she fluttered them open with visible effort; the wrinkled lids gleamed harshly blue in the sunlight falling through the screen. She strained with every movement she made, full of effort and care, as though movement were both painful and dangerous, as though one quick motion might shatter a limb or rib.

I remembered her as she had been as a young woman, when I was a very young boy, and she had loved to dance and had danced like an angel, as light and easy as a breeze, radiant with grace and beauty, if already touched with sadness in her look and bearing. Twenty years ago and twenty feet behind where she now sat, she had taught my cousins and my sister Sarah to dance while her son Peanut followed her about the parlor with quick awkward steps, and I stood in a corner and watched, too afraid of the house to make any noise. For the duration of the family reunion she spent all her time with the young people, avoiding her parents and sisters and even my father. The only adult company she would tolerate was that of my mother. Sully played the piano in the parlor and sang and made us sing with her; she jumped from the piano and danced and the rest of them danced too; Helen and Junior strode into the parlor from time to time and removed their children under various pretexts, but they always drifted back. The parlor had never been used by my grandparents, and was the coldest room of that cold house until the dancing filled it and Sully built a fire and opened the curtains to admit the southern winter light. My grandfather, curious, came by twice; the first time he did a quick buck-and-wing in the hallway and passed on into the living room; the second time Sully had singled out my sister to dance with alone, and the old man watched for a moment, tall and sternly handsome and expressionless in the doorway.

"It's amateur night," he said, and walked away.

I watched them, enthralled. Sully's eyes caught the fire, her pale face flushed rose, beads of sweat glistened, trailing down her face like dew and her hair flowed and swirled around her as she turned and turned, the firelight shining through it like summer twilight in the trees, her bare feet flowing through their steps as she moved like water, like water full of fire, spinning, panting in fierce insistent and determined merriment, her eyes glazy and dreamlike. She and Sarah together performed as in a ritual; they jostled into angles, strove into curves, their limbs and weaving bodies tangled like the tongues of fire that lit them.

My grandmother opened the door. She opened it slowly and stood in the doorway, her face as immovable and devoid of expression as a block of quarried stone, looking down her nose as though taking aim down the barrel of a gun, and although she stood perfectly still, it was as if she had flung the door aside and stalked forward with clenched fists. I was in complete awe of this woman with the hard lean face and angry eyes; and apparently the rest of them were too. She froze the dancers instantly; then they melted from their postures and the fire drained out. My grandmother glared at the fireplace. In memory I expected even it to extinguish itself under that gaze.

"We never had a fire in the parlor," she said; and this seemed to say everything, to deny hope of simple pleasure in her eternally frigid house with its empty fireplaces. She glared at the set of plastic revolving logs which Sully had removed and placed against the wall. "Captain Perrin always said it made such a mess. Besides, we'd all go up in smoke with nobody but these children in here to tend it." Sully must have been about thirty years old.

Irene turned and disappeared. The music fell like water, drop by drop into the cold, still room, sounding tinny and empty. We slinked out, all of us feeling chastised and guilty, none of us knowing why there should be guilt. Sully moved last and most limply. In the living room my grandmother ambushed us again, waiting in a severe upright position by the blank fireplace with a Bible in her hands, flanked by two copperplate engravings of Sir Walter Raleigh. She did not look at us. She needed glasses but was too vain to wear them and held the book out from her chest.

"Ecclesiastes, chapter seven, verse four," she announced. " 'The heart of the wise is in the house of mourning; but the heart of fools is in the house of mirth.' " She snapped the Bible shut and stalked away.

While we were in the living room getting religious instruction, the parlor began to burn up. In our state of near panic, no one had thought to cover the fire with its screen, and an ember popped out and ignited the carpet, which was destroyed. The walls and ceiling peeled and blackened in ghostly forms and had to be scrubbed down and repainted. Some furniture was ruined. The smoke poured out into the hall, providing an early alarm, and everyone ran around in circles trying to warn everyone else to run outside. No one was hurt and the fire was quickly put out. The old man never forgot the precise amount of damage, down to the last penny, and he did not let Sully forget it. None of us forgot; it was $317.68.

Sully, lying back in the lounge chair with her eyes closed, spoke. "I like a winter that can decide about itself," she said. The day felt as warm and pleasant as early spring, although it was early November. A breeze sucked through the screens. Sully looked asleep or dead.

"Four kinds of pills," she had said to my father the night before, when we picked her up and brought her to the house from the airport. She had been drinking on the plane. "One to go to sleep with, a tranquillizer because my doctor's sure I'd kill myself—which of course I would—and an upper so I won't get depressed from all the other pills. Tell your father what an upper is, Little Harlan."

Sully had a notion I knew all about what she referred to as The Scene. She had weaved on the front seat of the car as we moved down the road in the dark, her voice slurred and too careful. "That's why I look so old," she had said. "How old do I look? About nine hundred years old?" She laughed hoarsely. Her voice set your teeth on edge like fingernails scraping across a blackboard. "God, I guess I look about as old as Tiny. Was she born a slave? How *is* my sweet Tiny?"

Now, in the morning flood of light on the back porch, Sully

looked her age of fifty. Two years ago she had looked thirty-five. Then she had been as slim as she had been years before, dancing in the parlor; now she looked not thin, but emaciated.

She wore white pants and a white ruffled blouse cut square and low on her chest. When she moved, wrinkles gathered at the cleavage of her breasts, shiny wrinkles like old supple leather. Her red toenails appeared and disappeared beneath the lounge chair as she swung her foot back and forth.

We could hear Junior coming out again.

"I couldn't care less about what *ought* to be mine," Sully said loudly. "I want Tiny to get what's coming to her, and what *I* want is my goddamned diamond brooch."

Junior bustled fatly through the door, brought forth a set of table linen, matching place mats and napkins, shiny with use and frayed around the edges. They were yellow with a design of red hams and chickens. Some of the chickens were cooked and on plates and some of them were walking around loose on the place mats. "Do you want these, Sully?" Junior looked at them as she offered them, holding them at arm's length, appreciating them. "They're the cutest set," she said.

Sully deigned no answer. She looked through the shrubbery crowding the screened porch, across the back lawn to the fringe of woodland that set the residential section of Clifton Park apart from the town. "What kind of bushes are those long stick things under the trees, Little Harlan?"

Through the spaces between the trees, I could see the valley where the creek ran, flowing to the river beside which my grandparents had been raised, a hundred miles upstream. I could not see the creek itself.

"They're roses," I said.

Sully laughed, a flat harsh waver of sound. "Oh, God, *roses,*" she said.

"Sully," Junior said.

"Do you reckon I'm going blind? Oh, I'm so old. How old are *you,* Junior?"

"I was asking you about these place mats." She leaned against the door frame, the linen now dropped to her side, crumpled in her dimpled white fist.

"Look!" Sully said, perching suddenly on the edge of her chair, her first rapid movement of the morning. "The mockingbird's come."

Below us on the ground outside, a mockingbird landed in a flutter of ceremony. He chattered and flipped around on the ground, raucous and absurdly authoritative, searching through the grass and cocking his head at us from time to time, shining his black beady eyes at us. Every day for more than ten years a mixture of corn and millet and sunflower seed had awaited his arrival; at least my grandmother had insisted it was the same bird each year. She said she recognized him.

"He must be the oldest bird in the world," Sully said. "He's older for a mockingbird than I am for a person; Christ, he's older than *Junior*. How many human years is one bird year, Little Harlan? Like, you know, they say one year in a dog's life is like seven years for us."

Junior sounded like a storm approaching. "All right, Sully, if you don't want them, I'll give them to Tiny."

"The poor little bastard," Sully said. Junior jumped as though she had been flailed with the word.

"I'm a Christian woman," she said.

"How will he live now?" Sully said. "He never had to take care of himself before and when Tiny's gone from the house and winter comes, he'll be out in the cold all alone. He's lived all his life on handouts and he'll be thrown out in the cold with nobody to look after him and he'll freeze and he'll starve and he'll die."

The bird hopped behind the hedge, seeking, and Sully leaned forward, strained her neck to follow his progress around the privet. The sunshine illuminated her platinum hair. "He won't know how to feed himself. Look how fat the little bastard is now."

"She has to have something anyway," Junior said loudly. She sounded like she was making a threat. "I guess it might as well be these."

"Junior," Sully said, sounding tired, falling back into the lounge chair, "Tiny kept our parents alive for twenty-five or forty years, or something. Why don't we give her the Spode china and one of the silver sets and something to keep them in. Along with her house, of course."

Junior shook the glasses in the cupboard, giving herself a tinkling, musical accompaniment as she thudded back through the kitchen. Her voice raised slightly in irritated wonder. "She's really full of dope today. She's crazy, crazy as a bedbug. How did she ever manage to get out of that asylum, or whatever it was?"

"Am I really related to them?" Sully asked. She sat up to light another cigarette. The match waved in front of the cigarette, the flame circling around its tip and occasionally passing across it. Her hand waved erratically in the air. Finally the flame touched enough times to light a coal and she sank back into the chair.

"All I want is my brooch," she said again. "Mother gave it to me when I was born. I've got plans for it. That brooch is worth simply oodles of money." She glared at the wall in the direction of the dining room. "Not that I care, of course, how much it's worth. I've got money coming out of my ears. It's the sentimental value, you know." She looked at me for a moment, her gray eyes tired and dull; it seemed strange that within my memory those same eyes had danced with light. "Where do you reckon those bitches have hidden it, Little Harlan?"

"I don't know, Sully."

"If you knew, you would tell me." She looked through the screen at the mockingbird still searching the same territory, over and over without pause, without moving to new ground, hopping around and pecking at the grass, cocking his head up at us. "We ought to feed him," Sully said. "He doesn't know Tiny has a half a day off."

She followed the mockingbird's flight up into the bare pin oak. He shrieked at us from a high limb, changing his call. Her eyes looked sightless as she stared at him, and they filmed over with water, almost tearful. "He's just like me," she said. "You poor puffed-up bastard; why don't you give up and fly away to Florida." As she wiped her eyes with the heel of her hand, she smeared the blue makeup across her face. "They wouldn't even write me a letter," she said. "I haven't had a letter in over two years, not since the last time I came to visit. I didn't even know Poppy was in a home until your mother told me on the phone. And Poppy wouldn't answer any letters before that, except to say no, I couldn't borrow any money. I mean even before he went senile he never even bothered to read them. I wrote and wrote and wrote, and nothing came back. Sometimes I never even *men*tioned money, and he just assumed that's what it would be about.

"The last time I called on the phone, was it last winter? I don't know, but it must have been around Christmas, because when else would that son of a bitch I let father my child allow me to make a long-distance call? I talked with Poppy for a minute and it was like always, like he was talking about the weather to a stranger, and then I asked to speak to Mother. He said, 'Irene, Sully's on the phone.' And she said, 'Sully? Sully who?' and he said, 'Sully, your daughter Sully,' and she said, 'I don't have any daughter named Sully.' She was sitting right there by the phone, for Christ sake, she knew I could hear every word. She was practically shouting at me. Poppy said, 'She's busy now, she can't come to the phone.' Good God, it was Christmas!"

Sully covered her face with her hands. "My mother, and she wouldn't even speak to me on the *phone.*" When she raised her head and looked at me, the makeup had spread and diluted across her face, giving the whole area around her eyes a pale blue tinge. She leaned forward and whispered to me, husky and intense. "Listen, do you know, when I was sixteen years old what that woman said to me? You'll never believe it, not in a million years. Well, of course you will; you knew her. I'll never forget it as long as I live, which won't be forever. I'm suicidal, you know. I told her I was really glad she was my mother. I never should have told a lie like that, because God punished me right then and there. She looked down her nose like she was watching a bug crawl across a cow pile, and she said, 'You're not my daughter. They switched babies in the hospital when you were born. You're not my daughter at all.' I asked her how she knew that, how she could say such a thing. 'I can just tell, that's all,' she says to me, 'anybody could see it. It's as plain as the nose on my face.'" Sully buried her face in her hands again.

She was silent for a moment. "She was my mother and she raised me and God help me, I loved her. . . . She was alive, she breathed, she moved, she felt; and now she's mud. She was my mother, whatever else she was, whatever she did to me. And now she's nothing: a load of mud in a long box and tomorrow we'll cover her with some more mud and we'll go away from there and she'll rot and that's it, that's everything, that's all forever."

She sobbed once, like a hiccup, and took a deep long breath. "I wish Tiny were here," she said. She looked out beyond the porch and hedge and lawn into the trees, toward the water we could not see. She stirred lazily in her chair. "Rot," she said, almost whispering. "I think of cancer as being this green slimy stuff, don't you? This green gluppy slime that grows inside you like algae, oozing all around, taking over, rotting you from the inside out. God, it makes me sick to think about it." She sat and thought about it, brooding. "He's still out there," she said. "We ought to feed him. Tiny's going to be mad if we don't feed him."

Junior came out but she had nothing to offer. "Are you going to the funeral home with us, Sully?"

"Yes."

"You'd better get ready. We're leaving in a few minutes."

"What do you mean, get ready?" Sully said, her voice harsh.

"Are you going, Little Harlan?"

"No," I said. "I'm going with my father to see Poppy."

Junior went back inside; Sully glared at her back until she was out of sight.

"Get ready," she said. "She thinks I'm not dressed properly to see Mother, as if Mother could see me now or care what I'm wearing. She never thinks I'm dressed properly for anything. God, you should have seen her and seen Mother, too, the last time I came home. I was wearing a miniskirt. Oh, they practically *died*. Especially when I wore one to Junior's garden club meeting which they couldn't very well keep me away from, since it was held here. Of course Junior's just jealous because she's gotten as big as an elephant and couldn't possibly wear miniskirts." Sully giggled, a sudden startling girlish sound; she covered her mouth with one hand, delight gleaming quickly in her eyes and as quickly gone.

"I was just remembering," she said. "Your mother called me up and said, 'Sully, I have terrible news. Your mother just died.' And I said, 'Oh, my God, honey, what am I going to wear?' Elizabeth must have thought I was positively nuts. She didn't answer me for a minute. Ha! If it had been one of my own sisters, instead of your mother, that would have been enough to keep me from getting here at all. But of course Elizabeth could understand it when I explained."

Sully's lethargy had been slowly giving way to a jittery, tired restlessness and she chattered on, shaking slightly as she talked.

"See, I had been staying for a while with my little Peanut—I mean George. Hey! it's too bad he couldn't come so y'all could have gotten together. He said a thousand times you're his favorite cousin. Do you remember the summer we all stayed here together, you and Sarah and me and little Peanut—? Goddamn it—George. We all had a great time, didn't we?"

"Yes."

"Until I got kicked out of the house, which you wouldn't remember about. Probably I put too much jelly on a sandwich. Anyway, I was staying with George, only he was living with this bunch of hippies, like in a commune. That was before I went out to California again. And that first son of a bitch I married absolutely re-*fused* to buy me any clothes, so I still didn't have anything except clothes George's friends gave me. Can you imagine hand-me-down hippie clothes at Mother's funeral? And I thought, my God, the way Junior acted about miniskirts. . . ." Sully laughed. "So *naturally* it was the first thing to pop in my mind, what in the *world* am I going to wear. But Elizabeth must have thought I had gone bananas."

She sat for a moment with a smile playing over her face like a patch of sunlight coming and going. "Do you know why they're letting me go with them to the funeral home? They're afraid I'll handle some of the loot while they're gone. They hated me before I was born. Do you know why I can't paint now? Do you remember how really good I could paint? There was a time when all I had was painting. Well, I don't have it now, I can't paint anymore, and let me tell you. It's because of them. When I was a little girl and drew with crayons or painted some watercolor or something, they would make fun of my pictures. They would hold them up in the air away from me and laugh and make fun and then tear them up. What the hell do they know about Art? So that's why I can't paint anymore, don't you reckon? Why aren't you going to the funeral home?"

"I saw her before she died. I'd rather remember her that way. And I'm going to see Poppy."

"I want to see him too. I guess I'll get to sometime before I leave."

She frowned and shivered, her unclear eyes looking out into the sky above the trees, looking beyond the sky, focused on nothing. "What was it like?" she asked softly. "Was it real bad? Did she hurt?"

"They kept her pretty much doped up."

"Like me. Did she know? Did she know she was dying?"

"Junior didn't want to tell her," I said.

Junior had not wanted to tell her, but she knew, and she knew it more completely and intensely than she had ever known anything in her life. My mother opened the door to her hospital room and we entered, slowly, on tiptoe, breathing quietly. The room was dark. The shades were drawn. The air was close and smelled of medicines and flesh. My grandmother was asleep. We walked over to the bed and stood silently beside her, one of us on each side of the bed. Her arms were folded on her chest. The skin of her arms was loose and what little flesh remained under her forearms hung down like water in a sack. She barely made a hump under the covers. She looked like she was made of old paper. Much of her hair was gone. My father had told me before we went up to the room that she weighed seventy-five pounds.

Her face was yellow and the skin sagged from her cheeks toward the pillow. Her lips parted slightly and her breath hissed in and out. Yellow mucous ringed her lips in hard crystals and trailed from her mouth down her chin and onto her neck. The crust was like excrement fouling her face. Her neck seemed as small as my wrist, and its features jumped out at us, the larynx like a tumor, the veins and tendons sagging cords. My mother took a hand towel from the table and wet it from water in a pitcher on the table and wiped at her face and mouth and neck. Some of the mucous fell off in hard lumps and some of it, softened, spread around on her face.

Irene opened her eyes. She looked straight ahead. She did not first roll or turn or sigh, as people usually do when they awaken. Her eyes did not even flutter open; they simply snapped open once without blinking and she appeared to be awake. They were sunk in their sockets, burning deep from within her face. She seemed to be peering with hopeless expectation, looking deep and unwaveringly but with profound fear into depth piled on depth of black abyss, into the heart of the heart of terror; I felt, standing before the wasted remnants of her body, that she had become one fact, one feeling.

My mother leaned forward close to her ear and yelled, "Irene! It's us."

My grandmother slowly rolled her eyes at her and stared. She spoke in a low hoarse voice, a rattling whisper. "I don't want to die," she said.

"Nonsense!" my mother yelled.

"I want to be brave," my grandmother said. Tears rolled from the corners of her eyes. Her voice cleared as she spoke. It rose to a whimper. "I try hard to be brave. I can't help it. I call on the Lord, but I don't want to die. I haven't finished, I've got to help Tiny clear out the basement. I don't want to die." She cried, half-shutting her eyes. "Elizabeth," she said. "I haven't had anyone to say that to." She reached her hand out to my mother from under the sheets. It was like a slow-moving claw, all skin and bones, dry parchment covering a frame of sticks. I could not reconcile the shrunken figure in the bed with the woman I had known most of my life, and seen stout and apparently healthy six months before. My mother took her hand and held it and patted it. "O Lord," Irene said, prayed, her eyes closed again. "Let me be brave."

My mother kept patting her hand and leaned down to her ear and shouted, as though her affliction were not cancer but deafness. "You're going to be just fine, Irene," she yelled. "You're going to be just fine."

My grandmother gagged. She closed her eyes and sputtered and coughed, a baritone ripping sound in her throat. I feared for a moment I would see her die. She opened her lips and pushed out a wad of yellow mucous which slid down her neck onto the pillow, where it spread into a thick, slimy pool. She spat, her eyes closed, and I remembered the day she whipped me for spitting into some bushes in her backyard. My mother cleaned the mucous with the towel. My grandmother, her eyes still closed, said, "Water."

My mother picked up the glass on the table, already full of water, and held it to her mouth. The plastic straw made a little belching sound when my mother bent it to Irene's lips. She tried to drink. Water streamed down both sides of her mouth. She dropped her head on the pillow and raised it again to try again to swallow. She tried and tried. Each time she worked her throat, the water came streaming out. The pillow was soaked. My mother held the straw to her mouth. She waved it away with both hands, without lifting them from the sheet.

She lay for a moment with her eyes closed, perfectly still, as though already dead. I supposed she had fallen asleep. Then she opened her eyes and turned her head. "Why, Little Harlan," she said. She looked at my mother and then back to me. "I didn't know you were here too. It's so nice of y'all to come visit with me." It was as though she had been asleep for hours.

"We wanted to," my mother said. And it was true; death brings forgiveness.

"I've always loved you," Irene said.

To hear such words from my grandmother left both of us speechless for a moment.

"We love you, too, Irene," my mother finally said.

"It's a shame," my grandmother said.

"What?" my mother said. She was still shouting.

"I think somehow I never got around to telling you that before. I never went in for a whole lot of gushing, you know." Perhaps that was an apology for the frigid meanness of her life.

"I know," my mother said, patting her hand again.

My father came through the door, bringing a sudden surge of artificial light from the hospital hallway. When the door swung closed behind him, we were in half-dark again. He came soundlessly toward us, a shadow in shadow. My grandmother came as close to beaming as her condition allowed and she tried to sit up. He took her hand and pushed her gently on her shoulder to keep her prone.

"You just lie right there," he said softly.

"I was just telling everybody what a shame it is," she said.

"What's a shame?"

"Here I'm going to die, just when everyone . . . just when everything . . ." She struggled with her words; she was trying to speak words her life had never allowed her to learn. Despite her years of cold disregard for me as a child, at that moment I wanted to cry in sympathy. During her last few years she had suffered, insular, encased in her icy shell, and she had almost thawed through it.

"No," my father said. "You're going to be just fine."

"I know that's what they say," she said. "The doctors have all these many things to say. They say when I get over this last operation I'll be able to go home."

"That's right," my father said. "They tell me you'll be going home next Friday."

She nodded. "At least I can die at home. I'd hate to die here, among strangers."

"You're going to be just fine," my father said.

"I want you to bury me at Greenfields," she said, forgetting the plot I had gone with her to buy a year before. "Lovely Green-

14

fields." I could see her fading in the memory of her girlhood before the turn of the century. She looked at my father; through the dim half-light he returned her steady gaze. "I did have breakfast this morning," she said. "I didn't lose it, either." She almost smiled. "It's the first food I've held down in two weeks."

"You'll eat right when you get home," my mother said. "Tiny will stuff you like a goose."

"Won't that be nice. It's been such a long time."

"Well, let's hope when you get home Friday, it will be for good."

My grandmother looked away, and the fear in her eyes was so bare and so huge it wrenched my belly with nausea. "I imagine it will be," she said.

They were both right. They took her home Friday and she died two days later.

Sully's nasal whine jarred me back into the present and the un-seasonable warmth. "That might be the first sensible idea Junior ever had," she said. She frowned. "Except if it happened to me, I think I'd want to know. Mother always said she'd want to get ready, whatever the hell that means. Wouldn't you want to know?"

"I'm not sure."

"Come to think of it, since Mother *said* she wanted to know . . . what did your father think about telling her?"

"He wanted to. So did the doctor."

"Then how come Harlan didn't tell her? He shouldn't let Junior boss him around."

"He figured since she was the one always with her, the one who had to face it every day, it should be up to her whether to tell Irene or not."

"Well, I guess I'm glad they didn't. As long as she never knew anyway. Do you think right up to the time she died, she didn't know?" She raised herself slightly from the back of the lounge chair, hopeful.

"Yes."

Junior returned, wearing a black dress bought for the occasion of her mother's funeral. Sully looked her up and down. "That dress is *perfect* for you, Junior."

15

"Thank you," she said. "Are you going to come with us? We've got to be there in twenty minutes, and it takes you such a long time to dress . . ."

Sully heaved out of the chair, gasping, turning into narrow angles as she stood, and walked unsteadily into the kitchen. Her metallic, wavering voice floated out to the porch as she spoke to Helen at the dining-room door. "Have y'all got everything divvied up? Isn't it wonderful, to have all the gory details out of the way before the funeral even starts?"

Junior sank into the chair Sully had vacated and sighed a deep loud sigh. "I could probably put up with her if she hadn't been married a half a dozen times," she said. "Maybe if we knew for sure she'd been married each of those times, maybe then I could put up with her. At least she's not beautiful anymore," she said with satisfaction. "It's been years since anyone has said 'Oh, how beautiful your little sister is.' If you ask me, they did her a disservice letting her out of that institution. Anyone can see she's not capable of taking care of herself, and the kindest thing we could do—"

"You look very tired," I said.

"I am," she said. She smiled, or tried to, or pretended to try: a faint movement of her mouth. She leaned back in the chair, exhausted, just as Sully had done. But her thick arms and bulging middle threw out a look of fat good health after Sully's emaciated body. "I am so tired I am numb. I have never in my life been tired like this, down in my bones. The last six months have been a nightmare, never knowing when Mother would pass away, never knowing if it might be tomorrow or next week or that very moment. Carting her back and forth to the hospital, hoping one minute, worried sick the next." Junior bent her head and covered her eyes with her hands, held to her eyebrows as though she were shielding them from the summer sun. With one hand she flicked at the corners of her eyes. "Poor Mother," she said. "I don't think I could have stood it another minute." She took a deep breath and sighed again. "The last few weeks she was home, she almost drove me crazy, trying to get me to sell Poppy's stocks and buy Greenfields back into the family so she could go die in it. Can you imagine? I told her she'd be much more comfortable dying in a hospital with doctors around. Of course I told her she didn't have to worry about it anytime soon, anyway. 'There's nothing left but walls anyway,' I said."

16

Greenfields. When I was six years old we came to the family reunion—a lugubrious celebration which was never repeated—and we
stayed with my grandparents. I did not know them; did not remember them from my infancy. We had moved from town when I was
two years old. The reunion was timed to coincide with our moving
back to town, and I knew I would never again sleep in the only
house I could remember. The first night I lay shivering in the dark,
alone in a big bed in a big cold room, scared and homesick, despite
the fact that my parents were downstairs. It was the coldest house I
had ever been in. Christmas was approaching and there was a spin-
dly bit of shrubbery a foot high sitting on an end table in the living
room instead of the huge tree there should have been, bent against
the ceiling. My grandparents were frigid, reserved strangers unused
to children—as if they had never had any themselves—and I missed
my sister, asleep in another room; we had shared a bedroom at home.
Suddenly my grandmother came striding through the dark and shook
my arm. I had no idea what this stange, stern person was going to do
to me.

"There's one thing you must never forget," she said brusquely.
"Your great-grandfather was Captain T. Coles Perrin, and he was a
cannoneer under Stonewall Jackson. He lost a leg at Chancellorsville." She was trying to whisper, but her voice, high and harsh
and cold, filled the room. She seemed angry at me for not knowing
these things. The room was completely dark, unlit by moon or
stars. She was like a ghost by my bed, no more than a voice and an
outline. "And Greenfields is your heritage, your family house, that
Perrins lived in for two hundred years. It's yours. You must never
forget that it is yours. Do you understand me?"

She faded out of the room and into the hall. I heard each foot
slam down on each stair as she descended, and my heart hammered
in my throat.

"It's a terrible thing to say," Junior said, "but it almost was a relief
when it finally happened. It took Mother out of her misery. Because
she was in terrible pain the whole time, you know. Don't tell Sully
that; don't tell Sully anything." Junior never wanted to tell anybody
anything when there was a chance of a secret. She closed her eyes
and leaned her head back against the chair. She had dyed her hair to
mask the gray, which was streaking with white, and it had come out

17

a sort of light purple that clashed with the red vinyl of the chair.

"All those rents and stocks," she said. "Always having to be careful not to let her know anything. Sully wrote all the time; I had to *race* to get over here in the morning before she got the mail, go through it to see if there was anything from Sully and hide it away from her. It put Mother in such a tizzy. Of course she never wrote except to ask for money. God, she must have needed millions while Mother was dying. I guess she knew *I* wouldn't put up with any foolishness, and she had better act fast. Mother was always so soft-hearted, you know.

"Harlan, I watched her disappear right in front of my very eyes, she melted away, just melted like an ice cube—no, no, like dry ice, because ice turns to water, doesn't it? And she turned to nothing, vaporized like dry ice, leaving a sliver, and then that sliver died." Junior stretched her hands in front of her poked-out belly, palms up, a gesture of wonder, her voice astonished too. "And what in the world do I know about renting houses and apartments, or about stocks and bonds—debenture bonds, convertible bonds, first mortgage bonds, I still don't know which ones are which."

She turned her head to the sound of the petulant mockingbird and looked through the privet hedge. "Is that stupid bird still out there?" she said irritably. "I know Mother loved that bird, but I get so sick of Tiny carrying on about him. And now Sully!"

She reached forward and banged on the screen with the back of her hand. The bird did not fly away. "I had more trouble than you could believe these past six months, with Tiny. Of course she's been a good old thing to care for Mother and Poppy, and believe me, I know it wasn't easy, but I simply cannot get along with that woman. She acted like she owned the place; she thought she was in charge, if you can imagine that."

She banged on the screen again. "Scram!" she yelled. She glared at the bird, gave up, and leaned back in her chair. "And now we've got Sully to deal with." She shook her head. "When the two of them get their heads together, you never know *what's* going to happen. You'd think Sully was colored too." She turned her eyes to mine and looked at me with an air of commiseration. "She wasn't bothering you out here, was she?"

"No."

18

"It sure is sweet of you to get her out of our hair for a while. Do you know where your father has gone?"

"Not exactly. Some legal business about Poppy's estate."

"Oh, that. He mentioned something about a note that might be in the lockbox. I hadn't the faintest notion what he was referring to. Of course I'm the trustee and I'll be executrix when he dies. I would know if there had been a note I signed myself, wouldn't I?"

"I'm sure you would."

"Well, good. I knew I could count on you."

"I beg your pardon?"

"I mean if push comes to shove, you'll explain to your father, if I don't remember the note, there must not be one."

"I don't know anything about it."

"I mean, nobody could forget if they owed Poppy money, could they?"

"Definitely not."

"I knew you'd be on my side."

"Side?"

"I guess Sully asked about the brooch."

"Yes."

"Of course she did. If she finds out your mother has it, poor Elizabeth won't have a minute's peace." My mother had come reluctantly to the funeral, and had driven her own car, ready to make a quick getaway.

Junior leaned forward and whispered, "I think Sully's been going through my things, looking for it. Have you ever heard such a low thing in your life?" She rubbed her eyes with the heels of her hands. Her eyes were red when she took her hands away. "I wish we could just give it to her, take the easy way out. But Little Harlan, we can't. We simply can't. I finally convinced Mother she'd have it hocked before she got out of town, and I said, 'Mother, you don't want a family heirloom like that in the hands of strangers,' those were my exact words. I said, 'Look at how you feel about Greenfields not being in the family anymore.' Mother insisted it not be given to her. She said we should give it to your cousin Carolyn. We can't just let a family heirloom go down the drain, can we?"

"But I thought it was bought for Sully when she was born."

"Oh, no, Poppy bought it for Mother to give Sully later."

"It's not quite the same thing as Greenfields."

"And we have to protect Sully from herself, don't forget that. It's silly to give her a family heirloom, no matter how old or new it is, and let her pawn it." Junior fingered her own diamond ring, given, like Sully's brooch, on the day of her birth, but received in her case on her twenty-first birthday when, as if she were a worm becoming a moth, she suddenly transformed into an adult. The cluster sparkled on her hand in the brilliant morning light. "I better help Helen with those candlesticks while Sully dresses," Junior said. "Never a moment's rest." She gave the thin smile again, then pulled herself to her feet and lumbered inside.

I followed her as far as the kitchen and found the blue coffee can my grandmother had kept the birdseed in. The can was in its usual place atop the refrigerator, the same refrigerator that had been there on my first visit to the house and that Poppy had refused with loud vehemence to replace. The can was half full, not enough for all the feeders, but there was enough to take care of the mockingbird. Furniture had been moved, silver and china packed away; but that article my grandmother had most used and seemed to care about most in her last days, a dented can filled with seed, stood in its usual place, and the mockingbird waited as always for his handout of grit and seed.

As I was on my way out, I heard my mother call from behind. We went onto the porch. She whispered. "I hate to look at dead people," she said. "I wish I could figure a way out of going. If it were my own mother, I could explain it in good conscience and not go." Small, trim, and healthy, my mother's appearance was a slight shock after the elongated and emaciated Sully and Junior's lumpy bulk.

"What am I going to do with Sully's brooch?"

"I don't know," I said. "I don't have anything to do with it."

"It's not my family," she said.

"Maybe that's why they gave it to you. They figured you to be neutral."

"Junior knew Sully wouldn't look for it in my things. That's why they gave it to me."

My father drove up in his father's car. We watched him walk up the drive and mount the steps onto the porch. His face looked drained, gray, and sad. He was as tall as my grandfather had been until age stooped him, and he walked as his father had, moving across the porch in long loping strides, picking his feet up high as though he were crossing a plowed field. But my grandfather had grown up working fields; my father had been only a casual and reluctant visitor to manual labor.

"What's wrong?" my mother said.

"Nothing."

"Did she do it?"

"I don't know," he said. He looked down at the can of bird-seed. "I'm glad you thought to feed it. Tiny would have run us all out of here with a stick if she so much as suspected that bird hadn't been fed exactly on time."

"Did who do what?" I said.

"Nothing," he said. "Nobody."

I went out to the back lawn. In the bright light skipping off the grass, the day seemed like summer. The warmth on my skin and the smells rising from the earth were a relief after the clammy house. The mockingbird fluttered up into the lower branches of the pin oak and left off whistling a treble-noted flutelike call to shriek loudly and petulantly, hopping from one limb to another and back again, chang-ing directions each time he landed, but always turning his head to look at me.

After a while the back door opened and I looked up at the square, perfectly symmetrical and graceless house to watch Sully stumble down the steps, hanging on my mother's arm and walking carefully. My mother got in the car behind the wheel and Sully sat in the backseat directly behind her.

"They're all sons of bitches, Elizabeth," Sully said. "If I could make a living doing something, I'd never have anything to do with any of them ever again. If I could still paint, I'd paint for a living. Don't you think I could? Hey! What a great idea! Why didn't I think of this before. Don't you think I could do that? Be an artist at a beach somewhere, just loll around in the sun, painting the hell out of everything, seascapes, portraits, you name it. I bet I could, don't you?" She leaned forward anxiously.

"A hard life," my mother said. "I think it's a little late for you to start on something like that."

Sully slumped back into her seat. "What the hell," she said. "I never was any good at seascapes or portraits. Don't like sand, either."

I threw the birdseed out in a wide circle in the grass. The mockingbird quieted; settled on a limb, he tipped forward with his wings raised briefly, showing a flash of white, settled back again, ruffled his wings back into place, cocking his head from side to side. His eyes threw back the world as broken points of light. When I drew my hand from the coffee can, the seed dripped through my fingers. It smelled like hay. A thick growth of privet rose above my head, between the lawn and driveway, an extension of the bushes crowded in lumps against the back porch. I could feel the pleasant heat rising around me, trapped by the hedge.

"Elizabeth," Sully droned, "those bitches hurried me up to get dressed and out here, and what happens? Here we are waiting for *them*. Isn't it typical? What the hell are they doing, anyway?"

"They're packing the candelabras," my mother said.

"Oh, God, we can't be too careful with candelabras, can we?"

"It seems like a lot of care for just silverplate," my mother said.

"Personally, I wouldn't care if they were solid gold. I got more candlesticks than I know what to do with. You could light up St. Paul's Cathedral with my candelabras. Where the hell have they hidden my brooch, Elizabeth?"

"I have no idea, Sully."

"Of course you don't," Sully said, patting my mother on the shoulder. "If you did, I'd have it already. Did you know, Mother gave it to me when I was born." She spoke wistfully, as though she carried with her everywhere a nostalgic memory of the event.

Through the ragged spaces in the privet I could see them. Occasionally my mother's hand would flash out the window, a quick flick of ash would fall. Sully reached laboriously across her body with her right hand, holding her cigarette stiffly out the window. Her forefinger, the long curving nail bright red, gleaming in the morning light, came down slow and hard and the ash on the end did not fall; before she finished smoking it, the cigarette bent and tore and she tossed it out. It consumed itself on the cement driveway.

The mockingbird landed a few feet from me in the grass, just outside my shadow, and began pecking in the grass, snatching at the

22

seed. When I moved my head he broke into the air as if a blast of wind had flung him skyward and he dropped into the pin oak, no longer screaming because he twirled a sunflower seed around in his beak, bits of the husk showering down in a tiny cloud of confetti.

"They're all sons of bitches, every last man in this world," Sully said. "But both of them together beats either one of them alone. They're both trying to get me to marry them again. It's a very balanced arrangement." She leaned forward again, crossing her arms over the back of the front seat and resting her chin on her arms. The light bouncing off the cement made her dyed hair look white.

"Herman's impotent but he's very sweet. He makes me breakfast in bed and everything. George thinks he's queer but he's just impotent. It's a good thing because if he weren't, George wouldn't let him in the house. He never used to be impotent. God, he was *not* impotent, the son of a bitch. I don't know what's happened to him since we were married, he won't talk about it. Maybe he's just out of practice." The hard metallic voice without inflection filled the bright springlike air with ceaseless clamor. She made a noise that might have been a snort or a laugh or both at once. "What's happened to Herman scares George half to death; use it or lose it, that's what he says.

"Herman borrows money from George and when George goes to work, which is only three days a week because he's semiretired, which he uses as an excuse to be such a miserable cheapskate, Herman goes out and buys me presents. Isn't that sweet? If George found out, he'd kill him. He'd blow his head off with his shotgun, for sure. The bastard. I sit around the house all day, on call for him. The sex maniac. Fifty-eight years old and Jesus, Elizabeth, sometimes it's five or six times a day. And of course the son of a bitch is *hung* like a *stallion*. Which drives Herman crazy, I'm not sure why, do you reckon because he's impotent? George usually makes sure Herman is somewhere around when he gets his jollies. I don't know what they've got cooked up between them. Sometimes I'm absolutely positive Herman is watching from some hiding place.

"If George were impotent too, maybe I could keep on living with them. Let them watch each other while they leave me alone. Maybe George would turn sweet too and I'd get lunch in bed. Do you know how I feel, can you imagine it, just lying around the house, cooped up, practically a prisoner in the house which he *has* to keep reminding me is *his* house, waiting for him to come up and grab me and take it without a word? He doesn't even look at me. He makes me feel like I'm nothing but a hole for him to plug up."

She was silent for a moment, her forehead dropping onto her crossed arms, rolling slightly from side to side. My mother was biting her lip. "I hate them," Sully said. "Elizabeth, what the hell am I going to do?"

"I don't know. It sounds like you ought to do something. What happened to Herman's job out there, that Harlan lent you the money to move for?"

Sully waved her hand without lifting her head. "Hell, *I* don't know. It didn't work out, or something. Of course if he had one, George wouldn't let him near me. Herman said he thought he'd fly out here with me and George threw Herman's favorite begonia right through the T.V. screen. Listen! I thought up this plan on the flight out here, it's so great! Harlan could lend me the money to go back to college on. Wouldn't that be wild? I could get my degree and make oodles of money. I could even go on to grad school. I bet I'd be a fantastic architect, don't you?"

"I don't know, Sully. I think it might be a little late to start on."

The screen door opened and Helen and Junior came heavily down the steps, each maneuvering her bulk in the same fashion as the other. Sully raised her head lazily and stared at them.

"Here they come," she said. "The married virgins. Two sea cows on their way to tea."

Despite six years' difference in age, they looked like twins crossing the paved distance to the car. Their dresses matched precisely, though Helen's had been bought in Detroit and Junior's in town, as though they had conspired to look alike. Their hair had turned the same shade of gray in the same places, and white streaks bolted through the same respective spots, the only difference being Junior's purple tinge over the white. Their double chins hung like four soft pears and shook in double unison as they climbed into the car, Helen in front and Junior in back with Sully.

"I'm so sorry Harlan and Little Harlan couldn't make it, Elizabeth," Junior said.

24

"They could," Sully said in her nasal drawl, slow and toneless and vicious. "They're going to see Poppy. Have you seen him since you put him away? What the hell have you done with my brooch?"

"I just hope they don't get him riled up," Junior said.

Chapter 2_____

WE DROVE IN THE OLD MAN'S last car. Every other year he bought a new Cadillac until he retired, and then he had a chance to buy only one before they took his license away. The Cadillacs were the penurious old man's single ostentation. One afternoon when I was eight years old, he had one hand wrapped around my shoulder and his other hand upraised, holding a switch; he was going to teach me not to flush the toilet without sufficient cause. My grandmother inadvertently thwarted him, calling out from the living room as he bore down on me, "Flush the toilet, Beau, company's coming."

But he bought Cadillacs to go with his house and his clothes. Junior had wanted to have the last, almost virgin car. She told Irene she would buy it if she had to, she just did not want to see it rust away in the garage, thousands of dollars powdering slowly into junk metal. But the old man would not let them sell it when they took his license: when he was not balancing his checkbook for nineteen twenty-eight, he was liable to be out in the garage, hat on, cigar between his teeth, hands on the wheel, looking straight ahead. And when they took him away, my grandmother would not let go of it herself; it was as if a part of him stayed with her, a vestige of his presence lodged forever in the garage.

The first one he bought I clearly remember: its smell, its look, and my red tennis shoes dangling above the floor. He was very proud of it. Along with the house, it was an outward show of his recovery from the loss of his second fortune. He bought it the year we moved to town, some months after the family reunion, and he asked me to go for a ride in it. "I ain't completed the deal on it yet," he said. "I need a expert rider's opinion on it."

I was six years old and I took him very seriously. "All right," I said.

We got in and he drove through Clifton Park. He pointed out the various features of the car. "Watch your feet," he said. "That carpet is one hundred percent virgin wool." My feet would not reach the floor, even when I perched on the edge of the seat. He ran the windows up and down with buttons at his left hand. He was dressed in a gray suit and he wore a straw hat with a band around it. The cigar stuck out of one corner of his mouth. He sat straight—his shoulders were as straight across as a board—and he looked down at me, grinning. "How you like it?" he said. He wore a fat bow tie and his shoes were polished to a high gleam, as bright as his new car.

"It seems to vibrate," I said.

He thought that was the funniest thing he had ever heard. I know he did because he talked about it for the rest of his life, told it as a joke over and over; in the car he threw back his head and roared with laughter. His laugh was heavy and deep and abandoned; I imagined he laughed the way a bear would laugh.

When we returned to the house, he told everyone what I had said about his six-thousand-dollar Cadillac. "He says I ought to maybe look around a little more," he said, grinning down at me. "He says it *vibrates.*" And he whooped with laughter again.

When I was twelve he had his third or fourth Cadillac and I took another ride in his car I can never forget. My parents were out of town, and I was staying with my grandparents for most of the summer; Sully was between marriages and was staying there too, with her son, Peanut. I had a date with the first girl I dated; not the first date, perhaps the third or fourth, but she was the first girl. Before he left, my father arranged for my grandfather to take me in his car on the date. The old man had already found out about the girl; her name was Jane Allman. He would call our house in the afternoon when I got home from school. Whenever I answered he would speak in a high singsong falsetto, breaking his attack with laughter in the middle. I was afraid to hang up on him. When I was not at home or did not answer, he would leave messages for me in Jane's name; my mother never passed them on, but my father always did.

He was excited; certainly more so than I was, for I dreaded the whole idea of the three of us together in his car. When it was time to go, he called me from downstairs. He had been ready to go all afternoon.

I came down the stairs, nervous, and worried about what Poppy might do or say, and strenuously concerned about my cowlick. He was dressed in his best, which was very dressed up; he looked tall and handsome and distinguished, and I felt scruffy beside him.

He beamed at me as we went out the door. "Did you wash your face?"

"Yes."

"Get behind your ears?"

"Yes sir."

He stopped suddenly. "Where's your flowers at?"

"What flowers?"

"Here, here," he said. "You can't go courting without no flowers. I never heard of such a thing."

"I don't want any flowers."

"They ain't for *you*, boy, they're for that little gal of yours."

"I mean I don't want to give her any flowers. She'll think it's stupid."

"I see you got a few things to learn about women," he said. "We're going to get you some flowers, or you ain't going."

"I think you're right," I said. "I don't feel too good, anyway. I'll go call Jane."

"Here, here," he said. He dragged me by the elbow to the car. "You sit in back," he said. He drove to a florist shop and jumped out of the car. He came back to the car with a tremendous bouquet and handed it to me. He was as happy as a child with ice cream.

"How's she going to hold them in the movies?" I said.

"Pin 'em on her chest, if you ain't chicken."

"I'm not chicken," I said. "I'm just not going to pin them on."

He chuckled. "He's chicken," he said.

"I'm not."

"And soon's she opens the door, you say to her, 'Lawsy, Miss Jane, if you ain't just as cute as a speckled pup.' You say that. I'm going to ask her did you say that when y'all get in the car."

"I've got to go home," I said. "I don't feel good."

We pulled into the Allmans' driveway and he got out and

opened the door for me. "Yessuh, Mist' Jackson," he said. Then he looked at my empty hands. "Hold on a minute, where's your flowers?"

I had left them on the backseat. "I'll give them to her in the car," I said.

"Nossuh," he said. "You got to give them to her at the door."

So I took the flowers to the door, looking behind me, watching him watch me, grinning by the open back door of his Cadillac. I breathed heavily, wondering what Mrs. Allman would do to me when I tried to pin flowers on her daughter's chest. It suddenly occurred to me that I did not have a pin, and was even going to have to ask for one.

But Jane took the flowers from my hands and thanked me for them and glowed over them. "How did you think of such a sweet thing to do?"

"It's nothing," I said. She put them in a vase.

When I started walking her to the car, my relief sank away at the sight of the old man standing by the door. He swept it open for us with exaggerated flourish. I could feel my cheeks glowing hotly. "Yessuh, Mist' Jackson," he cried. He winked at Jane, beaming at her. "His chauffeur, ma'am," he said. He closed the door with another flourish and got in and we drove away.

"The boy told me you was just as cute as a speckled pup," he said. "He said he was going to tell you that."

Jane sat in the middle of the car and Poppy peered at her in the rearview mirror. I scrunched against the window and stared out of it. I was afraid to look at Jane to see her reaction.

"Did he tell you that?"

"Not yet," she said.

"He will," he said. "If he don't, I say so right now."

After that the old man let me alone and talked to Jane the whole way to the movie. Jane was immensely entertained. I thought the two of them ought to run off together. After the movie was over we went outside still holding hands and there he was, smack in front of the entrance, the engine running and he standing beside the back door again, waving his straw hat at me and grinning. I dropped Jane's hand. He had traffic backed up for four blocks; horns were blaring at him and drivers yelled angrily; he paid no more attention to them than he would have if he had been deaf and standing in his living room.

Night had fallen and it was dark in the car; I did not think the old man could see in the backseat, so I took Jane's hand again. He said nothing about it. Until he and I got back to his house. He began with "You should have seen them two lovebirds . . ." and went on from there, year after year, and never stopped talking about Jane Allman until they put him in the hospital.

My father parked and we turned from the car and there Poppy stood or perched at the front door, staring out upon the world. He bent slightly forward, shoulders hunched, his head cocked like a curious bird. We watched him watch our approach, his face pressed to the glass; the closer we got the slacker his jaw hung, his mouth parting a little more with each step we took. A dressing gown, blue trimmed with a thin line of darker blue, hung on him as on a clothes hanger. He stepped back as my father pushed open the door and examined us like specimens of something.

"Do you know who we are?" my father asked.

"Seems like I seen you fellers somewheres before," he said, ready to be amiable. "Do you live here?"

"Now, Jackson," my father said. "Old man. You know me."

He hesitated, leaned forward to closely study my father's face. "Course I do," he said.

"What's my name?"

The old man considered a moment, regarding my father up and down, then lighted up. "Why, you're my little boy!" he said.

"How about him," my father said, pointing to me.

"Hello, Poppy," I said.

"Do you know who he is?"

"Can't say as I do," he said, mildly disappointed.

"It's your grandson. He's come to see you."

"If you say so," he said. He looked out the glass door; the sun slanted across his eyes, a clouded blue. His face shone, smooth and polished, as though it had been sanded, the wrinkles he once had faded away now into an infantile smoothness and placidity. He stared out on the bright November day. "I was just on my way home," he said.

30

"Do you want to go to your room?" my father asked.

"I reckon that'll be all right," he said.

We started walking down the hall. The old man swayed slightly forward with each step, as though to propel himself with the momentum of his upper body. From side to side he briefly looked, up one wall and down the other, his gaze stopping above the heads of the patients lining the hallway in benches and wheelchairs, staring at us as we proceeded. We left a wake of turning heads, a faint rustle. The old man appeared neither to see nor hear them, as if he were walking down a street looking at himself critically in store windows, as indeed he had done the last time I saw him before they put him in the hospital; but then he had been alert, had thrown his shoulders back and admired his strut, and he had been popping his cane down on the walkway with a jaunty percussion instead of the dirgelike rhythm his scuffling slippers now gave our progress down the hall.

I sniffed the closed air, trying to isolate the odor mixed in with the antiseptic hospital smell, and the old man jerked his thumb at me. "Who'd you say this feller is?"

"He's your grandson."

His shuffle slowed; he watched me intently, rolling his eyes sideways at me as we walked. Finally he stopped.

"He's who?" he said.

"Your grandson Harlan."

"Harlan?" He looked at me closely. He bent to my face. "That's my name," he said. He looked back to my father, puzzled. He looked worried. "How'd he get my name?"

"He was named after you, he's your grandson."

The old man started to walk again, taking half a step, then stopped. "You sure?" he said. "He ain't some hitchhiker?" He looked away from my father at me again. "You got to be awful careful with hitchhikers. Don't you think he looks kinda shifty?"

We resumed our walk and he asked, "Where is it you're taking me?"

"We're going to your room," my father said.

"What!" the old man said, stopping again, his mouth dropped open in astonishment. "Why, this can't be the way to my room! My room ain't this far from anywhere!"

"It's not much further now."

31

"Why are we going to my room?"

"So we can sit down together and have some conversation."

"Conversation? About what? *I* ain't got nothing to say."

"We'll think of something."

"Ha. It won't be interesting."

We turned a corner into another corridor. "Why can't we just talk here," the old man whined. "I'm tired, I want to sit down. You can *talk* anywhere. I been talking all my life."

"Your room's right down this hall, not twenty feet away. You can sit down there." When my father spoke he sounded sad and amused at once.

"I can't make it that far. I want to sit right here."

"There aren't any chairs here. The closest chair is in your room."

"That's all right," my grandfather said. "I'll just rest standing. What's that bush under your nose?"

We rested. My grandfather stood in the middle of the hall, looking tentative as a perched bird, as though he might fly off at any moment. My father leaned against the wall, concrete blocks painted yellow. He folded his arms and studied his father. In a moment the old man said, "What are we all doing standing around here for? Where are we going anyway?"

My father hefted himself away from the wall, pulling at his mustache now that his father was looking at him again. He took the old man by the elbow. "To your room," he said, guiding him down the hall.

"My room's somewheres else," my grandfather mumbled to the wall. "You can't get to my room from here."

We turned then into his room. "Do you want to sit on the bed?" my father asked.

It was a narrow iron-frame bed with a green spread that almost matched the green chair that I sat in. The frame of the chair was also metal.

"I reckon it'll be all right," my grandfather said uncertainly. My father held him by the elbows and helped ease him toward the bed. When he was about halfway to the bed in a wide crouch, legs spread wide apart and bent, he said, "Hold it! Hold everything." He stayed crouched, staring at the bathroom door.

"What is it?" my father said.

"I have to spit," he said.

My father pulled him erect and led him slowly into the bathroom. As he passed through the door, the ceiling light in the bathroom went on and gleamed through his white hair like a halo. I heard him hawking and then spitting. I heard a soft plop in the toilet. Then he hawked again, scraping deep in his throat. I examined the room while he was in there spitting. The metal clothes chest was the same drab olive color of the bed frame and chair frame. It looked insubstantial, as if it would crumple underfoot like an empty can. The walls were a lighter green, matching the color of the bedspread and upholstery on the chair, the interior color of public buildings like dormitories and Y.M.C.A.s.

In the bathroom my grandfather made a greater effort, whooping and rasping. Then he said, "Hey! It's Christmastime."

"Not yet," my father said. "It's just the middle of—"

"It *is*," the old man said. "I know it is. I heard it on the Muzak."

They came out of the bathroom and my father helped the old man onto the bed, letting him down as he crouched, his knees bent and legs bowed. He looked around to locate himself, as though aware that he was a transient in this room who would never live anywhere else, and he wanted to get one last look while he was still here. His eyes made a minute scrutiny of every object in the room, circling slowly until they rested on me. He started, jerked his head back, and arched his body in a moment of surprise. Suddenly, for the first time, he recognized me; his eyes were clear, mischievous with light. "Now looky here what the cat drug in," he said.

My father was behind him and could not see his face. "That's your grandson," he said.

My grandfather began to brush his hands together in a peculiar way. They were like shapely animals with their own life and purpose. He brushed off his left hand with the fingertips of his right in quick, jerky motions. He stared down at them with his mouth open, completely absorbed. His eyebrows rose and fell.

"Do you want to wash your hands?" my father asked.

The old man stilled his hands, studied them. Lying inert in his lap they looked like something dug up out of the earth.

"I reckon they need it," he said, his voice mournfully fatalistic, almost a whisper.

My father went into the bathroom and together we listened to the water run. He kept brushing his hands while he looked at me. We kept silent the whole time my father ran water in the bathroom. When the sound ceased my grandfather leaned forward, his hands still going, and whispered, "Water."

As my father emerged, my grandfather shouted without turning around, "This feller in here don't say much, do he?"

My father took the old man's hands and began to wipe them gently with the wet cloth. My grandfather watched closely, his face bent down. "Don't do it too hard," he murmured. "The folks around here always do it too hard."

As soon as my father finished, the old man began to brush his hands again, as though brushing off crumbs. I could hardly keep from brushing my own hands the same way.

"Why, now they're all wet," he said, his voice full of surprise and hurt and rebuke. My father was already coming out of the bathroom with a towel. He dried his father's hands, and the old man turned them over and over, gazing down at them open-mouthed and with wonder, as though waiting for them to break into pieces and fall on the floor. He abruptly looked up as though he had heard something and began to look around the room again. Shortly his hands began to brush themselves once more. His eyes rested for a moment on the clothes closet, the door of which was open and where one pair of pants and one shirt hung.

"Do you need some more clothes?" my father asked.

"I don't know," he said.

"If you need some more I can get them for you," my father said. "I'll be glad to get you some more."

The old man kept staring open-mouthed at the closet, his hands working, his eyebrows going up and down in puzzlement.

"Do you wear the ones you've got?"

He reflected for a moment. His hands paused in midair while he thought. "I believe so," he said.

"I can get you some more."

"They'd just steal 'em," the old man said. "They steal everything." His eyes sparkled for a moment as he spoke, and he looked angry. Then his eyes faded again into dull, empty blue.

"Who does?"

"I don't know."

"Has anyone been to see you lately?"

"Ain't nobody ever come to see me."

"Don't you remember me and Irene coming a couple of months ago?"

"Can't say as I do. You might have been here." He screwed up his face and his hands paused once again while he thought. "I believe I remember you might of come here once, a long time ago. Irene never has been here."

"Poppy, she's been here a hundred times to see you."

"No she ain't," he said. "Why don't she come? Is she sick? Is she all right?"

"She's fine," my father said. He looked out the small high-set window at the empty sky.

"Then why don't she come?"

My father looked across to me. "She was here not too long ago," he said. "A few months back."

"Who was?" the old man said.

"Mother. Irene." My father looked frustrated and amused and sad.

"Irene, Irene," the old man said, his eyebrows moving up and down. He seemed to be trying to remember who Irene was. "It's somebody around here belches all night long. You can't sleep unless you're stone deaf."

"Are they treating you all right?"

"I don't know," he said. "I guesss so." He was staring at the wall, his empty eyes like two pieces of blue china, his hands brushing with that quick slow movement like a pulse.

"Is the food good?"

"I guess so."

Once more while we sat in silence he looked at me and his eyes came alive, gleaming. They had been lifeless even when he talked about my grandmother. "This feller here don't say much atall; he don't say hardly anything." He coughed and went slack again, like a light turned off.

"We've got to be going," my father said. "We'll be back after lunch."

We got up to leave and the old man stirred as though to follow.

"You'll be back, won't you?" He looked up at my father. "You ain't going to be gone long?"

"We'll be right back," my father said, his hand on his father's shoulder. "We won't be gone an hour."

Chapter 3 _____

ALTHOUGH IT WAS EARLY FOR LUNCH, we were hungry, and because of the extraordinary springlike day, feeling the sun fall bright on our skin, we decided to enjoy the warmth while it lasted and eat outside. The others might not have returned to the house yet anyway, and Tiny would growl for hours if we fixed lunch in her kitchen before she arrived.

"I can hear her now," my father said. "Do you want to eat at the park?" The park commemorated an insignificant engagement of two patrols during the Civil War which local heritage and mythology had elevated into an important last struggle against Sherman's invasion.

"Yes," I said. "By the lake."

"Good," he said. "I haven't been there since you were a boy."

"I took Poppy there a few months before we put him in the hospital. It wasn't long before he beat up Irene. You remember, I told you about the trip to Johnston?"

"Yes."

"I took him to the park the day before I was supposed to go to Johnston and he asked if he could go with me."

He turned down Ashland Avenue and I knew my father was heading toward the Appetizing Delicatessen. We had not been there together in many years; visits there had been a big event in my childhood, which culminated when I was sixteen in an orgy of five delicatessen sandwiches, a quart of milk, and a piece of cheesecake while my father and the proprietor stood by watching me in what I thought was unnecessary awe while they exchanged money not for food but in payment for small bets.

"It was strange," I said. "There I was taking Poppy out to feed the ducks, doling out little chunks of bread for him to throw in the lake, the way you used to do for us. It was like a dream that warps things around in subtle ways. He was my charge the way I used to be yours; not a simple switching of places, because he's *your* father. Do you see what I mean? My father's father, and me. . . . And he was under my care like a child out of school . . ."

"Just like he's under mine," my father said. "Good practice for you for my old age. Get you used to it."

"I'm serious."

"So am I."

Poppy had talked to the ducks, teasing them, and he threw bread at them, tossing it at the tops of their heads, reminding me of the summers in his backyard when he would squirt watermelon seeds at me. He chuckled every time he hit one of the bobbing heads, just as he used to cackle with glee when one of the watermelon seeds popped me in the eye. It had been warm that day by the lake too, but the middle of October is often warm in our country. Despite the warmth, the air was crisp and lean with autumn cleanness, and smells and sounds seemed to carry farther than they had the month before. The lake stretched away from us right below our table, as flat and smooth and glossy as a china plate. On the far side two hills rose up, wooded, the woods gray and lavender and marked still with brilliant hues here and there. The smell of smoke came across the lake. There were tables scattered up and down the hillsides and at some of the tables there were fireplaces for cooking. Between the half-denuded trees we could see the tables.

The old man threw his last piece of bread and looked at me, knowing it was almost time to leave. "I guess you ain't coming back here tomorrow," he said. "I guess if you was, you wouldn't want no company."

"I'm going to Johnston tomorrow," I said.

"Who's going with you?"

"Nobody."

"What?" He pulled his head back and raised his eyebrows. "You ain't going all the way to Johnston *alone*. Why, it's fifty miles to Johnston!"

"Well, I was," I said. "But why don't you come with me."

"I reckon I better," he said. "You ain't going to try to make it in that little robin's-egg car of yours, are you?"

"Yes."

"Well, I don't know," he said. "You ain't going to wreck it halfway there, are you?"

"Not if I can help it."

He picked up the remnants of his peanut butter and mustard sandwich, which he energetically maintained kept his sinuses clear, and was suddenly as absorbed in the sandwich as he had been in the ducks. He leaned down to it, his wrists still on the table, and attacked it with his mouth as though he meant to hurt it, snapping off lumps and chewing furiously with his mouth open, making considerable noise, his body hunched over his food. It reminded me of countless lunches at his house. He always ate as though he feared someone was about to come along and deprive him of nourishment. He stuffed the sandwich in his mouth, gulping quickly. I could see the food sliding down his gullet; just like the ducks and geese.

"Well, then," he said, wiping his hands on the table, "I don't see why I don't come with you." He gulped down his milk. "Only they wouldn't let me go."

"Who wouldn't?"

"Irene and that nigger girl friend of hers."

"I'll talk to them," I said.

"All right," he said. "Only don't tell them nothing about Johnston. Say we're going to a ball game. They wouldn't let me go to Johnston to pick up a cashier's check for one million dollars."

"What ball game?"

"It don't matter. They don't know nothing about baseball. *Any* ball game."

I told my grandmother we were going to Johnston; even if he did not remember, she would know there were no baseball games played in October in a medium-sized town in North Carolina. Even the World Series was over.

"But don't tell him you know where we're going," I said to her over the telephone. "He's having too much fun fooling you."

"I don't know if he should go," she said. "Are you sure this isn't any trouble for you?"

"No, we'll have a good time. I'll enjoy it too."

"I don't know," she said. "It might get him all excited."

"It'll be good for him," I said.

"What if he sees some of our old friends? I'd be embarrassed to death if they saw him like he is now. I don't know."

"I'll pick him up around ten," I said.

He was waiting on the back porch when I arrived and I could see him stand as soon as he saw me walking up the driveway; he hurried to the screen and peered out anxiously. He opened the screen door for me when I reached it, sweeping his arm to beckon me inside, bowing at the same time with a broad grin, eyes alight. He looked years younger than he had the day before. The wrinkles across his forehead jumped up and down.

"They *think* they don't let me have no whiskey," he said. "But I got some orange juice in the icebox I been saving for you. Let's us have a drop, split it before we go."

Tiny yelled from the kitchen. "Little Harlan, don't you let him talk you into giving him any of that juice." She came out to the porch, a short taut woman with bowed muscular legs; because of her arthritic hip, she listed from side to side as she walked. "I had to fight wid him all morning to keep him from drinking that one last glass. He drunk enough to give a ahun kettle heartburn. He drunk a whole pitcherful. I says to him Little Mist' Harlan like his orange juice just as much as he do. I says you won't gone take him to no ball game if he drank ever last drop of that juice."

"Let's split it," I said. "Can't he have another half a glass?"

"Now what I tell you!" the old man yelled. His face turned red and he shook his fist, spotted with the liver-colored markings of old age, at Tiny. I knew that when he got here he'd say—" He spun quickly to me, pointing his cane at my chest, his head lowered and his eyebrows raised. "What was it you said, exactly? I wouldn't want to misquote nobody." He turned back to Tiny. "Say that," he said. "I been burning up all morning to have that orange juice, and I could have had it half a hour ago when I really wanted it. I probably don't even want it now, for all you know. You just want me to die of thirst. If I was in the desert and hadn't seen a drop of water for a year, you wouldn't let me have any. You'd talk about heartburn. The only reason you've lived so long is to watch me die. I ain't even going to drink it now, I don't care what you say."

"Don't you let him have it," my grandmother said, her head rising behind Tiny's head, superimposed above her with white hair and face, like a photographic negative of Tiny's face.

"Don't want it anymore," the old man grumbled. "Been waiting around here all morning on this boy that never been on time anywhere in his life not even to go to the john, everybody huffing and puffing 'bout this and that and one thing and the other, talking on about how no, no, we got to *save* this here valuable orange juice like it was the last drop on earth and it was liquid gold, looking to see did I have any matches, a lot of huffing and puffing about my—"

"Would you hush up for five seconds, Beau," my grandmother said.

"—suit," he finished. He sat down and thumped his cane on the floor, glowering at Tiny. Although he had treated her with more beneficence than my grandmother had, he had ordered her around for decades, and was furious at being under her care and direction. His cane was thick, carved, and painted to resemble a totem pole. He had won it at a county fair twenty years before, putting a shot in a contest against competitors a third his age. "You ever seen this here stick of mine," he said. He twirled it between his palms.

"I believe I've seen it a couple of times," I said. It was almost as old as I was.

"How come you never mentioned it, then?"

"It's a fine one."

"Bet you can't guess where I got it at."

"He's heard your old joke a thousand times, Beau."

"Where'd you get it?"

"Stanley's Jewel Box, ain't it a gem." He cackled and slapped his knee.

"That's not funny," my grandmother said primly.

He turned to her in astonishment. "Why, it's the funniest thing you ever heard in your life!"

"Heah yo' orange juice," Tiny said, handing me the glass. She put her huge palm against the back of my neck and pulled my ear to her lips. "Be careful!" she whispered. She lurched back into the kitchen and my grandmother went into the garage. I gave the juice to the old man. We listened to Irene rummaging around in the garage.

"Stay out of my automobile," the old man said in a low voice, which he knew that she could not hear, as she was hard of hearing and refused to wear a hearing aid. He held his cane in one hand, leaning forward on it, paying no attention to me or the juice I had set on the table. He strained farther and farther forward, staring into the garage. My grandmother was around the corner and he could not see her. He appeared to be glaring at a broken-handled shovel leaning against the far wall. After a moment he yelled at her. "What you fooling with out there?"

"I'm just looking for something, Jackson," she said.

"Well, *what?*" he said, stomping his cane. *"What* are you looking for?"

She did not answer. He roared at her, half-rising from his chair, his face moving quickly through a series of angry expressions. "Are you messing with my bidness papers? Don't you go messing with my bidness! You'll ruin ever'thing!"

She came up the steps out of the garage, closing the door behind her. The old man sat back and quickly shoved the glass of juice midway between us on the table.

She waved her arm above her head. "I found it," she said.

"Found what?" he said. "You expecting some kind of prize for it?"

"D. Harlan Jackson, Senior," she said.

He saw what it was and started leaning back in his chair away from it as she approached. He glowered. "I know my name," he said. "Whatever you and some of these others around here might think."

She leaned over him and grabbed his lapel and clumsily pinned on the name tag. It was an old one from a sales convention. There was a big HELLO! at the top, and at the bottom his name was typed in.

"Quit that," he said, glaring straight ahead. "What are you trying to do to me." He did not try to stop her. When she finished she stepped back and admired the tag as though it were a bunch of flowers she had just pinned on somebody. He lunged forward and grabbed the juice and gulped it down. She did not remember until he finished it.

"Jackson! That was for Little Harlan."

"It's all right," I said. "I gave him half of it."

You're going to have the heartburn again tonight," she said. "Don't come wake me up and complain about it." She shook her head, looking down her nose at him. She turned to me. "I've got to go to a UDC meeting. Come tell me about my camelias before I go."

"A most growed man going to college to learn about *flowers,*" he said. "Whoever heard of such a thing."

"We've got to be getting along too," I said.

"This'll just take a minute."

"U–D–C ," the old man said. "Un-tied Dames of Corpulence." His face lit up with glee as he remembered suddenly the name he had given the group before I was born.

"Beau," my grandmother said. "That's not funny."

"I ever tell you what my pappy done in the war?"

"He doesn't want to hear that now," she said.

"She don't like to hear about nothing but heroes running up hills, getting their legs shot off, and bleeding on everybody. She thinks Private Perrin won the whole shebang. She don't even think they lost."

She turned to me and said, as though she had not been drumming it into me for fifteen years, "He was a captain, of course. He could have been a colonel but he wanted to stay close to his men."

"My pappy joined when he was fifteen years old," Poppy began.

"It was your grandfather, Beau."

"Shows how much older she is than me. Her *daddy* fought in the war. More'n a hundred years ago! Ha!"

"He was quite advanced into middle age when I came along," she said.

"Anyhow I always called grandfather Pappy. He went off to some big battle or other. I ast him was he scared."

"This is the silliest story. Come look at my camelias."

"No, he said, he won't scared. I says, 'Pappy, you was mighty brave.' He says, 'Naw, I warn't brave, neither. I was hiding behind a tree.'" The old man rocked with laughter.

"It's not something to make fun of," Irene said. She was beginning to lose her temper.

He chortled some more. "Then he run off and come home. He never had no slaves, he said. It won't none of his business." He regarded my grandmother with satisfaction. "And she don't even think they lost!"

"Overpowered," she muttered as she pulled at me and we went down the steps toward the camelias.

"You see?" he yelled after us. "You hear what I mean?"

Around the corner of the house she stopped in front of the camelias. She looked very small; she had always been stout and seemed tall. Powder made her face dull and flat, and less expressive.

She had never worn makeup before the last year or two. The powder blurred but did not obliterate the age spots. Her body was shapeless as though stuffed like a chair instead of full of living flesh. I tried to remember when I had grown taller than her.

"Don't leave him alone," she said. "Don't let him out of your sight for one minute."

"I won't," I said.

"And watch out for his cane."

I looked at her for a moment with curiosity, linking her words with Tiny's enigmatic warning. I envisioned him attacking people with his cane.

"What?"

"He loses it all the time. It has his name and address on it, but I don't know if anyone would bother to send it back from out of town."

"I'll make sure he doesn't lose it."

"Don't let him out of your sight. Don't let him go to the bathroom alone. If you have to go, take him with you."

"Okay," I said.

"You have to treat him like a baby," she said. "He can't be trusted to do anything for himself. He still tries to take care of business interests when I'm not here to stop him. Last Thursday I came home and four angry people were waiting on the front stoop for someone to yell at. He rented all of them the same apartment. He's done that several times. He's tried to sell some of his stocks. He loses checks that come in, or sometimes he deposits checks and thinks that they're lost. Then he yells at me and chases me around the dining room, says I stole them. Two weeks ago he went to visit Mixon, thinking he was still alive, and got lost." The Mixons had lived three houses down on the other side of the block.

She picked at a leaf of the camelia in front of her. "If it weren't for Tiny I could not live." I had observed her changing relationship with the servant she had so long abused, but her expression of the change came as a surprise. "Could not live," she repeated. She looked away to the invisible creek. "I used to live farther up on the river it goes to," she said. "Isn't that strange." We walked back around the corner and as we mounted the steps she spoke in a high voice, so the old man would hear. "So you think I should just leave everything as is?"

"Yes."

"Well, that's what I always do." she said.

"Are you ready to go, Poppy?"

He stood and walked fast at the door. "I been ready since before you got up this morning," he said.

"He's been ready since seven o'clock," Tiny said. "He was waiting at the door when I came in."

Both women were beside him, smoothing his coat, Tiny adjusting his tie.

"Here, here, what are you doing to me?"

They went at his pockets, one on each side. "Get out of my pockets!" he said. He looked at me, looked down over their heads, drawn up out of his stoop to his full height. He looked disgusted. "They been looking for matches all morning," he said. "I reckon they're planning to try to burn the house down while I'm gone."

My grandmother withdrew a cigar from the pocket inside his jacket.

"Here, here," he said.

She waved it at me. "Don't let him light it," she said. "He can carry it around with him, but don't let him set it on fire."

"Quit playing with my see-gar," he snapped. He snatched her hand and took the cigar. My grandmother patted him on the shoulder as he stalked out the door; it was the only physical show of affection I ever saw her make for anyone.

He slowed as he approached the car. He held out his cane toward it, as if to fend it off. "Do it bite?" he said. He circled slowly to the front of the car and stooped slightly while he stared at it, his cane pointed between the headlights. "I ain't going to pedal," he said. "I'm too old to pedal all the way to Johnston."

"I'll do the pedaling," I said. "Let's go."

He opened the front door and stood there waiting to see what would happen. He had been in the car every day while I went to college in town, the year after they took away his license. He eased himself into the front seat and slammed the door quickly behind him. He cut his eyes over at me as I started the car. He was trying not to grin.

"Does it vibrate?" he asked.

He pointed out landmarks as we drove through town. The first outside the residential section of Clifton Park was the cemetery. "There's the graveyard," he said. A few blocks down he pointed again. "There's the old folks home," he said. He chuckled. "Convenient, ain't it?"

"There's Bob Meekins' insurance agency."

"Yonder's the curb market."

"There it is," he said, as though it was his and he were proud of it. "There's the post office."

Two blocks past it he turned to me and said in a high wail, his mouth open wide in surprise, "Why, you drove right past it!"

I nodded my head.

"Ain't you even going to stop?"

"Not today," I said.

He shook his head. He turned and looked through the back window, squinting at the post office receding behind us. "I never heard of anybody going downtown and not stopping at the post office," he said.

When we were out on the highway, he said, "I reckon we can stop in the post office on the way back." He settled in his seat and watched the countryside pass by. "I know all kinds of folks in Johnston," he said. "I'll introduce you to some of my old friends."

"Okay," I said. "I'd like that."

He thought for a few minutes. "How many do you reckon are left?"

"I don't know," I said.

"Do you think I'll find a lot of them?"

"I don't know. I wouldn't count on it. You haven't lived there in forty years."

"But I been there on business. I ought to be able to run down most of 'em what's left. A bunch of them hang around the lobby of the Roanoke Hotel." He watched the hills roll by and the empty fields that spread low between their swells, the white farmhouses rising starkly out of the land. The woods were like thin smoke clinging to the hills. "They'll all remember, don't you reckon?"

After a moment I said, "Of course they will."

"That's right," he said. "Just about everybody in Johnston knows me. Whatever happened to that little gal of yours?"

"Which girl?"

"That little blond-headed one I had to carry all over town for

46

you. That time I took you to the picture show and picked you up. You got married to her yet?"

"No. I haven't seen her since that day."

"What? You can't fool me. She's got her hooks in you and you'll get married off to her and have about five or six little chaps running around between your legs before you know it. I seen you two spooning in the backseat. If I recollect right, she was sorta pretty. Wouldn't win no beauty contest, but nobody started barking when she walked down the street."

"She did win a beauty contest."

"No!" he said. "That little gal? Why, she ain't old enough."

"She won the contest years after that time we went to the movies."

"Ha!" he said. "You have too been seeing her."

"I read about it in the newspaper," I said. "I haven't seen her since that date. She said she didn't like the car."

"She did not!"

"That's right," I said. "She said it vibrated."

He grinned and twirled his cane between his hands. "Good riddance, then."

The old man drew out his cigar and ran it under his nose. He placed his cane beside him and held the cigar with both hands, studying it. Slowly and with great care he unwrapped the cellophane. He bit off one end of the cigar and spat it on to the floor. Then he leaned back and stuck the cigar in his mouth. Very softly he spoke to the window; I could barely hear him.

"I sure wish I had me a light."

I handed him a pack of matches. He took them without looking at them. He bent over the match as he struck it, as though hiding the cigar from the world beyond his window. Smoke filled the car as he puffed. When he was satisfied with how it was lit, he cracked open the window and tossed out the match. When he drew on it, his eyes closed and he smiled. He looked very pleased with himself.

He held the cigar in his right hand, poised between his thumb and two fingers as though he were going to write with it. His fingers flowed from his hand, long and tapered and graceful. His fingernails were always clean and neatly trimmed. But his hands looked like they had worked hard, too. The cigar was long and tapered like his hands.

"Listen," he said. "Did I ever tell you about that calf?"

"No," I said. "What calf?"

"Why, that calf me and Creed Simms—or was it Silas Mutch, Junior? Why, no, it won't neither of them. By George, it was my cousin Lyle! That's who it was, it was Lyle. That calf me and Lyle carried across the river to Silk Hope. I didn't never tell you about that?"

"No," I said.

"Why, I can't imagine. You ain't never heard that story," he said quietly. He drew on his cigar and looked at it lovingly as he let the smoke stream slowly out of his mouth. "I tell you what," he said. "I'll tell you about that calf."

"Fine."

"It was a calf me and my cousin Lyle Jackson carried across the river to Silk Hope in what was left of a little wooden skiff. Lyle, he was a more or less permanent resident of our house even though his own folks lived eight miles off. We sorta held him in escrow. I believe this happened the year he come at Christmas, and lingered. Until March. Anyhow it was one Christmas he come, riding a mule. Mama went out to the door to see who was it coming, we could hear the mule a long ways off. It was Christmas Day, and what sort of person would be riding up on a mule on Christmas? By God! Would you believe it, it was Lyle!

"Mama went outside, she says, 'It's Lyle!' She says to him, 'Much Christmas down your way, Lyle?'

"And he says, 'No'm, not a whole lot.'

"And she stood there on the porch a minute, and she just looked at him a minute and then she says, 'Well, git off that mule and come on in!'"

The old man heaved with laughter, slapping his hand on his knees. "You ever heard anything like that? He said, no'm, and she says to git off that mule and come on in.

"Well, that's how come Lyle to be there that March, I believe. Maybe the Christmas mule was another time, but he was somehow there that March.

"We must have been eight or nine years old and we was big buddies. Him and me and Silas Mutch, Junior. Do you remember your great-great-grandaddy? He was the one sent us. He had a calf he wanted to sell to get the money to buy his seed and fertilizer to plant with. This was right at eighteen ninety, and let me tell you something, cash didn't grow on trees. He give me and Lyle a dime to cross the ferry with. We were supposed to take that calf and ride her across the ferry and into town and sell her to the butcher and be home for dinner with the money in my purse.

"We put the rope on her neck and started leading her down the path, which twisted and turned almost straight down the side of the hill to the river. The river was swollen with rain and the snow melting in the mountains. From time to time through a clearing, when the bank along the path was low—it was rutted into the hill like a ravine—I could see the river and the ferry rocking against the near side. I remember it just as clear as anything; it's like I am looking out the window at it right now. The river looked like a sheet of lead laid out in the valley, and the sky was the same color, it was about to rain. But we were supposed to be back before dinnertime, we weren't worried about no rain, just two little eight-year-old tads, we thought it was *fun* to get rained on.

"I don't know if it was me or Lyle thought of it, but looking down at the ferry we agreed that instead of paying out that dime to cross, we would take the calf across on a boat we would scrounge up and buy us some candy. We never seen candy once a year, much less a dime, for that matter. Candy! The big treat for us was once a week, Pappy would gather us all in the living room after supper and give everybody a apple.

"The way we planned it was, all we had to do was borrow one of the old skiffs somebody always had lying up under the willows. We'd just go sailing right by Silas Mutch Junior's daddy's ferry and tell him to go fish, we had our own boat. We dragged that calf down the path in a hurry, all overcome, and by gum, we *did* find an old skiff lying up under some old black willows.

"But that calf, she didn't want no interfering around that boat, which anybody could tell belonged to somebody, it wasn't no relic that floated up on the rising river. Maybe the calf had a conscience. But we didn't let it bother us none, because we had to use it to get back across the river, didn't we? Silas might not even let us ride one way if he saw us cheating him out of his fare, rowing a calf across on the trip out. That Silas was terrible about fares.

"Why, years later, when I was courting, I come up from the Silk Hope side in a buckboard. I was sixteen and courting so it had come to get pretty late on, after midnight, and I whistled for Mister Silas. He yells over who is it, and naturally he recognized me helloing back at him, as me and Silas Mutch Junior was thick as ticks on a yard dog. He pulled his ferry on across and there I was sitting in the buckboard, grinning like the cat because I only had fifteen cent when the fare was a quarter by then for a horse-drawn vehicle of any sort; and I was thinking I had gone a round with Mr. Silas and done won it, because what was he going to do, go all the way back and leave my fifteen cent in my pocket?

"I handed over my change, grinning at him. Likely he saw my teeth shining in the starlight. He said, like he never seen money before, like it was going to poison his hand, 'What's this?' and I says 'That's my fare' and he says, 'Harlan, you know it costs a quarter to take a buggy across the ferry.'

" 'It ain't nothing but a buckboard,' I says, 'and anyhow I ain't got but fifteen cent.'

" 'Why, then, you ain't going across,' he says. 'You're already over here now, Mr. Silas,' I says, 'and here it is after midnight with no one else to come along. Now what you going to do? Leave me here and lose *all* that whole entire quarter, or take me across and just only lose ten cent?'

"*Durn* if he don't commence to pull that ferry out in the river, fading off into the night with a rippling sound, and I yelled at him, 'You can't leave me on this side the river all night' and he yells back to me, 'Any fool ain't got but fifteen cent to his name, it don't matter which side of the river he's on!' " Poppy banged on his knee and rocked back and forth, gurgling and chortling. "You ever heard the like of it? You know what, it reminds me of the time up in Ashe County when me and my cousin Lyle Jackson went to sneak a peek at Bald Mary with her bonnet off. We was—"

"Wait, wait," I said. "I want to hear about the calf."

"Calf? What calf?"

"That you were taking across the river to sell for your grandfather."

"Oh, you've heard that story, have you?"

"You were just telling it to me. You had the calf about in the boat."

He reflected for a moment. "I believe you're right," he said. "We had to lift her up to put her in, did you know that? Waded out into the river that even in July was like flowing ice around your shins, that calf hollering for Mama like she hadn't been suckled in a week. Did she fight? Boy, let me tell you, she *fought*. Lyle was getting butted on the front end and I was getting kicked on the rear. We splashed and tumbled about and finally got her in and tied down to a seat so she wouldn't rear about and drown us.

"The river was running strong, swelled up with rain and almost ready to flood, with whitecaps which I never seen on the river but twice or three times in my life. The boat bucked and swayed and scared that calf half to death; I wasn't feeling none too pert about it, myself. She yanked so hard she gagged and I was afraid she'd choke herself to death so I asked Lyle to untie her and as soon as he did she jumped four feet straight up in the air, carrying Lyle up with her, and just then a great crack of thunder like everything that ever was had come apart at once busted out right over us and as soon as she touched down, knocking the boat one way, she jumped again, right out the side, flipping it over the rest of the way and we all went in. The wind was blowing hard and the whitecaps slapped at us like the river was trying to beat us to death. Lyle went under and I thought, Lord, he ain't never gone have much Christmas nowhere again, but he come right back up. Soon as I seen he was all right I took out after the calf, who was disappearing downstream like two eight-year-old demons was trying to drown her. She was the same color as the river. It had looked gray like the sky from up above but when we got right down in it, it was muddy, exactly the color of the red clay fields.

"Lyle caught up to me and we were just barely keeping the calf in sight—it was black as death under those thunderheads—until at last she tired and we caught up to her. We both tried to hitch a ride, but that tired her out even more, she stopped swimming, and looked about to drown so we had to carry *her*. You understand, that calf represented every nickel my grandaddy could raise for us without selling something we couldn't part with; if we didn't have that calf to sell, we wouldn't eat next winter. There we were, out in a stormy river with a savings account, maybe drowning it.

"Halfway across, it commenced to rain; no, it didn't rain, water come out of the sky in a solid sheet. We got lost. We didn't know which way was Silk Hope and which way was home. I swum in front, pulling the rope, and Lyle kicked from behind and pushed and we both prayed we were going straight and would wind up on one side or the other, we didn't care which anymore. It seemed more and more impossible with every minute that went by, and finally after the river pushed enough muddy water down my throat so I thought I'd never be thirsty again, and getting numb all over, and crying and cursing the day I was born and the day God made cows, we suddenly come up a bank, half froze and shaking and weak and near blind and a week past dead. It was even the Silk Hope side. We were standing on it and still couldn't see the bank. We drug that calf through the woods and finally it stopped raining, just as we walked up to the butcher's shop in town.

"The butcher—a big round man named Linden Otey who had a dog once that died from eating a jar of false-teeth cleanser, and he swole up like a balloon and popped—took one look at that calf and said, 'Boys, I got to take off three pounds for all that water and mud.'

"When we got home—on the ferry, we sure as sweet Jesus won't gone to swim again—Pappy asked about the missing money. We told him the calf fell in the mud and got kinda scummed up, a little bit, and Linden Otey knocked off three pounds. 'That's the most foolest tale I ever heard!' he said. 'If you ain't man enough to tell the truth, at least tell a good lie.' And he whipped us. You know what he said we done? Took that extra quarter and spent it on candy!"

The old man drew long and slow on his cigar. It was almost gone. "That's what it was like, growing up in the country, there wasn't no money."

He looked through the window at the town he had moved to when he left the country, his eyes faraway and dreamy-looking. He took his last puff on the cigar and threw it out the window. "I don't think he should have whipped us, do you?"

"No."

He sat up suddenly. "Why, we're in Johnston," he said in amazement.

"That's right. Here we are."

He pointed to a long brick building, three stories high, rundown and apparently abandoned, its empty window frames staring out like empty eyes. "Look! Looky there! You see that warehouse?"

"Yes."

"That was the first place I worked when I come here. In two

years I owned it. Did you know that? Five years after I bought it, I was the biggest tobacco broker in the South, and do you know what that means?"

"What?"

"That means in the whole world." He craned his neck to watch his old building as we passed it. "In nineteen twenty-seven I made four million dollars."

"What?"

He nodded his head. He grinned. "I done all right, didn't I? Course by then it wasn't all in tobacco."

I knew he had been, on paper, the sole owner of eighteen miles of Florida coastline, but I had never thought in terms of dollars. "I don't see how you could lose that much money," I said.

"Shoot," he said. "It's almost as easy to lose as it is to spend. I lost it just like everybody else. I was worth over twelve million on paper. Stocks and land. Stocks wiped out in three days, had a two percent margin. I paid a grand total of nothing down for the Florida land, just gave notes for the down payment, and borried more against the land as the value went up. Those bastards took everything I had. A man come to the house and tried to get my wedding ring. I swallowed it. 'Come back tomorrow and look in the toilet for it,' I says. 'If somebody hasn't carted that off too.'

" 'Fellow,' he says, 'you want it that bad, you keep it.' "

I parked the car and helped him out and we started walking toward the Roanoke Hotel. "How'd you make money the second time?"

"Worked hard and saved my money," he said. He thumped his cane as we walked, excited. "I reckon they'll all be there," he said. "I bet a lot of them are still alive."

"How did you lose it the second time? I never did understand that."

"There wasn't nearly so much, for one thing. I wasn't even what I would call rich. I don't remember too much about it, it all happened so fast. Mortgages!" he exclaimed. "Mortgages done me in. I had everything mortgaged, trying to make money too fast. Greedy. I folded myself up by trying to do too much too soon. There was a big boom during the second war, after it. I missed the boat by six months. Boom came, I didn't have a nickel. You listen to me. Don't never owe a penny, you'll keep out of trouble. Don't mortgage a pack a matches, pay cash all down the line, and not much of that. Don't buy a quarter tin of shoe polish when spit and mud will do."

"But you got the second money back."

"Oh, no, no. I never seen that kind of money again."

As we approached the hotel he began grinning a wide grin, his eyes taking on a youthful sparkle, his step light. An elderly couple came out of the revolving door. The man smiled and his wife, hanging on his arm, did too. The man lifted his hat. "Mr. Jackson," he said politely. The old man nodded back, tipped his hat too. When they were gone he turned and watched them. He stood very straight, looking proud. A childlike wonder and delight spread across his face. "Did you see that? I ain't even passed through here in ten years."

We pushed through the revolving door. He looked alertly around the lobby. "I know just about everybody in Johnston. The ones I don't know, they know me." He was trembling with excitement. He nodded to everyone in the lobby and naturally they nodded back. "Look at this! I don't know a soul here, they all know me! Why don't I just wait here," he said. "You go on about your business, I don't want to get in your way. You don't have to hang around here for me to do my visiting; you just leave me here while I wait for my old friends to pass through."

He leaned toward me, leaning over me, a head taller than me. "I won't go nowhere," he said. "I'll stay right here in the lobby. I won't even go to the dining room, not to speak of outside." He looked around the lobby again. "Look! There's Wilson," he yelled, pointing his cane. "By George, you remember Wilson, don't you? He used to come to ball games with us."

"Yes, I do."

"Do you think I could stay here?" He pleaded like a child. "I'll stay right here in the lobby." He pointed to an armchair beside Wilson. "You see that chair. I'll set right there till doomsday or you come back. I won't even stir around in it to stretch."

"All right. I don't see why not."

He started quickly for the chair, stepping high, his handshake ready before he covered half the distance.

"You stay right here, now," I called to him.

Without slowing or looking back, he gave a quick nod.

54

My affairs in town consumed two hours, and when I returned I was worried before I looked across the lobby at the empty chair. I could feel my stomach drop, and then he grabbed me by the elbow from behind. He was still excited, but he seemed more in control of himself. "Everybody come in here to lunch," he said. "Why, you seen Wilson with your very own eyes!"

"Yes. Did y'all have a nice talk?"

"He's not hardly hisself anymore. All kinds of other fellers come in here. I don't think you'd know them. Johnson, J. W. Peters, a half a dozen others."

We went outside. He squeezed my arm as we walked. He swung the cane and tapped it on the pavement. "I guess I saw just about everybody. They say old Hubie Person's still running his place up on Broad Street. Can you believe that? He's older than I am. He was always one of my best accounts. You know what I'm going to do? I'm going to go back into business. What do you think of that?"

I did not know what to say, and said nothing.

"You know what, you and me ought to set up into our own place, just you and me. Go into one of my houses, a couple of happy old bachelors, no damn worritin' women grabbing at you all the time. And I'll go right back into business. Let's go stop by and see Hubie Person right this minute. I was going to go see him, but I didn't want to leave the lobby and get you worried if you come by."

"Let's have some lunch first," I said. "We'll go by after lunch."

"Fine," he said expansively. "Just fine." He watched himself in the store windows as we walked toward the restaurant. He tapped his cane and held himself very erect, curved slightly backward, checking the line of his shoulders in the reflections jumping from one glass front to the next. From time to time he looked ahead to see where he was going. He looked ahead once and stopped dead in midstride, his cane pointed out, caught in the middle of one of the long circles he had been swinging it in. "Would you look at that?"

An enormously fat man approached us; he looked as if he had been blown full of air or helium. He was abreast of us, and Poppy yelled exuberantly, "S'pose you was as fat as that!"

I pulled him by the arm as he turned to watch the red-faced man, huffing and rocking laboriously down the walk, and we entered the restaurant to eat lunch.

My father and I had picked out various cheeses and two kinds of sausage, apples, and a bottle of white wine. The slices of cheese and sausage were arrayed on the wooden planks of the picnic table. The bottle dripped beads of water. The scent of the cheese and sausage and the two apples rose on the warm air into my face. The white Pekin ducks swarmed around us while two Canada geese stood out of the crowd, their long black necks rocking back and forth, their heads turning quickly to each move we made.

"I wonder what would have happened if he had never retired," I said.

"Sometimes he's lucid even now," my father said. "Some days he can remember almost everything."

"They treated him like a baby. I still don't know which came first, the way he acted or the way they treated him."

"Usually though he just remembers the past, the earliest days of his life. Sometimes he can't remember the next day that I saw him the day before."

"Is he ever worse than he was today?"

"No, that's the worst I've seen him. Of course he deteriorates steadily. One thing, no matter how bad off he is, on any given day, he's got spirit. Even today, he had spirit sometimes."

He sighed. "It's hard to think of my old man dotard." He cut some long slivers of cheese with his pocketknife and laid them in his mouth. "But it comes to all of us; it will come to me soon, it will even come to you."

"I guess every time you come down here to see him you think of the day we put him in the hospital."

"Yes, I do." He cut slices of apple and put them on pieces of cheese and spread them on the table between us. "There wasn't any way out of it, though." Across the lake the gray and black trees rose to meet the sky and sank in reflection into the lake. The light skipped off the water, making tiny winks of the ripples that without the glare would not have even been noticeable. My father poured more wine and stared out over the lake too, over the rim of his glass.

"What was it this morning, about someone doing or not doing something? That you were going to tell us later."

"It's some bad news, probably. Some bad news about Junior."

"Something she's planning to do to Sully? She hinted around to me, said she wanted to protect Sully from herself."

He shook his head. "No, it's something that may have happened. I have to look into it more this afternoon." He finished his wine. "I wish I could take the old man home with me. But I don't see how I could, do you?"

"Why don't you tell him Irene is dead? I was wondering about that."

"It's the kind of thing he wouldn't remember. Why bother him with it, if he's just going to forget it." He looked again at the woods rising from the water's edge. "Do you remember riding Blackie over there?"

We could see the road where my sister and I had ridden the pony that Poppy gave us. It was paved now and I regretted the dust that had bothered us then. "Yes. Of course."

"I think they take pretty good care of him there, don't you?" He leaned forward, his blue eyes startling under the gray hair. He was the same age Poppy had been when I first knew Poppy. "Don't you think it seems like a good place, for what it is?"

"Yes."

"I wish I could take him up to Virginia with me, anyway."

"Why don't you? You could see him every day."

"He's been moved around a lot. Maybe a place near home wouldn't be as good. He's used to where he is, and I hate to shift him around anymore, bother him more. These were the first people willing to handle him on a permanent basis, outside of an insane asylum. No other place can handle his violence."

"But he's not violent anymore."

"He tries to run away. Also, I've got to be coming down here more now anyway. At least once a month, unless I can find a lawyer to operate his estate for me."

"I thought Junior was doing all that stuff. She took over from Irene when she got sick, didn't she? How come she can't do it, since she lives right here in town?"

"She was going to, but we'll have to change that, it looks like. That's what the bad news is about. And I've got to get back to find out for sure. Do you want some more wine?" I shook my head and he pounded the cork into the bottle. He took one last look around. "Nobody ever knows anything for sure," he said.

Chapter 4 _____

THEY RETURNED SHORTLY AFTER WE DID and they had Tiny with them.

Tiny and Sully entered the kitchen together, Sully's long arm draped over Tiny's shoulder like a rope, leaning heavily against her. "You tell us what you want, Tiny," she said. "You're just as much family as any of us."

Tiny stood holding her uniform in a grocery bag, squeezing it with both hands. "I can't think about it just now," she said.

"I think you better think about it anyway, honey," Sully said. "I know how you feel, but I think you better think about it pretty quick while there's still something around to think about."

"You hush, Sully," Tiny said, glancing quickly at Junior and Helen.

"I'm sure we'll find something suitable for Tiny," Junior said, smiling with her mouth.

Tiny glared at Junior. "You gone change before dinner?"

Helen and Junior started out. "You tell us if there's anything we can do to help you with, Tiny," Junior said from the doorway, moving toward the stairs.

"Help," said Sully, snorting. "How could she help? She hasn't cooked a meal in her life. How do you reckon she got so fat without even knowing how to cook?"

"I'll think about what I might need, honey," Tiny said. "Now you go upstairs out of my way and change with them."

Tiny came up to her shoulder. Sully bent and kissed her on the cheek, and Tiny patted Sully on the back.

"I'm so glad you're here, Tiny," Sully said.

Sully went upstairs and Tiny disappeared into a closet in the

58

hallway that served as pantry and laundry room. She came out wearing her blue uniform, faded to a soft hue, almost gray, patched and resewn so skillfully that the repairs barely showed.

She saw me sitting at the dining-room table. "Why, hello, Harlan," she said, smiling, the gold tooth on one side of her mouth gleaming. "Ain't it nice to see you?"

"It's nice to see you, Tiny," I said. I went into the kitchen and we hugged one another. She kept her face turned away but the smell of alcohol billowed through the room as thick and obvious as a cloud of smoke.

She moved to the sink, quickly but jerkily, with a side-to-side lilt that threw askew her wig. It slipped down on one side and almost touched her ear. The back of her neck shone like polished wood, like a piece of walnut rubbed by generations of hands. Small beads of sweat gleamed against her skin.

She shook her head as she washed the dishes they had left from breakfast, a slow contrast to the quick, jerky efficiency of her working hands and arms. I sat in a chair by the red table. The room seemed to warm up as Tiny worked. In the kitchen with Tiny while she cooked had always been my refuge against the cold house. "My, my," she said, over and over. "My, my."

She turned her face briefly to me, her hands continuing without pause to wash and rinse and place dishes in the rack. Her hands were large, the knuckles swollen huge; her thumbs bent back so far they looked broken.

"And tell me what I gone do now, Harlan," she said. "Who gone take care of Mister Jackson in that home all by hisself, what I want to know."

"Don't you worry about a thing, Tiny," I said. "You've worried over them long enough."

"I am not going to *worry*," she said. "But I sho gone *wonder*. I can take care of myself; it's some of these other folks I'm wondering about."

She walked backward, carrying a dishrag and a plate, dripping a line of water and suds to the middle of the floor, where she stopped and stooped and peered at the staircase. She slowly moved her eyes up the stairs, jerking her head upward step by step. She reached the top and looked for a moment through the ceiling as though she could see into the room where the women were changing clothes. Then she snapped her head suddenly to face me, knees bent, the tight knots of muscles on her calves bulging as she leaned toward me. She whispered huskily, urgently, "How everybody?"

"Everybody's just fine," I said. "Under the circumstances."

"The circumstances ain't too good," she said. "It's a terrible thing." She shook her head and walked back to the sink to rinse the plate, dripping a second, thinner line of water along the floor.

"Are they treating that little girl all right?"

"No."

"I heard about that brooch," she said. "I didn't hear nothing else on the way over here. Even your mama couldn't hush her up. I seen the dining-room table." She shook her head, rinsing the last plate. "That's all I'm gone to say. I ain't mentioning one mo' word about it to nobody."

"Here comes Junior," I said.

"I might make that one 'ception," Tiny said.

"I've decided we don't need a hot meal today, Tiny," Junior said as she entered the kitchen from the dining room. "You don't need to go to all that trouble for us."

"*You* decided?" Tiny said. "I been cooking hot meals in this house every day for thirty years. I reckon I can cook one more."

"Oh, no, Tiny, you don't need to go to all that trouble today."

"I can't help it if you so lazy you ain't cooked a lunch in twenty years and got to where you don't like a hot meal at noon," Tiny said, clattering bowls and measuring utensils together on the counter. "I don't want no bickering about it. I goes to trouble when I needs to go to trouble, and these days are days when folks around here need hot meals for sure. If you want to bicker about something, you go find Sully and talk to her about that dia-munt necklace of hers."

"That will be enough, Tiny," Junior said.

Tiny pointed a bag of flour at Junior, a white cloud puffing from the open top. "Out," she said. "You git out of my kitchen this minute." She did not speak loudly but her voice quavered, high-pitched.

Junior stood in the doorway, chin lifted and peering down her nose in precisely the posture my grandmother had taken thousands of times. She pointed her finger at Tiny. "Listen here," she began in a harsh nasal whine, and Tiny moved on her, flinging the bag of flour on the counter behind her, striding forward with her oversized hands balled into fists.

Junior retreated into the dining room.

Tiny began sifting flour into a bowl. She used a strainer instead of a flour sifter and she joggled it over the bowl and the flour snowed down. "I don't work for that *strange* woman," she said fiercely, speaking into the bowl. She poured milk in without measuring it. "I don't work for nobody now, and if I did, it sho as my sweet Lord wouldn't be for her." Tiny reached up with her free hand and straightened her wig as it slipped down over her ear, leaving a faint white hand traced on the coarse hair. "She been trying to order me around for months."

Tiny rolled the dough on the counter with her rolling pin. Her whole body moved back and forth as she rolled, her muscles flexing and relaxing, her body still strong despite her drinking and her arthritic stiffness. It was painful for her to walk and she was afraid of falling down, but working at the counter, she looked nearly the same as she had always looked, from as early as I could remember, spinning the pin over the dough with quick easy motions, flipping the flattened mass around and sculpting a perfect circle.

She used to make biscuits at the same time she made the coffee. Sometimes she made corn bread instead of biscuits, and sometimes the corn bread was pan-fried, as thin as paper and lacy around the edges. The lace corn bread was so light you did not actually eat it; you put a piece in your mouth and let it dissolve. As a child I always stayed in the kitchen while she cooked and felt the room gradually warm up. When she was younger she moved with a dancer's grace and I used to watch her ballet of meal preparation, as she glided through the kitchen, pulling out dishes and food and pots and pans without ever looking at them, always doing two things at once, doing everything at once, it seemed, the coffee and biscuits last so that they would be fresh and hot, and when they were done, everything else was done at once, suddenly and miraculously and apparently without effort while she cheerfully conversed with me. She let me ring the bell for dinner. By the time we were gathered at the table, the food was there waiting. Usually I would try to help Tiny carry it out. It both pleased and embarrassed her. After dinner my father and I would carry out our dishes, and his assistance practically mortified her. We ate there once a week for eight years, and she never grew accustomed to my father's helping her. As soon as she no longer heard the silverware clinking against the china, she would bounce on her bowed muscular legs into the dining room to forestall him. As we carried our dishes into the kitchen, she would say, "Here, now, Mist' Harlan— No, wait—here—you got set. I'm bringing in coffee and dessert and I don't want you to miss— Here, now, let me take— No, no, y'all are awful sweet but don't— Well, thank you, thank you."

They paid her five dollars a week until my grandfather retired and my grandmother began to thaw out. She also received a bonus of five dollars at Christmas, and two weeks' paid vacation. She never took the vacation; she worked and took the extra money. My father regularly assaulted Irene about the wages she paid.

"How do you expect her to live on five dollars a week?"

"She has a husband," my grandmother said. "I don't see why he can't work."

"He left her ten years ago!"

"Well, that's certainly not *my* fault," she said. "And besides, she eats here. She gets bus fare when I don't pick her up in the morning."

"Five dollars a week is a crime."

"I can get help anywhere for five dollars a week."

"You could in nineteen thirty," my father said.

"Well, even if it costs more now, you're paying for younger women. They can do more."

"What?" my father said. "Tiny works like a dog. You couldn't find five people to do the work together Tiny does alone."

"For heaven's sake," my grandmother would say. "You *know* we give her a house rent free."

"What's she going to do when she can't work anymore? Who's going to take care of her then? You don't even pay Social Security for her; they don't know she exists."

"We'll take care of her. I'll be around. The Perrins have always taken good care of their coloreds. We'll keep paying her the same she makes now when she can't work anymore."

"You're older than she is!"

"I don't see what difference that makes," my grandmother said, looking down her nose and drawing her head back, a haughty pose she took when she was offended or when she went to United Daughters of the Confederacy meetings.

Although Tiny would not allow herself to be browbeaten in any other way, she complained about money only once. My grandfather rented a cottage at Nags Head and took more than twenty people. Tiny did all the cooking and cleaning and laundry every day. Being at the beach was much different for me from being immersed in the frigidity of my grandparents' house, as though that coldness were something they could not carry with them but had to extract from the house itself; and as a result I spent little time with Tiny and most of it with my cousins in the water and the dunes, Sully our leader in finding things to do. She was married to a man I saw only then; I cannot remember him, but I remember she paid no attention to him whatsoever. She courted her son; one of the few times she saw Peanut after they took him from her.

I did go into the kitchen from time to time, just to talk to Tiny for a few minutes and tell her what we were doing. Whenever I entered the kitchen she was there, and every time she was bathed in sweat. It ran off her arms onto the floor and her uniform turned from light blue to almost black with moisture.

Once I went into the kitchen for a quick visit and my grandmother was there, wearing a dress. She never put on a bathing suit the entire week. She and Tiny stood in the middle of the room fixed in their places, looking at each other. Tiny was holding a pan by her side and she was trembling. She spoke very slowly and she worked her mouth to get the words out. She dipped her head with each word and her jaw when she opened it stayed tautly down until she raised her head to make it rise and form the words.

"If I . . . thought . . . I won't . . . getting paid for this week . . . I . . . sho wouldn't . . . be in heah . . . sweating . . . sweating like a . . . hoss."

"We're paying for a vacation for you!" my grandmother said. "You've got a whole week at the beach for nothing! Most people have to pay a fortune to come to the beach. Why can't you see that?"

"Because," Tiny said. "If you don't pay me . . . I . . . gone walk out right now."

They stood and stared at one another, Tiny's arms crossed now and my grandmother reared back, looking down her nose. Tiny took a step toward the door. "An' you won't never see me again when you get home, neither."

"Oh, all right," my grandmother said. "But don't you let me catch you on that beach during the day."

My grandmother opened the swinging door that led to the huge living room. I could see the front wall of glass. "I'll get Mr. Jackson to give you the money," she said. "Or would you rather we sent it directly home for you? You won't be able to send it until tonight, yourself. You'll be working."

"Yes'm," Tiny said.

She glared at me as the door closed behind my grandmother. "I ain't got time now," she said. "Go play."

I followed my grandmother into the living room. Most of the adults were there, gathered around the front wall of windows which opened out to the ocean. The windows were propped open with sticks and a breeze came through but it was still very hot.

"So I had to tell her I'd pay her, Beau," Irene said. "So go send her husband five dollars or she'll leave."

The swinging door banged open and Tiny stepped into the room, small and black and furious against the white door still slowly swinging back and forth. She glared at Irene, then at Poppy. She still held the pan in her huge fist.

"Changed my mind," she said. "I ain't gone be run like a slave in this heat for twenty or thirty people for no 'mount of money. My grandaddy was born a slave but I won't and I got no plans to be one."

My grandfather did not answer. The others, indolent in the heat, looked away from the scene. My grandmother stared at Tiny, outraged.

"I got four, five times as much to do here as back home," Tiny said. "And it's twice as hot. I'm going home."

My grandfather looked down at her from across the room out of his calculating eyes, coldly amused, or pleased with himself. He held Tiny in his gaze while he stood still and then pulled his thin billfold from his pocket. He walked over to her as he took out a twenty-dollar bill and popped it between his hands. He always carried new bills and he liked to pop them. He held it out to her and she looked down at it.

64

"Take it," he said. "And I'll send the five dollars to Jameson. That makes five times as much money as you make at home, for five times as much work."

Tiny stared at the bill and finally, slowly, she reached out her great hand and took it. She looked at it again and then wordlessly put it in her pocket. I could not understand her look of defeat.

Poppy took out a ten-dollar bill. "And here's ten dollars for it being twice as hot."

"Beau!" my grandmother said.

"And take the rest of the day off and Saturday too."

"Beau!"

"Junior, get in there and fix supper." The old man went back to the windows and sat and looked out over the ocean. Tiny looked at the ten in her hand and at him and she turned slowly and went back into the kitchen.

"Did you see that?" my grandmother said. "She didn't even say thank you. She didn't say so much as pea-turkey."

The raw biscuits sat in lumps on a baking sheet. Tiny turned; a tear rolled thickly from each eye, shining on her face, leaving a pair of bright trails down her cheeks.

"The last thing she said to me," Tiny said, "was I don't know what I'd do without you. And then she said, 'Take care of Mister Jackson.' She knew she was going to die before they ever took her to the hospital the last time. She come home to die." Tiny put the sheet of biscuits into the oven. "She might have been a mean woman but she got . . . softer and softer. Sometimes I didn't know myself why I stayed here with them, but the last five years, why I *couldn't* have left. We got to where we was like sisters. She fixed it so I could have my house. She put it in her paper."

She sniffed again. "You better go on in there and see they don't roll up the carpet or pull up them floorboards before we're finished using that room. And tell 'em they made such a mess out there, they gone have to eat on the porch."

I went in as Helen entered from the living room. Junior sat at the table, staring at the litter around her. "We've hardly started," she said.

"Isn't it awful," Helen said. "I'll never get all these things to Detroit. It's going to cost a fortune. I wish somebody else would take some of this stuff." She sighed, her eyes darting from object to object on the table and all around the room.

"Well, Tiny should get some of it," I said.

"Of course she should," Junior said.

"And she *will,* Harlan," said Helen. "She will."

"We've been having a little trouble with her," Junior said to Helen. "Naturally, she's upset like all of us are, but I don't see why she has to bite somebody's head off when they try to make things easier for her."

"Who gets the silver service?" I said.

They looked at one another. "I remember, Mother promised that to you, didn't she, Helen?"

Helen seated herself beside her sister, rested her chin in both palms. She looked at the piece of sky that showed above the air conditioner, wrinkling her eyebrows so that they almost touched. "You know, I think I remember something like that."

"It was Christmas before last," Junior said.

"I believe it was," Helen said, her puzzled look slowly dissolving.

"I remember it perfectly now," Junior said. "It was during a commercial while we were watching *A Christmas Carol.*"

"How could I ever forget?" Helen asked, her voice a bright bell tone, smiling at her sister.

"Who gets the corner cupboard?" I asked.

Junior looked to Helen, cocking her head to one side. "I remember Mother saying she wanted Young Irene to have it," Helen said. "I remember exactly what she said. She said, 'I want Junior to have the corner cupboard.' Those were her exact words. I remember it because it was at the same time that she said she wanted Carolyn to have the diamond brooch because if she gave it to Sully, Sully would pawn it, and I was the only girl not to get diamonds when I was born to pass on to my daughter."

"Well, we certainly remember *that,*" Junior said. "How could we forget it."

"Here she comes," Helen said urgently. They both sighed deeply, like they were about to submerge in water.

Sully swayed into the room. She sat at the table with them, weaving slightly as with one hand she grabbed the back of the chair and eased herself into the seat. "Junior," she said in her sweetest, smoothest voice, smiling serenely, "what is all that shit in your suitcase? Those sterling spoons and that little gold box from India?"

Junior blushed. "What are you talking about? What have you been doing rooting around in my suitcase?"

Sully turned and yelled at the closed kitchen door. "Tiny!"

"And why do you have to use that dreadful language?"

Tiny appeared, standing askew to the door frame. "Are y'all going to eat?" she said. "You made such a mess in heah, you gone have to eat on the porch."

"Didn't Mother give you that gold box, Tiny?" Sully asked. "That little gold box from India with elelphants on it? I guess it's worth about a million dollars."

Helen, smiling at Tiny, said, "I'm sure she gave it to Young Irene. Don't you think she did, Tiny?"

Tiny looked from Helen to Junior, pushing her lips together, scratching the base of neck with her forefinger. Then she turned and winked at Sully. "I reckon she did," she said. "I reckon she give it to that Junior."

"I'll be glad for you to have it," Junior said. "I believe Mother *did* give it to you." She rose from her chair. "I'll go get it for you right now. I put it away so it wouldn't . . ." She paused with an air of significance, carefully looking at no one. "Ah . . . get mis*placed.*"

"That was right clever of you, Junior," Tiny said. "You got a head on you as long as a stovepipe." She turned back into the kitchen; passing through the door she said, "I got no use for no gold box." We could hear her muttering to herself in the kitchen.

"We'd better start packing, Helen," Junior said. "We'll never get done."

"What about those sterling spoons?" Sully said.

"Oh, shut up, Sully," Junior said as she moved to the corner cupboard.

"It's all right," Helen said. "*I* know all about the spoons."

"Oh, boy," Sully said. "That's a relief." She observed them with a faint sour smile as they opened the cupboard.

"Let's start with the crystal," Helen said, reaching for one of a group of tall stemmed goblets. "What do you remember about these, Junior?"

Sully looked at me, her smile spreading. She raised her eyes to the ceiling and rolled them around.

"Why, Helen," Junior said. "Mother gave those to you."

Helen clapped her cheek in surprise. "Oh, Lord, of course she did. I'd forgotten all about it. That was years ago when she and Elizabeth made a trip to Baltimore. That was before Carolyn was born."

Sully snorted. "They're Elizabeth's," she said. "Little Harlan, those glasses belong to your mother."

"Oh, no," Junior said, smiling, "I distinctly remember that Mother picked these out for Helen to have, I remember exactly what she—"

Sully rocked the table with a slam of her fist. Heirlooms rattled dangerously together. "They were never Mother's!" she shouted. The vein in her neck swelled and pulsed and the thin strings of mucles stood out in sharp relief. "They've always been Elizabeth's! She bought them, paid for them; she just let Mother *use* them. If you remember so goddamn much about the trip to Baltimore, you will remember *I* was there." Sully glared at her sisters, her face going red.

"Don't you use that kind of language around *me*," Junior said. "I told you before. I'm shocked that you can talk like that with Mother not even in—"

"Oh, of *course*," Helen said, reaching out to replace the goblet and taking a glass from another set of crystal. "It was *these*. How stupid of us, Young Irene. But like I said, it was way before Carolyn was even born."

Sully stomped to the door. She whirled and said, "What relation do you bitches think the rest of us were to her?" She ran up the stairs.

"I'm going to Detroit," Helen said, starting for the door as if she were going to walk there holding the glass all the way. "I'm going right now. What's the first flight out of here?"

"You can't go, Helen," Junior said. "We haven't buried Mother yet."

Helen sat down. "Harlan, what's the first flight out of here after the funeral? I can't stand one more minute of this than is absolutely necessary. I'm not strong like Young Irene. Roy and

Carolyn have a flight right after the funeral; I'll leave with them." She sat perched on the edge of her chair, staring at the glass still suspended in front of her, a few inches above the gleam of mahogany.

"Let's pack your glasses," Junior said quietly. In silence they began wrapping the second set of glasses in newspaper, packed them into a box.

"What was she doing poking around in my suitcase?" Junior said. "What right has she got?"

"She was looking for her—for Carolyn's brooch," Helen said.

"Did you notice how Tiny wouldn't take that gold-plated box? Do you know why? Because she thinks if she doesn't take anything else, we'll have to give her that house she never even paid rent on." Helen did not reply and no one spoke for a time while they continued wrapping the glasses. There were at least two dozen.

Then Junior said in a low voice, "Mother told me not to tell anyone this, but I think it's time you knew. Do you know why she was in Baltimore when they went up there?"

"Why?" Helen asked, her voice pitched to Junior's.

"They went to get *her*. Mother and Elizabeth went to get her away from that sailor's she's *supposed* to have married. They annulled it because she was only fifteen, too young to get married without Mother and Poppy's permission. So it was never legal, so she was never married at all, she was living in sin."

"The hussy," Helen said with satisfaction.

"I don't see what all those men have seen in her," Junior said. "They won't see much anymore. She looks like a ghost. She figures just because she was married to those two at one time before, it's all right to live with them now. Both at once, can you *imagine?* I guess she thinks that because she lives in California she can do anything she wants to. I'm telling you, anybody can see she needs to go back to that place until she gets well. If she ever can."

They were each wrapping a last glass, and my mother came into the room. "Oh, those are my glasses," she said. "I bought them in Baltimore years ago when I got those tall stemmed goblets."

Junior opened and shut her mouth; she and her sister looked at one another and wordlessly they began to unwrap the crystal.

My mother pointed her finger outside. She went to the door

and opened it and looked back. The fresh springlike air stirred in the room. I watched Junior and Helen unwrapping the glasses. My mother beckoned again with a crooked finger and she tilted her head. I followed her outside and around to the back of the house. We stood under the dogwoods, away from the porch. No one could hear us there. The dogwood trees were older than the house, their trunks bigger than my waist. Their branches cast patterns like puzzles on the grass.

"I wanted to see what they're going to give Tiny," I said.

"A one-way bus ticket, if she's lucky," my mother said. "Do you know what's happened? Did your father tell you?"

"No," I said.

"He went to make sure about it, but I'm sure," she said. She plucked one of the fat gray buds ringed with purple, dormant and dead-looking but fat with the promise of new life in spring. She rolled it between her thumb and middle finger, shredding off the outer scales. "It's incredible," she said. "I've got to tell somebody." The undefined mass of whitish green came apart and she dropped the bud. She looked past the trees that separated Clifton Park from the little valley. She was shaking her head. "Junior stole thirty thousand dollars."

"What?"

"That's right," she said.

"Junior? *Junior?* Where? What did she do, hold up a bank?"

"She took the mortgage for her house out of your grandfather's lockbox."

"What was her mortgage doing in there?"

"Didn't you know he loaned her the money to buy it with? When that idiot Colson she married left her, Jackson bought the house for her."

"Good God, I can't remember when she didn't have that house. That must have been at least twenty years ago. How much did a house cost twenty years ago?"

"Damn few of them cost thirty thousand dollars," she said. "She didn't pay back a nickel of it. Jackson told her she didn't have to, it would just be taken out of her share of the inheritance when he died. So she stole the note when she started handling the estate for Irene. As soon as they signed over power of attorney to her, she lifted that note. She knew she wouldn't get very much when Jackson dies unless she did take it."

"How do you know this? How did you find out?"

"Your father's not sure of it. He went to check the lockbox and check with the lawyer. What happened was, he went to Dick Stanley's Jewel Box to see about selling Sully's brooch for her and putting the money in trust. Junior's right about her pawning it, whatever her motives about it are."

"For Christ's sake, it's hers; why can't she wear it or pawn it or do whatever she wants to with it."

"For one thing, your father can't keep shelling out money to her every few months. But I admit I kind of side with you."

"I'm not on any side, I just—"

"But I'm just holding it for safekeeping. It's not mine to give or keep. I wish I could pass it on to someone else to worry about."

"Well. So what did going to Dick Stanley's have to do with Junior stealing thirty thousand dollars?"

"Nothing. Your father didn't even see him. But his daughter Rose was there; she manages the place for him now. She started hanging around there as a little girl, she was there when Junior worked there."

"Junior? I didn't know Junior ever worked anywhere."

"She didn't work there long. They caught her stealing."

"No," I said.

"Yes, she took jewelry and cash. At least they thought it was her that took the jewelry after they found out she had skimmed five thousand dollars in three months."

"Jesus Christ," I said.

"They just told her that they knew, and they never told anybody else. They didn't even try to get the money back. Dick didn't want to embarrass your father. I think maybe he dated Junior in college, too. But I'm not sure about that; she's older than I am, of course."

"Of course," I said. "This is incredible. I can't imagine Junior doing anything like this."

"You've seen what they're doing in there."

"But outright theft is different. Even the embezzlement is different from taking the mortgage note. It's hard to see Junior doing anything like that; she's inherited the Greenfields complex, the magnolia syndrome, from Irene."

"Just the outward show of it. And the outward show is just money and talk. You've got to realize that the Colson fellow had just left her and she had three kids to raise, and Dolly was born after he left."

"I can remember that. But Poppy gave her money."

"Anytime he gave anybody money he had a death squeeze on them. And do you know what he did to her? I just found out today. Your father's known about it all along. In the note your grandfather stipulated that she would have to start making payments on the house if she ever got married, and would have to pay back the money he gave her every month. That's why she never remarried."

"You always said it because nobody would marry her."

"Well, that's true too. Sully had already been married three times by then. Counting the one they annulled. I guess your grandfather didn't want Junior getting married every few months too. One in the family was enough. Of course Junior wouldn't have. Sully had more than extraordinary beauty; she could make men do whatever she wanted to. Junior couldn't have found six men fool enough to marry her."

"Do you know for *sure* she took that note?"

"Your father already asked her about it. She said she didn't remember seeing it in the lockbox. That was a mistake, not that it would matter; the lawyer has a list of every document that's supposed to be in there. That's where your father's gone now, back to the lawyer's office to check the list. And Junior has already admitted by omission that at one time, at least, there was a note. Your father asked her because he wanted to wait to check everything to give her long enough to put it back, and then everything would be smoothed over. . . . I thought that was dense; and your father's not usually dense. This whole thing has him all confused."

"It seems like a good idea to me, too."

"Don't you see? If he lets her put it back, he won't be able to stop her from being trustee. And executrix, when Jackson dies. I argued with him about it for half an hour. She could raid the estate and leave nothing but bad memories."

"She wouldn't do that."

"Harlan, she just stole thirty thousand dollars from it; she embezzled five thousand and who knows how much jewelry. I finally convinced your father he better do something about it. I guess Sully overheard us; that must be how she found out about it."

"Oh, no," I said. "Don't tell me Sully knows."

"I'm not sure how much she knows, but she knows something."

We both looked at one another, both thinking the same thing. I said it first. "I wonder why she hasn't said anything. She could shut Junior up for good."

"I don't know," my mother said. "But I think she's planning something. She's in this situation with those two men, and it's driving her crazy. She's talking about Herman, which means she's about to ask for money again. Maybe she wants to borrow it against her inheritance, I don't know. I think the worst part—"

"Good God! I haven't heard the worst? There's more?"

"The worst part is your grandfather putting that condition to the mortgage about Junior remarrying. That's too mean even for him. Your grandmother must have thought that up. Thank God you take after my family and not this one. As Irene would have said, you don't have a drop of Perrin blood in you. And thank God for that."

"Blood is blood," I said. "And now she doesn't have any, either."

My mother shivered. "Please don't be so particular. I just saw her. Junior is left in a terrible position, which is why she's done this thing. She's been supported most of her life by your grandfather, and now all of a sudden she's losing that, and her house being deducted from her share of the inheritance would leave her very little to live on. She'll have to sell the house, and even then, she'll have less than eight thousand a year to live on. That doesn't fit with her Greenfields complex, as you call it. She can't imagine living on that kind of money; I can't either, for that matter. She's scared. That's why she's gobbling up all the furniture in there, to sell it. Well, not all of it; she's leaving the junk for Helen. The way she's carrying on in there, not even Junior's that bad." She reflected for a moment. "Well, maybe she is. Maybe she would be doing it anyway."

"She's parceling out a good deal of it to Helen, it seems."

"She's fooling Helen. Helen wouldn't know Queen Anne from modern Danish. She's lived her whole adult life in Detroit."

"Is anything else missing from the lockbox?"

"Your father doesn't think so, but he's checking everything. Did you know you have a note in there?"

"No, me?"

She nodded and smiled. "It's for four dollars and something. For some flowers for Jane Allman."

"It's not valid," I said. "I never signed it."

"It doesn't matter anyway. You're not in his will, so you've got nothing to lose."

Chapter 5 _____

LATE IN THE AFTERNOON relatives began taking over the house. Helen and Junior drove to the airport to fetch Helen's husband, Roy, and my cousin Carolyn. Sully and I were sitting again on the back porch, although shadows instead of sunlight fell in slanted columns across the screen, and the air was growing chill. Junior's two sons came up the steps in single file, their faces blank and morose, their bodies seeming to float pudgily around an inner core itself soft and yielding. During the summer I had spent at my grandparents' house, Junior had brought them over every day and left them there to play with Peanut and me. Richard and Hollis spent their days with us sitting on the couch in the living room, breathing. They watched television when one of them summoned enough energy to rise up and walk over to the set and turn it on. Sully and Peanut and I spent all our time outside working on our project, an elaborate apartment house for purple martins. Sully disappeared in the afternoons and Peanut and I would try to get Richard and Hollis to go down to the playground with us to play basketball. They never went; it was either too hot, or it looked like rain, or "Lassie" was coming on television, or one of them had on new shoes. My grandmother, looking haughtily down at me and Peanut, kept telling Sully that Richard and Hollis were the best children she had ever seen. She said she never even had to tell them to wash their hands.

"That's because they never get them dirty," Sully said. "They sit around like little statues."

"So much the better. Cleanliness is next to godliness; and next to cleanliness comes quiet children."

Because they spent all their time on the living-room couch, Richard and Hollis found out where Sully was disappearing to in the afternoons. They heard her telephone conversations in the den when she forgot to close the door. One day with feigned innocence they asked their mother why Sully went to a married man's house every afternoon, was she his maid? A white maid? And Junior told my grandmother, and my summer and Sully's life fell apart.

My grandmother's outrage whitened her face. She made certain we would be present when she confronted Sully, and she glared down at Peanut as if it was his fault.

Sully could not say much with us there. "He's not married, he's separated," she said.

They sent us to bed early. Peanut, confused and frightened, managed to escape quickly into sleep; I could not keep my eyes closed. After a while, I crept through the cool dark and cracked the door open and slipped back into bed. Their voices came up the stairs. "If you ever want to see another nickel of your father's money you'll do exactly as I tell you," my grandmother said. "Isn't that right, Beau?"

"You can't do this to me." I could barely hear Sully.

"You'll sign these papers relinquishing custody and pack that boy off to his father and in September he's going to the school in Switzerland and he flies straight there without stopping to see you."

"He's a terrible father! He doesn't even like him, he never has."

"No wonder. How does he know whose son it is?"

"He beats him. He beats him." Sully sounded as if she was trying not to cry.

"A boy needs a good whipping every once in a while," my grandfather said. "Especially one like him."

"You get to see him at Christmas and two weeks in the summer. Don't talk to me about how bad a father he is, after the way you've been carrying on. Right under my nose! It's the most disgusting thing I ever heard of in my life. You don't have a drop of Perrin blood in you."

The old man snorted. "Blood is blood," he said, "but don't blame her on me."

"Your plane leaves at seven in the morning," my grandmother said.

"Poppy," Sully said.

76

"What?" His voice rose into the room, harsh and cold and intolerant; he already knew what she would say.

Sully sounded as if she was about to choke on her low words. "I need the money now. I've got to have it right away."

"What for?"

I couldn't hear her reply.

"To live on?" the old man roared. "To live on? People work."

"Just enough to get by on for a while."

There was a long silence. "How much do you need?" he said at last.

"I don't know, exactly."

"Don't know, exactly. That's some way to run your life. Don't know exactly. Well, you figure it out. You figure out how much you need to the penny, item by item, then we'll talk about you getting it. And you're going to have to send me receipts for every nickel you spend."

"How can I do that?"

"If you want any money, you'll figure a way to do it. Are you going to send receipts, or not?"

Again there was silence, and I strained to hear.

"Speak up, girl," Poppy said. "I can't hear you."

"Yes."

"And don't go getting the notion you can take the money and disappear with Peanut. You'll be gone before he wakes up, and you won't get any more money in the mail until I hear from his father. You understand me?"

Soon I heard Sully's footsteps on the stairs. She softly entered our room and went to Peanut's bed. She stood still for a long time. He was asleep on his back, his mouth parted slightly; the dim, milky moonlight fell in a square through the window on his chest and face. I watched her white gauzy form listen to him breathe in sleep. She knelt beside him and bent to his face. She took his hand and pressed the back of it against her cheek. He did not stir. She was crying. Her back was shaking. She sounded like she had hiccups.

"Sweet angel child," she whispered. "My pet, my joy."

I looked at their faces lit by the faint moonlight, blurs of white in the dark, their features unclear but easily visible, her face anguished and almost unrecognizable, his calm and serene in repose. "Oh, God," she whispered. "Oh sweet Jesus let me die."

Richard and Hollis walked across the porch, still single file. Hollis went to a chair and dropped in it as if he had not sat for a week. He worked in a bank.

"Hey, y'all," Sully said. "How in the world are you? Where's Dolly?"

"School," Hollis said. His brother Richard stopped beside him, looking around with puzzlement. His puffy eyes squinted as he looked for a chair. There was another chair at the opposite end of the table, but it made Richard nervous to be so widely separated from Hollis. He sat instead on the table, looking blankly out to the patch of woods beyond the back lawn.

"What are you doing these days, Richard?" Sully said.

"Nothing much," he said. He looked down at Hollis to see if he had said the right thing, but Hollis was looking at the woods too.

"It's tough to find a job these days, I know," Sully said. "How's things at the bank, Hollis?"

"Fine."

"Are you vice-president yet?"

"No ma'am."

"Well, I guess you'll be vice-president someday," Sully said.

"I guess so," he said. "Is Mama over here?"

"She went with Aunt Helen to get Uncle Roy and Carolyn," I said.

"Oh," he said. He stood up. "Well, I guess I'll go on inside." Richard slipped from the table and followed him. They went through the kitchen and I watched them through the window, moving slowly and morosely, still in single file.

"Vice-president," Sully said when they were gone. "Fat chance." The sun had fallen behind the trees and houses and in the fading light coming from behind her head Sully's bleached or tinted hair, almost white, shone like moonlight, brighter than her face. "Don't tell them Tiny left food in the refrigerator before she left, or none of the rest of us will get any supper." She leaned forward suddenly. "Don't they have anything to drink around here, Little Harlan?"

"I don't think so," I said.

"If George was like either of those, I'd take him out somewhere and shoot him, I swear I would," she said in her thin nasal drawl. She looked out on the lawn. "I wonder where the little mockingbird sleeps. Do you think he sleeps in a nest?"

"He probably roosts. I don't know."

"Do you know Pea—George has got his doctor's? His doctorate, or whatever. Did you know that?"

"Yes."

"Can you believe it? You know how smart he always was. And he was working for the government. Some very hush-hush stuff about some kind of secret things. Atomic things, or poisons, or something. I never did get it straight. Anyway, he quit, and the government simply doesn't know *what* it's going to do without him."

"I didn't know he had been working for the government."

"I didn't tell you? It must have been Elizabeth I told. Well, George quit because he didn't want to work with anything destructive. Don't you think that's *wonderful?* He had this very high-paying important job, making absolutely gobs of money, and he told the government to take it and stuff it." She reclined back deep into the lounge chair. "God, I wish I had a drink. I'd be fine, if I could just have one drink. So George went to live in the commune. I told you all about that. He's looking for a job that doesn't have anything to do with killing people. I think that's a good idea, don't you?"

"It sounds like a very good idea."

"I told him I thought it was. We're very close, you know. He writes to me, and everything." She fumbled in her pocketbook on the floor. "I've got a letter in here somewhere that he wrote me. He writes me all the sweetest things." She waved the folded paper at me, smiling. "See? He writes to me all the time." She put the letter back. "Are you going to stick around for The Miseries?"

"The miseries?"

"You know, when all these people that didn't know Mother come filing through to pretend like they did, and cry on everybody."

"I guess I'll stay for a while."

"I don't blame you for going out. Where is it you're going again?"

"The Pickwick. It's a bar."

"Oh, yeah, I heard of that place. Bunch of artists and writers, right? I love places like that. I'd fit right in, wouldn't I? Because I used to be an artist. But I guess it wouldn't look too good if her own daughter went out to a bar the night before her funeral, would it?"

"Maybe not."

"I think it's fine for you to get out. Have a drink for me while you're there."

"I'll have to have a beer for you. We're in North Carolina."

"Oh, yeah, I forgot what a backward state we're in. I don't feel like I'm in civilization in a place where you can't go to a bar and have a drink. Listen!" she said, sitting suddenly up again. "How about bringing me a couple of beers back with you? Since it's just beer, maybe you better make it three."

"Are you supposed to drink with all that medicine you're taking?"

She grinned, her small, perfect, white teeth whiter than her bleached platinum hair. "Of course not," she said. "It's fun, do you think they'd let me drink, when it's fun?"

"All right," I said. "I'll bring you a couple."

"God knows I'm going to need it after tonight. Junior found all the old photograph albums, and she's going to have a show when everybody comes over for The Miseries. What an incredible idea! Could you bring maybe three or four beers?"

"Don't you think maybe a couple would do for tonight? We'll probably all be up early tomorrow."

"I guess you're right," she said. She signed. "Well, you and Sarah are the only niece and nephew worth a damn. You think I shouldn't have more than two, that's what I'll have. Listen, I absolutely *adore* Sarah's paintings. I think it's wonderful she went to Europe to study art. You know what Junior said? She said she couldn't understand why anyone would go study when they'd already finished school, when they weren't even *in* school anymore." Sully suddenly burst into laughter, rocking back and forth. "Oh, Lord, do you remember when Junior and Mother and Tiny went to Sarah's opening? Tiny had drunk enough liquor to founder a mule."

"Yes," I said.

It had been the work she did for her Master's degree. Irene and Junior went together, and I picked up Tiny and took her there. The

80

paintings were all abstract expressionist, and neither Junior nor Irene had the faintest notion what to do or say. The School of the Arts was supported by many wealthy people, and the graduation shows each year were fancy, swarming with elaborate aristocracies. My grandmother was embarrassed enough that my sister painted something besides flowers or faces; when Tiny came in she almost died. Everyone there knew my grandmother and knew very well who Tiny was. Tiny was drunk. She rolled around from picture to picture and my grandmother tried in the small gallery to stay away from her and pretend she did not know her. Tiny kept trying to catch up to her. She was as amazed as my grandmother was at the paintings; she had probably never seen a nonrepresentational painting. She would try to scurry up to my grandmother, Irene moving constantly away, and then she would stop in front of a painting, weaving back and forth. "My, my," she would say, wide-eyed, almost falling down. Junior escaped, but my grandmother could not; she was one of the patrons, and her granddaughter one of the exhibitors. Tiny chased after her, stopping to say "My, my," at each one, until Sully came in and pulled her out of the gallery and took her home.

"Poor Tiny passed out on the way to her house," Sully said. "I never have figured out why you let her go." She giggled. "But I'm glad you did, it was a riot."

"I couldn't tell her what to do," I said. "She never would have forgiven me if I'd tried to stop her from seeing Sarah's show."

"Good grief, they're back!" Sully said. We could hear them all coming in the front door. Sully spoke in a husky whisper. "Listen, Harlan, do you know what the hell is going on around here?"

"I'm not real sure about it."

"Neither am I, but something sure as hell is. I know your father's not going to let Junior be trustee."

"I heard something about that."

"She thinks I've been kicking up a fuss about my brooch. She doesn't know what a fuss is until she sees me get that brooch from her. Just wait until the funeral's over. I'll be damned if I'll hover like a vulture over the furniture, but just wait if I don't get my brooch. I know I can count on *you*. Do you know what that bitch said to me this afternoon?"

"What?"

"She said she didn't see why Sarah's not here for the funeral. Can't see why she can't just up*root* herself from Florence and fly over here for one day. For Christ's sake. It looks like her own daughter won't even make it from sixty miles away. Probably Junior wouldn't fork over the five bucks for bus fare."

"I'm sure Dolly will be here."

"Oh, yeah," Sully said. "I forgot—she likes parties."

"I guess we should go inside now. People will start coming over soon."

"Yes, and it's getting dark. I can't stand to be in the dark."

She stood and hesitated for a moment, balancing herself on her high-heeled gold-colored sandals before she started walking. We went through the kitchen and down the hallway to the larger central hall that paralleled the stairs. We turned right to go to the living room. Sully made a face at herself in the mirror that hung there, a mirror that had a name: Harrison's Revenge. We could hear people buzzing in the living room and Sully whirled suddenly, almost falling. "God, not yet, not yet; let's sit in the den for a while so I can work up to it."

Sully entered first and turned on the light. "Boy, this brings back memories," she said. She sat on a sofa upon which hounds stilled forever in motion chased one rabbit while another rabbit—which in childhood I always imagined to be brother of the first—crouched in a posture of absolute fear, looking up at the bellies of two hounds pouring heedlessly over him. The scene was repeated in squares over and over on the sofa, like a recurring nightmare. I took the chair my grandfather had always used: a wooden chair, simple and elegant in design, the back a curve filled with spokes. His grandfather paid a country carpenter to make it in the eighteenth century, and it glowed with generations of use. When my grandfather retired, he retired to the room, and particularly to the chair.

"This room gives me the heebie-jeebies," Sully said. "Whenever I needed a little loan, he brought me in here and held court."

Before he had retired he had used the room to work in, and after retirement to pretend to work. When I was very young, I would drift toward the room when Tiny was too busy for me. Besides daydreaming about the hounds and rabbits, the only entertainment in the house was listening to the old man answer the telephone, although it was a risky occupation. I watched him work while I waited for the phone to ring. After a minute he would notice I was there, and he would look up and say, "Well, you'll have to be quiet if you're going to come in here." He sat in my great-great-grandfather's chair, and I would sit across from him on the sofa, very still, tucking my feet hard against the sofa, since they did not touch the floor and I needed the contact to remind myself not to swing them. I watched him as he worked, the cigar on the table beside him, balanced on the ashtray, the smoke rising in a straight silver ribbon. I waited for the telephone to ring while he bent to his papers, a pencil poised over the sheaf as his eyes ran over the figures like they were looking for targets to pin wriggling against the sheet. His eyes were set deep and wide in his face and when they looked up at me from his work I could not look away. He would look into my eyes, holding my gaze, looking deep inside like he saw dirt all the way through me on the back of my neck. "Quit that fidgeting!" I would hold my breath and lock my feet against the sofa even harder, feeling them prickle under the pressure. His lips were full and wide and sharply defined; as though they had been carved out of wood and inlaid in his face. His hair was streaked with silver and brushed straight back on his head, brightening his eyes. After a few more moments he would look up again. "Can't you quit that fidgeting?"

"I haven't moved."

"Don't talk back, it's rude. You was *thinking* of moving, anyhow."

"I—"

"I said don't sass me, boy! I got eyes all over my skin, I can see everything you think."

"But—"

"Scurrying around here like a little rat. Go tell somebody they want to see you. Go on, go, go."

Sometimes the telephone rang before he ran me out, and he would glare at it so hard I almost felt sorry for it, although I was glad he wasn't glaring at me. He would let it ring several times, leveling his malevolent gaze at it before he snatched it off the hook and yelled into it, "All right!" Poppy was a grown man the first time he used a telephone, and he never overcame his suspicion that it was somehow a dangerous instrument. When he conversed on it he always yelled, as though his voice were being carried through a hollow tube, and the farther off the caller, the louder he needed to yell.

After he retired he did not run me out of the room; he desperately encouraged anyone's visits. He retired the first year I was in college, and I came to visit frequently. During that first year, he roamed the house, slapping his hands together. "Free at last!" he would exclaim. "I can do anything I want. Let's you and me go to a ball game tomorrow."

"I've got to go back to Johnston after lunch." Somehow I usually managed to arrive at lunchtime.

"Well, maybe next week," he would say. "I've got some business to attend to anyhow." They made him retire because on his way to work one morning he fell asleep at the wheel of his car and woke up late in the afternoon, still at the wheel, the car out of gas in the middle of a cornfield.

We would sit down to lunch and the old man would turn on the television to watch reruns of the old Groucho Marx program. He sat at the head of the table and from there he could see the television in the living room. He turned it up loud so that he could hear it, but not loudly enough for Irene to hear it. Groucho didn't know it, but he and the old man were having a contest.

"You don't *look* married," Groucho said to the couple.

"They ought to go somewhere and practice," the old man said.

"Would you like to go backstage for a while and come back after you've had a little practice?" Groucho said, his eyebrows going.

"Ha!" the old man said, hunched over his plate, shoveling in lace cornbread. "Did you hear that? I said what he said, only I said it first."

The young woman was an amateur singer trying to become professional. She asked Groucho if he could sing.

"I used to be a pretty good singer before *tunes* come in fashion," the old man said.

"Certainly I can," Groucho said. "You've heard bullfrogs sing, haven't you?"

"See?" the old man said. "What I said was ten times funnier than what he said. Ed Sullivan ought to come snatch me right out of this chair." The old man never took his eyes from the set, unless there was some food on the table he wanted. Then he would stare at the serving dish without speaking or moving until Irene noticed him.

"What is it you want, Beau?"

He would not answer; if she did not guess, he would lean forward and glare harder at the food or salt, or whatever it was he wanted. "Beau, what *is* it?"

No answer.

"Tiny, Mr. Jackson needs something," my grandmother would call.

Tiny would come from the kitchen, stand looking at him with arms akimbo. "He want the coleslaw," she would say, or the pickles or salt or corn bread; she could always tell.

Then my grandmother would pass it to him and he would take it without saying a word and Tiny would go back into the kitchen until she was called back later to figure out the next item when he began glaring again. This behavior began in the second year of his retirement.

By the end of that second year, Poppy had deteriorated to a considerable degree, and at the same time, barriers fell, and the latent hostility between my grandparents began to emerge openly. That Christmas Poppy gave Irene an envelope, containing $8.16 in cash; he would say nothing about it, and she fumed and then exploded. He refused to open her present to him, and she grew angrier still. She began going out more than before to bridge parties and club meetings; the old man followed her on occasion, and when he did not he called her every few minutes to find out when she would be coming home.

One day as he followed her down the sidewalk, she turned and snapped at him, "Stop following me!"

He stomped his foot and began to cry. "I'm not going one more step until you tell me why you treat me like a fool!" he yelled.

During the third year, the old man would always be in the den when I arrived; he could no longer keep up with Groucho; he aged, and Groucho in reruns stayed always the same. I would go into the den and watch him working in his grandfather's chair, both of us remembering in our own ways earlier times. Sometimes he would be balancing his checkbook for a month in, say, nineteen twenty-eight, and sometimes it might be accounts receivable for nineteen fifty-two. He wore wire-rimmed reading glasses with thick lenses that would have softened his eyes even without their aging; his hair was completely and brilliantly white, but still brushed straight back on his head. He looked up when I entered. "I'm glad you're here. I can't seem to get this thing straight." And he would bend over the papers or checkbook or ledger, squinting as if the whole problem were merely one of poor vision. "Can you make heads or tails out of this?"

"I don't know anything about it."

"Well, what good are you, then. Go on and eat lunch."

"You come too."

"I got to figure this thing out. Why can't folks around here understand I'm a busy man?"

During the fourth year, Irene could not take the cold air of the house anymore. It was as though her own blood and body temperature had once matched the temperature around her, like a reptile, but now, slowly metamorphosizing into a warm-blooded creature, she noticed the slightest change in temperature and could not bear it. Or so it seemed to me then; perhaps it was the first symptom, not uncommon among cancer patients, of the malignant cells that ate away her flesh and life.

For Irene the little bits of coal that had been introduced a few years earlier to replace the revolving plastic logs were no longer enough, and she and the old man began a running battle over the thermostat. They never spoke of it to one another, but it continued day and night without cease, and was a constant source of ill feeling between them. Because the old man was so rapidly failing, she usually had the upper hand, but when the old man sneaked a change in the setting without detection, he would gloat for days.

Most of the time, though, he was in the den all day, every day, even at night, smoking his cigar and going over and over the old figures with greater and greater urgency. He had every business receipt since the days when he lost his first fortune, a whole bedroom upstairs full of them crammed into drawers, under the bed, in the closets.

He woke up in the middle of the night to worry over the figures, going downstairs in his robe and pajamas to work on them. He fell asleep there in the wooden chair. He fell asleep during the day, too. His license had been taken away after Irene found the bumper to his car in the backseat. He said a man with a straw hat had given it to him, he didn't know why; but immediately a policeman appeared at the door with a dozen citations, including one for driving on the wrong side of the road for a mile and a half, and the news that the tickets would be served if he did not relinquish his license that day. So he had nowhere to go outside of the den, and when I arrived there during lunchtime his head would be on his chest; he would start when I walked in. "I think I've got it." He would raise his head and go over the papers, his pencil poised to strike. "Well, where was it?" he would say, petulant and irritated. "I had the durn thing a minute ago. I was just about to figure it out."

He would look up at me, glaring, his blue eyes still clear, with the glasses raised to his forehead, but anyone could have looked away from his gaze. "You made me lose my place."

Once when he fell asleep the cigar fell and set the rug on fire. Tiny smelled the smoke and ran to the den and back to the kitchen and back again to the den with a bucket of water. She sloshed it over the smoldering carpet. The old man awoke. "Here, here," he said, "you can't wash in here now. I got work to do."

"You sit like he did," Sully said. "You sit up straight as a board and cross your legs the same way and hang your arm by the table, ready to bash the phone to pieces if you don't like the way it rings. Just like he did."

"I was thinking of him."

"Me too. I was remembering his goddamn *in*quisitions whenever I needed a little loan for a little while. Listen, I think I want to go see him the next time y'all go, all right?"

"Sure."

"If I can take it. I think it's terrible Junior never has gone to see him, don't you?"

"Well, she has her opinions."

"Boy, does she ever." She leaned toward me, conspiratorial, her eyes at once vague with fatigue and throwing off a slight gleam, brightened with anger. "Have you heard them talking in there? Junior's running on about how hard she's worked these last eight months."

"It hasn't been easy, taking care of your mother."

"I'll have to admit the bitch loved Mother. No harder than loving herself. The trouble is, she thinks she's the only one who did love her. She acts like she was an only child." Sully weaved in the sofa, her words slurred as though she were slightly drunk. "She ought to go to a brain surgeon and get the inside of her head redone. Only it wouldn't do any good. The best surgeon in the world's got to have something to work with."

We sat in silence for a time. Sully studied her parents' wedding picture. Irene, youthful in the photograph, had a sort of harsh beauty, like a bust carved in marble, smooth and hard, her high cheekbones shining. Her eyes looked like they never closed. Her nose was an exclamation point in her face: long and thin, a classic nose, but marred by a slight bulge at the end, the dot below the exclamation point. Her hair appeared to hold up her face, so tightly was it pulled back into a bun. In the photograph, her wedding portrait, she held the disapproving pose—chin high, looking down her nose as though aiming at my grandfather, who was smiling, young, and cheerful.

"Listen to them in there," Sully said. "Of *course* it's a sad time, everyone knows that. Why does she have to make it sound like a national emergency that's happening to her? Harlan, what am I going to do?"

"We'll have to go in there in a few minutes. You'll just have to grin and bear it."

"I mean about Herman coming."

"Herman? He's coming here?"

"If he doesn't, I'll never get out from under that bastard George."

"Well. I don't know how Herman is going to fit in around here, but if that's what you have to do, go ahead and do it."

"But if he *does* come, which I'm sure he's on the way, George is going to kick me out."

"But if you want to get out from under George—"

"If I don't have a job for Herman, he'll be gone in an hour."

"Maybe he shouldn't come."

"But then how will I get away from George? George is driving me to an early grave. That son of a bitch is strangling me to death."

"Maybe you should just leave both of them."

"And then what? Then what the hell am I going to do?"

"I don't know."

"I don't either. Except I've always wanted to open a restaurant. I'm a terrific cook, did you know that? Hey! I'll bet your

88

father would lend me the money to open up a restaurant, don't you?"

"I don't know."

"Boy, this would be great!" She struggled forward off the back pillows of the sofa, her face suddenly alight. "You know what I would have for my main specialty? This fabulous mussels and pecan dish I invented. I'll get some tomorrow and you tell me if you think it would make a restaurant go. Boy, would it ever!"

"I don't think my father would put up that kind of money."

She thought for a moment, still excited, and then her face drained empty and sad again. "Christ, I can't do anything." She looked like she was about to cry. Suddenly she stood and tottered against the telephone table. She picked up the phone and dialed. She listened for a long time. "That little queer! He probably got on the bus and couldn't find his way off. Maybe he and George are— Hel*lo*, George, sweetheart, I just called to see how—" Her face went suddenly white and she sat beside me on the arm of my great-great-grandfather's chair. "What?" She listened again. "What do you mean? . . . I didn't, I swear I didn't. . . . George! George, wait! . . . Listen, you just— I did not, you son of a bitch! . . . Wait, George." Her voice grew suddenly weak and plaintive. "George, I promise you."

She listened for a moment longer and looked at me, her eyes full of terror. "He hung up," she said, surprised, almost whispering. She dropped the phone into my hand and walked back to the sofa, fell into it. I hung the phone up. "You know what that son of a bitch did? He told George he was coming here. He told him I asked him to! I told him not to breathe a word, I knew this would happen, I knew it." She covered her face with her hands. "Herman told him we were getting married again. That son of a bitch knew exactly what would happen."

"I don't really understand this."

"Oh, George hates for me to be near him unless he's there. He loves it when he *is* there, twisting the knife in poor Herman's gut. Poor Herman, my ass! That son of a bitch!" she yelled. She stood up, her fist clenched, and fell immediately back into the sofa.

My mother came in. "Sully," she said. "There are visitors out there. Are you all right?"

"Oh, Jesus, I hope so," Sully said low and hopelessly. "If this doesn't work out, I'm dead, oh, my God, what have I done."

"What in the world is the matter?"

"He's trying to force me in a corner."

My mother looked at me, bewildered. "Who is?"

"Herman. As soon as you get a few wrinkles they treat you like dirt." Sully had calmed and quieted herself, but the arm she was leaning on shook.

"Is there anything I can do?" my mother said.

"Can you make wrinkles disappear?" Then she waved her hand and looked again at the wedding picture. "No, Elizabeth, not yet. I guess I can still take care of Herman." And then she smiled, weakly and with sour irony; whether at the portrait or her own words I could not guess.

"Do you feel like coming in now?" My mother leaned over her, wanting to do something.

"Oh, Lord," Sully said. She rolled her eyes to the ceiling. "I guess I have to. Do I look all right?"

Chapter 6 ⎯⎯⎯⎯⎯⎯⎯⎯⎯⎯

THEY WERE SUBDUED AND TALKING QUIETLY, sitting in a wide circle around the living room. Junior wore her black dress and she sat next to Helen on the sofa. Helen's husband Roy and their daughter Carolyn sat on the other side of her. Everyone stopped talking as we entered and then immediately began droning again. The men stood for Sully and we went around the room shaking hands and speaking to people. Sully called every man there "honey," and fluttered her tired eyes at them. She walked as though she were picking her way across ice in her gold sandals.

"How's the boy," Roy said, winking at me. "How's the old football."

"Football?"

He looked down at the top of my head. "Oh, yeah, you're not the one plays football, are you? What is it you play?"

"Mahjong."

"Right!" he said. "So. How's it going?"

"Hello, Carolyn."

"I'm getting married!" she said. "Can you believe it?"

"Here's a picture of Mother when she was state chairman of the U.D.C.," Junior said.

"He's the nephew of the fourth richest man in Idaho!"

"And this one," Junior said, handing another photograph to be passed around, "was taken at a family gathering right here in this very room."

"So you've got to come to my wedding. You will come, won't you?"

My father took me away by the elbow and introduced me to friends of his parents I had somehow never met, and I said hello to the others I had known. Sully and I both circled the room to speak to everyone. People spoke in low voices to their neighbors, casually glancing at the photographs that Junior passed around. Sully sat in the seat Roy had vacated.

"You sweet old thing," she said, blinking her eyes at him. "Letting me have your seat after that *long* trip."

"Been sitting all day."

"Dolly's coming," Carolyn said when I completed my tour. "She's going to be a bridesmaid."

"Now this is a photograph I love," Junior said. "Mother's wedding picture." It was not another copy of the portrait in the den, but one I had never seen, of my grandmother alone in her wedding gown, looking, again, almost pretty, but the severity was already imprinted upon her face. Looking at the photograph, I realized with a shock something that had never occurred to me in years of absent gazing at the wedding portrait in the den: that I was looking at eighteen ninety something, into another world; and the woman in the photograph had sat beside me on the sofa and together we watched men land on the moon. Poppy dozed in another chair. He did not seem to care much about it, which seemed at once odd and understandable. Until his late boyhood, he had never traveled by any mode not available to Moses—a phrase that came from his grandfather. Poppy used to tell me, "My grandpappy always said when he was born it won't no way to go but the way Moses went: foot and mule." Raising his head occasionally as we all watched the dreamlike motions of Neil Armstrong, he said, "The moon! How are they going to get any fool to believe that. Why, look at it, that's Arizona."

"I don't know, Beau," my grandmother said.

"Huh! They ain't fooling me. It's just a show to scare the Russians. If they can go to the moon, where's God? Do you think God would let them fly through Heaven like that?"

"I don't know, Beau," my grandmother said doubtfully.

"Huh. Wake me up when Lawrence Welk comes on."

"It's two A.M.," I said; but he was already asleep.

"Here's a picture of a trip to the mountains. Law, Helen, just look! I was fifteen years old." This photograph, like the others, went from hand to hand around the room. A corner had been snipped off; Sully was not in the picture.

"Let me tell you something, Richard," Roy was saying. "You want to start high up in the business world, go out for some sport in college. I played football."

"I finished last spring."

"If Dolly doesn't hurry up I'm going to absolutely pop. I've got to tell someone about my dress."

Sully was watching the photograph album as Junior flipped through it to choose pictures to pass around. Sully looked more and more glum. I moved closer to see better.

"Here's one of Helen's wedding. Just look at Mother. If she doesn't look like she thinks *she's* the one getting married."

Some photographs she passed over. One of Bald Mary, who, when her husband bounced a four-dollar check, disconsolately shaved her head out of the enormity of her shame, and the hair never grew back. She was never mentioned again in the family, not because it occurred to anyone she might be insane, but from the embarrassment of having a bald woman perched in the family tree: a second cousin. She passed over Olena Marable, a prim, straitlaced, and sweetly puritanical woman who—so Poppy said—employed euphemisms for every part of the human body, going so far as to call a nose the olfactory organ, an ear a hearing mechanism, and so on; at the age of seventy-two she offered the use of her body to the son of the sheriff in Silk Hope for the night, to try to entice him into buying four place settings of Brindle's Genuine Bavarian China so that she could qualify for Brindle's Grand Adventure to Curaçao. She was arrested by the sheriff for prostitution and was never heard of again, as if she had never existed.

Every few minutes someone left, and every few minutes some new people came in. Some did not stay long enough to see a complete circuit of one picture. Someone called to Junior from across the room. "Junior, we haven't seen one of Sully yet. And she was such a beautiful girl."

"Haven't come across one yet," Junior said. And she had not: there was not a single photograph of Sully; there was a portrait of Lafayette, the significance of which few people in the room understood; there was a print from a daguerreotype of Captain Perrin that was made to resemble as closely as possible a photograph; there was a copy of one of the Raleigh copperplates hanging beside the fireplace;

93

but there was no sign of Sully, until Junior picked out one more photograph. "Here's a seated portrait of the children," she said. "A studio portrait." This picture was also cut; but coming from the sharp, new edge of the picture was a wrist and hand, and Helen was holding the disembodied hand in her lap. Junior passed the photograph around and Sully rose and walked to the far corner of the room.

"Look!" Junior said. "Here's one of Muffy in a red sweater. If that isn't the cutest thing."

"Who the hell's Muffy?" Sully muttered to the corner, bringing a momentary, hardly noticeable halt to the conversations.

"Mother's dog, of course," Junior said.

My grandmother had hated dogs all her life. She wanted to buy one for protection. Poppy had almost exploded. "Buy a dog! *Buy* a dog. Whoever heard of buying a dog. I'll go get you one at the pound, you have to have a dog." He came back with the sorriest-looking cur he could find, a yellow animal with its ribs like a washboard under the short coarse fur, limp ears, and a drooping tail. My grandmother fell in love with it instantly and the dog hated her until it ran away. Muffy tolerated Tiny, who yelled, "Git, you rag!" whenever it crossed her path, but when my grandmother fed him, saying, "Here, Muffy, here, my little pet," he would sit on the kitchen floor and pull himself across to her on his haunches, growling and snarling, teeth bared. Irene was scared to death of him, as much as she loved him. She would put the bowl down nervously and he would suffer her one quick pat on the top of his head, and then she had better move and let him eat; between bites he would turn and growl at her, and at the end of the meal he would chase her from the room. One Christmas she gave him a red sweater, and Tiny managed to get it on him. Irene took a picture of it; he went into the backyard and ate it off. Sometimes he would corner her in her chair in the living room when she ran out of tidbits of meat with which she tried to win his affection; then she would stand in the chair and yell for Tiny. When the dog ran away, Irene went to Atlanta on a shopping spree to console herself. "That dratted dog cost me over four hundred dollars!" Poppy said to anyone who would listen. "I could have opened a kennel for that kind of money."

The picture of Muffy completed its tour. The door chimes

rang like church bells and my father opened the door. "Why, if it ain't little Harlan!" a voice boomed. "I'd a knowed you anywheres!" I could not see around the corner.

"That's right," my father said. "Come on in."

He stepped into the hall and although I had never seen him before, I recognized him immediately.

"I'm Silas Mutch Junior," he said, gazing up into my father's eyes like he was in love, pumping his hand up and down. He was dressed in overalls and he wore a wide coat and a tie. He had on shiny black shoes he might have worn at his wedding forty years before, and white socks. "I ain't missed a day of work in my life," he said. "I'm serious."

My father walked him into the crowded room. Silas took off his hat and turned it around and around in his hands. My father introduced him to the people and he bobbed at each person. He spread his legs in a wishbone and dipped his knees each time and he bobbed his head. He grinned a wide warm grin to each person, grinned until the introductions were over. Then his face transformed instantly and took on a grave mask of mourning as he took a short step forward into the middle of the room and sucked in air.

"Now," he said. He looked up. "I just want to say." He studied the floor again. Just when I thought he was not going to say anything, he jerked his head up again. His eyebrows jerked upward, too; it was as though he were attached to them rather than they to his head, and they were pulling him around. Although no one moved, it seemed as though the whole room were leaning toward him. Everyone was listening to his booming voice. "That I come to pay my respects to a fine gentleman. One of the finest it was ever my . . ." Here he studied the floor again, his face screwed up with thought. "Pleasure to know. . . . And now, I would like to observe a moment of silence in his memory."

He looked down to the floor for a full minute, his hat in his clasped hands before him. There was total silence until he raised his head and looked at Junior. "Little Miss Irene," he said, "if you *ain't* the spitting image of your mama. I never had the pleasure to meet her, but I seen her picture a thousand times before your daddy married her. I thought at first you were—" He looked around at my father. "Where *is* Irene?" he said. "Why, I wanted to tell her I come to pay my respects. Did you know we played together back in the long ago when we won't nothing but a couple of little tadpoles." He put his arm on my father's shoulder. "Harlan, I'm might sorry he passed away. You're going to miss him, I know you are."

"Well, he's still alive, Silas," my father said.

"What?" The hat stopped twirling in his hands for a brief moment. "Why, I heard . . ." He stared down at his feet. He turned one foot this way and that, examining it. He turned his head and dropped one shoulder very slightly, his back bent, and looked up at my father from underneath his chin. "You say he's . . . he's still alive."

"That's right," my father said. "It was—"

"Why, that's the best news I heard in a *long* time. But . . . but . . ."

"It was my mother who passed away," my father said gently.

Silas stepped back a couple of paces. He looked hurt. "No!" he said. "That's terrible. I *wish* I'd got here sooner. I been telling your daddy for years, I wanted to come meet his little bride. He told me all about her. I feel like I do know her. Well," he said. He looked at the floor again and shook his head. "Let me say this," he said. "I guess it's just as well I come anyway. I want to pay my respects to one of the finest ladies . . ." He looked down once again and wrinkled up his nose and frowned, studious. He turned to the others again. "To one of the finest ladies it—it was—never my pleasure not to know."

He smiled and bobbed at each person around the room as he walked backward toward the door. He turned to my father and put on his hat. "Well, I reckon I got to be getting on," he said.

"You're not going back to Silk Hope tonight, are you, Silas?" my father said. "It's two hundred miles."

"It don't take long," he said. "That bust moves right along."

"Won't you stay and have some supper with us?"

"No, thanky, I'll get me a snack at the depot. They got—Wait. Hold everything. Where's your daddy?" He looked all around him.

"He's in a home, Silas. Had to put him in a home."

"Why, I know just how he feels. I'm ninety-one, myself. I reckon I got to be getting on. A home? That bust pulls out of here in a half hour."

"Well, it was mighty nice of you to drop by."

"Naturally I come pay my respects. A home, you say." Silas shuffled his feet. "It won't nothing . . ." He shook my father's hand again, pumping it as though he were drawing water from a well. "Y'all come now, you hear?" He backed out the door.

As soon as the door closed behind him, people buzzed together in knots, talking and laughing about Silas. I joined Sully and Roy by the table in the corner. Roy was laughing so hard tears were in his eyes.

"Don't laugh at him," Sully said. "I like him."

"I like him too," Roy said, still laughing. "I can't help it."

"Go get me a piece of celery."

Roy walked away to fetch it. Sully waved her hand at the table. "Welcome to the Mausoleum," she said.

A round white cloth with lace edges was draped over the square table, leaving the corners bare. On each corner sat a porcelain Confederate horseman astride a mount. One across the table was charging us with saber upraised. In the center of the table was a pedestal with miniature flags; highest in the middle the Confederate Stars and Bars, flanked by the State Flag and the American Flag. Flat on the table in front of the flags lay a gray book, its covers faded and scuffed, the gilt gleaming only in traces on the edges of the impressed title and legend, which read: REMINISCENCES OF A CONFEDERATE ARTILLERY OFFICER. Separating the title from the author's name at the bottom—CAPTAIN T. COLES PERRIN—was a design of a drum and two crossed flags, enwreathed by the words FIRST IN FREEDOM, LAST IN BONDAGE, the gold of these rubbed almost entirely away.

My father joined us. He gave Sully a stalk of celery. "Roy said you wanted this."

Sully picked up the Confederate flag and waved it at us, grinning. She held it in front of her chest so that the crowd behind us could not see her.

"Why did she care so much?" I said.

"It formed her," she said.

"But she wasn't even alive."

"One way to look at it is this: it didn't even start until it was over. She was born just a few years after Reconstruction. People hated that more than the war itself. That and the war, particularly the war, was the only topic of conversation for thirty years. Everyone had been in it or touched by it. Your great-grandmother never talked or thought about anything else. Captain Perrin lost his leg, and she never forgave the Yankees for it; neither did your grandmother."

"We grew up with it too," Sully said. "Junior still can't look a Yankee in the face."

"Do you remember when Poppy brought a Yankee to dinner on business?" my father said to Sully. "Maybe you weren't old enough."

"God, you couldn't forget that in a million years," Sully said. "She wouldn't speak to him for a month."

"But his grandfather fought in it," I said.

"He didn't come from a family that lost anything by it: no plantation house, or slaves or indolence. And some people were simply insane about it, and others reasonable. Maybe the women were more bitter because they didn't get to fight in it, and they resented their poverty and loss of material and ease more."

"Men like money just as much as women, honey," Sully said. "You've talked to Herman."

"I don't know when Dolly's going to ever get here," Carolyn said, joining us. "Have I told you about my dress, Aunt Sully?"

I looked at the daguerreotype of Captain Perrin staring down from the wall with bitter almond eyes. Below him on the wall hung a bronze plaque that read IRENE PERRIN JACKSON at the top, and at the bottom in smaller letters, PRESIDENT OF THE UNITED DAUGHTERS OF THE CONFEDERACY, GENERAL BRAXTON BRAGG CHAPTER, 1958–. She had died in office.

On the table two photographs, reproductions new and shining, looked at each other across the gray book like sentinels guarding it. One was Lee, the other Jackson. Smaller portraits in oval frames were set like a necklace laid out in a wide circle around the center attraction. The light glared from some, making the faces invisible, but from others the faces looked up sternly or sadly into the air. From the circle of generals there radiated outward in symmetrical fashion a variety of objects: ashtrays with Confederate flags painted on them, musket and minié balls, Confederate bills, a Confederate hat made of lead, about the size of a quarter, a white unused pencil with The Flag on it and the legend in red, SAVE YOUR CONFEDERATE MONEY, BOYS, THE SOUTH WILL RISE AGAIN. The new and old marched together from the centerpiece toward the four horsemen, making a cross on the table like the cross of stars on the Confederate flag.

I looked up at the other wall at the lithograph of Greenfields, the house heavy and imposing, surrounded by gardens and fields and woods, wistfully pictured, light and airy and graceful. Beside it was hung a photograph of the house in ruin, just before the turn of the century, just after it had burned. The bare branches of trees showed in the margins, the windows of the front wall stared blank and empty and dark like Captain Perrin's eyes, and I could see the boxwood maze in front of the house.

Chapter 7 _____

FOR MOST OF MY LIFE I had the impression that Greenfields had belonged to my grandmother's father, whom she referred to always as Captain Perrin. I found it did not the day after Poppy beat her up.

I heard Tiny screaming before I reached the top step. I flung the door open and myself across the porch and then through the inside door. The old man's hands squeezed my grandmother's throat; he held her up; she looked as though she were doing a dance on the tips of her toes. The veins on the back of his hands stood out like knotted cords.

Tiny was screaming and beating at the side of his face without effect, she on tiptoes too, reaching up high to hammer at his temple, swinging furiously with both fists, yelling all the while, the motion of her arm not a punch but a long swing as though she were throwing rocks at his head, her fist bouncing off his temple as off a brick wall, her wig jolting with each blow.

The old man stared through space, his mouth open and working, his throat going up and down, as though he too were yelling but no sound issued. His eyes stared wide and unfocused; his whole face gleamed bright red. My grandmother was turning blue, her eyes bugged out fishlike. From where I stood or ran—I knew I was running, my legs were churning, but I seemed to stay forever in one place, saw the action unfold with dreamlike, maddening slowness—the blue of her face looked pale blue, a whitish blue, a color out of a dream, an impossible color. Her arms by her side waved limply, tried to raise against him, her fingers curling and uncurling and curling again like dead leaves.

When I neared them the sensation of churning forward without moving ceased abruptly; I jumped and slammed my whole body as hard as I could against my grandfather's locked arms and his grip came apart and we all four went down on the floor.

I jumped up. Tiny was putting her wig back on and scrambling to her feet. The old man lay on his back, looking at the ceiling, his mouth open and working, a thin string of saliva oozing from the corner of his mouth down his cheek and into a little pool on the carpet, his eyes staring deep into nothing, his hands strangling thin air.

My grandmother lay on her side, her breath rattling in her throat, her eyes closed, her face improved now from blue to bright red. Tiny and I grabbed her at once, and we carried her out of the dining room and through the hall and up the stairs. She seemed light in my arms. Her head, extended beyond the crook of my elbow, bobbled as we mounted the stairs, unsupported and uncontrolled. Her eyes were closed. The lines of wrinkles around her mouth were dead white. As I carried her I suddenly realized that never before, not even once in my life, had I had my arms around her.

We put her on her bed under the pale sky-blue lace canopy. The blood coming from the corner of her lips colored the white satin pillowcase.

I left Tiny to undress and care for her and ran back down to the dining room to pick the old man up off the floor. I bolted through the door and there he sat in his chair, placid, reading the obituary notes in the newspaper. He looked up at me in pleased surprise. "Why, looky here. Where'd you come from?"

He studied my head for a long moment, squinting. "You been putting Vigoro on your hair, boy?" He looked around him, growing suddenly petulant. "Where's Irene? I got to go to the post office. Have you seen her?"

"She's upstairs," I said.

"I told her I need the car key," he said furiously. "What's she doing pooting around upstairs? I got places to go, people to see, don't she know I'm a busy man? I can't stand around here all day with a finger in my mouth, waiting for a durn car key."

"You can't drive," I said. They had taken his license away the year before.

"Can't drive? What you mean, can't drive?" he said. "I been driving cars long as they been making them."

101

"You don't have a license."

He leaned forward over the table, his eyes suddenly shining, looking conspiratorial. He reached into his pocket. "That's what *they* think," he said. He grinned hugely as he pulled out a tattered folded card and showed it to me. It was a license from nineteen twenty-seven. I took it from him.

"Where'd you find this?"

"Always had it," he said. "I tell you, I been driving since eighteen ninety-two."

"This license isn't good anymore," I said. "It says right here, 'Not valid five years after date of issue.' "

He snatched at it. "Let me see where it says that," he said.

I put it in my pocket. "I'll drive you to the post office."

He began to pout.

"Are you all right?" I said.

"No," he snapped. Then very sadly and slowly he said, "I don't feel so good anymore, I never feel good. I feel older than anything."

"Do you hurt anywhere?"

"No," he said irritably. "It ain't nothing in particular, it's just this all-over *old* feeling. I lay awake at night, feeling old, remembering things and just feeling old. I remember my grandmama giving me strawberries and cream one day, I was four years old. They was the biggest, reddest, juiciest strawberries I ever seen in all my life. The juice ran out and turned the cream as pink. I remember before that. I remember one winter morning my pappy—grandaddy—breaking the ice off the pump. I look out into the room and, why, I don't see the room, I see him. Just as clear as I see you."

"I'll be right back," I said. "I've got to go check on Irene. Then I'll be right back and we'll go to the post office."

"What's wrong with Irene?" he said. He leaned forward, concerned and worried. "Is she sick?"

"She's not feeling well," I said.

"Well, whyn't you say so in the first place." He rose. "I better go see what ails her."

"No, you wait right here. We've got to go to the post office. I'll be right back."

I ran up the stairs. My grandmother still had her eyes closed. Her face was beginning to swell and the bulge on her lips looked worse. I noticed for the first time a puckering and discoloration around her eyes.

"The doctor be here in a few minutes," Tiny said. She was wiping constantly at the pale wrinkled forehead with a wet cloth. "I reckon she gone be all right, but you know how vain she is. She gone be fit to be tied at having two black eyes."

"You think she'll be all right? Did she wake up? Has she said anything?"

"She woke up for a minute. She didn't say nothing. She started to crying and went back to sleep. She gone be all right, don't you worry. How about Mister Jackson?"

"He doesn't know. He has no idea what he did. He doesn't even have a mark on him to wonder about."

Tiny nodded. She wiped all around Irene's face, gently and continually. "He didn't get hurt at all, I bet."

"I don't think so."

She shook her head. "I don't know what to do with him. I think you better call your daddy and get him to come down here."

"I will. First I have to take him to the post office."

"That's what it was all about," Tiny said. "She wouldn't give him the car keys. You be careful now, alone with him in that car. Don't let him grab aholt of your neck too. I don't know who would shake him loose then." Tiny began to cry. "She'd be dead if you hadn't come in. I might as well have been beating against the side of the house."

"He's strong for an old man," I said.

"He still strong for an anybody. Before you was born, he picked up the front end of his Packard and held it while your daddy changed the tire."

"I thought it was just a Ford."

"Done that, too. Only the Ford, he drug it out of a ditch."

"Nobody could do that."

"I know," she said. "But he done it anyhow. It can't nobody climb up a telephone pole upside down with nothing touching but his hands, neither. That's impossible too, but that didn't bother him none."

"I can't believe it."

"I seen it with these two old eyes, a lot younger then and seeing plenty."

"If anybody else told me, I sure wouldn't believe it."

My grandmother opened her eyes. She did not look at us. We both bent over her.

"I have to go home," she said.

"You're here. How are you feeling?" Tiny said, almost whispering.

"I have a headache," she said weakly. "Do I look all right? I've got a bridge club tomorrow."

"You look jus' fine," Tiny said. "But you ain't going to no bridge club meeting. The doctor be here in a few minutes."

"You leave me be and take care of Beau."

"He's all right," I said. "I'm going to take him to the post office."

"That's so sweet of you, Little Harlan," she said, her voice drifting away. She went back to sleep, or fell again into her daze.

"This is the first time I ever rode to the P.O. in a golf cart," the old man said after I got him into my car. "I reckon it'll get you there, though."

"That's right," I said.

"Don't you think it *vibrates* an awful lot, though?" he said, exploding into chuckles.

On the way back, he shook his head. He shook the circulars and junk mail in his hand, his voice plaintive. "Would you look at this? I'm s'posed to be retired. Look at all this work they keep loading on me. I reckon you better drop me off at the office, I'll do it there."

"They tore the building down."

"Oh," he said.

"We better go check on Irene."

"That's right, I forgot she was sick." He stared out the window as we rode. "What was it you said was ailing her?" he said after a while.

"She doesn't feel well, is all."

"I think I better see what's wrong with her. But on the way, how about stopping off at Parkview Terrace? I want to see an old flame of mine."

"I didn't know you had an old flame."

"It's a whole lot you don't know."

104

"That's true," I said.

"I could tell you all kinds of things you don't know. I forgot things you never even guessed about."

"I believe it."

"You don't believe me?"

"I said, I do believe you."

"You'd be making a bad mistake not to," he said.

"But we better go straight to the house," I said. "To check on Irene."

"She'll be all right as long as she don't mess with no doctors."

"I imagine the doctor's been there and gone by now."

"What?" He reared against the window, pulling his head high. He glared at me. "And what if he kills her?"

"I don't believe he will."

"I never heard of such a thing," he said. "She don't need no doctor. I keep telling you, she's just feeling a little poorly. She don't need no doctor."

When we returned he had been and gone.

"He says she'll be fine," Tiny said.

"How much is he going to charge for what we already knew?" the old man growled. "I told Harlan it ain't nothing wrong with her." He started off for the den. "I can't stand here jawing with you two all day. I got work to do. I don't know why nobody can see I'm a busy man."

I told my father over the telephone.

"Oh, Lord," he said. "What are we going to do."

"I don't know. But you've got to do something."

"I guess I'll have to shake loose and come down there."

"I think you better," I said.

"You better call Junior and get her to help out over there."

"I've already done that."

"Good. I'll be down tomorrow, as early as I can get there. Let me speak to your grandmother."

"She can't come to the phone."

"Is she all right?"

"The doctor said she would be."

He was silent for a long time. "He beat her up pretty bad, didn't he?"

"He tried to kill her."

"Can you control him until I get there?"

"Yes. I think he's all right now anyway. Like I said, he doesn't have any idea of what he did."

"That doesn't mean he won't do it again. You sleep there tonight."

"I will. I think Junior might too."

"Okay. I'll see you tomorrow."

When Junior came she bustled into the house like a whole crowd of busy people. "What's this all about, Poppy?" she said. "What mischief have you been up to now?"

The old man glared at her. "What are you talking about? What brings you here this time of day? It ain't suppertime. Did you come to pay your rent?"

"Where's Mother?"

"She's upstairs," I said. "Lying down."

"What's all the hoo-rah about?" the old man said. "She's just feeling poorly. I been trying to tell them that. Then they drug in some kind of witch doctor. What'll happen now is anybody's guess."

Junior dropped her blue overnight bag at my feet. "Run that up to my room, please, Little Harlan." She turned to my grandfather. "Poppy—"

"Hush up now," he snapped. "Lawrence Welk's about to come on the T.V."

I shook my head at Junior and pointed upstairs, put my finger to my lips, started up the steps, and waved to her to follow.

She sighed heavily and lumbered up the steps behind me. "What's the big secret?" she said.

I whispered to her, "Poppy doesn't know what he did. It's completely blanked out on him."

"Well, it couldn't be too bad, then," she said. "I didn't see how it could be. He's so old he couldn't hurt a fly." She started rolling toward her mother's room. I hopped in front of her.

"Before you go in there—"

She tried to step around me. "Just let me see Mother," she said. "I'm going to miss my garden club meeting. It starts at eight. I don't see why I had to come over here at all."

"You better be prepared before—"

"Oh, I know how she is. I know how she exaggerates these things. Don't worry, I know how to handle her."

106

"All right, go in," I said. "Go on in, then!"

She opened the door and stepped inside. *"Mother!"* she screamed. "What happened to you?"

She was still asleep from the sedative the doctor had given her. Junior ran to her. "Call an ambulance," she yelled at me. She began shaking her mother violently. She did not wake up. "Oh God, oh God, she's dead."

"She's under medication," I said. "The doctor gave her something to make her sleep."

My grandmother stirred in her bed but did not wake up. One side of her face was swollen now to nearly twice its normal size, puffed and mushy-looking, like the flesh of a ripe melon. Her black eyes were like a raccoon's mask. Most of her face was discolored. There was still blood on the pillowcase.

Junior, sitting beside her on the bed, stared down at her. "We've got to do something about Poppy. This can't ever happen again." She had tears in her eyes.

"You're right," I said.

"Why did he do such a thing?" She fumbled in her sleeve and withdrew a handkerchief to wipe her eyes. "Wake up, Mother," she said very softly.

"The doctor said she'd probably wake around eight. Then at midnight she gets another pill if she can't sleep."

"Oh, no, my garden club meeting's at eight," Junior said. "Well, to *heck* with the garden club. I just won't go." She put her pocketbook down and took off her coat. "I'll sit with her awhile," she said. "I want to be here when the poor thing wakes up."

"There's nothing you can do for her, until eight," I said. "Why don't you come down and have supper with us?"

"No, I'll just stay here," she said. "Send Tiny up with something."

"Okay," I said. "I'll see you later. I'm spending the night."

"Oh, thank you," she said. "I don't think I could stand to be here alone tonight." She looked down at her sleeping mother. "Why is this happening to me?" she said in a high-pitched whine.

My father came onto the back porch, moving slowly and heavily, his shoulders beginning to stoop. He looked up at me. His eyes for a moment looked old, unclear, like his father's eyes, the same cloudy blue. "How's Irene?"

"She doesn't look good, but she's all right," I said. "I believe she's right sore, but she won't say so. Tiny's making her spend the morning in bed. I think she'd be up and about if she weren't embarrassed about her looks."

He nodded. "Never been sick a day in her life," he said.

"Where's your grandfather?"

"In the den. He's balancing a checkbook."

"Good God, we better get it from him quick. He'll snarl up their affairs so it'll take an accountant a week to straighten it out."

"I don't think it would matter too much. It's for nineteen thirty-four. He says the bank made a twelve-dollar mistake, and he's going to get the money back."

"With interest, probably."

"That's exactly what he said."

We went into the den. My father stood in the doorway looking at his father.

"What are you doing, old man?"

He looked up at my father, startled. "Now look at this!" he exclaimed. "What is this, old-home week? First that boy comes wandering through, and then Junior spends the night, and now here you show up out of the woods." He turned his head away to try to hide his grin, looked out the window past the woods toward the creek. "What brings you about?"

"Can't think of any good reason," my father said. "You doing any good these days?"

"I think I'll live, but it don't make much difference to me."

"You're not feeling good?"

"Well as common."

"But *how* are you? Are you feeling . . . healthy?"

"Nothing extry, thank you."

"Old man, what's *wrong?*"

"It's my blood," he said. "I seen it on the T.V. about this tired blood and I can feel it creeping all over my insides." He shook his head. "Tired, tired, tired," he said sadly. "It's all used up and I ain't making no more of it, is what it is. I have cut myself a dozen times in the past two weeks and never noticed because I don't bleed no more, because the most of my blood is gone and what's left don't hardly move."

"Of course it moves, old man."

"Then how come it don't come out when I cut myself, tell me that," he said. "Tell me how come whenever I stand in one place more'n a minute, my feet get all mortified. It's the molecules. They been stirring around, stirring around, for years and years, and they're wore out. The blood bank said where they'd send me some new blood when they have a surplus on hand. But I don't want it. No telling what kind of blood you might get. Especially I don't want no damned nigger blood. Overnight I would turn as black as early-morning thunder. I don't know where to get me any new blood, since I surely ain't taking none off the blood bank." He began to cry. "I'm too old." He looked at my father, studied his face. He had control of himself again, suddenly. "You got a old man for a son, you know you're ancient, don't nothing make you feel older. I told that boy there, I lay awake at night sometimes, just feeling old. You'll find out, day after tomorrow."

"What's happening day after tomorrow?" I said.

"He'll find out next week," he said to my father. Then to me: "That's about how long it will seem backwards to now when you reach where I am."

"You look right perky," my father said.

He grinned again, shyly. "I'll last another few days, I reckon," he said. "I'm glad you come ambling by. I got something to talk to you about."

"What's that?"

The old man pushed his glasses back on his head and grew very serious. He leaned forward, tapping his checkbook with the end of his pencil. "This here bank's trying to cheat me outta twelve dollars and nineteen cent," he whispered. "I finally figured out how they done it."

My father leaned over the checkbook. "That's for nineteen thirty-four," he said.

"What difference does that make?" The old man reared back in his chair. "I don't care if it was thirty-two B.C., they still owe me the money."

"That bank busted in nineteen thirty-six, for the second time," my father said. "It was your bank."

The old man stared, speechless, at my father for a moment. Finally he said, "I never owned no bank, what are you talking about?"

"You did too, old man! That bank of yours failed twice, and you had to pay double twice. Don't you remember? That was the last money you had, the only money that wasn't mortgaged against something. That's what ruined you."

"Speak for yourself, boy," the old man said. "I ain't ruined."

"You lost two fortunes on that bank."

The old man looked uncertain, stared off into the air. "I seem to recollect something about a bank. I had so durn many things going. . . ." He turned again to my father. "I had two banks, didn't I?"

"No, just the one. You owned it twice and it busted twice."

The old man glared down at the checkbook. "I believe you're right," he said. "And this bank here, it was the one? It was mine?"

"Yes."

"I be durn," he said, turning pages over and over. "My own bank owes me twelve dollars and nineteen cent." He checked the addition and subtraction down one page of stubs, his lips moving. "Now this looks all right here," he mumbled. He looked up at us, from my father to me and back to my father. "Now wait a minute. If it's my own bank, it would seem like I could get my money back. Don't it?"

"But the bank's all closed up."

The old man stared at the checkbook a minute more, and then he began to howl with laughter. He whooped and hollered, and threw back his head and slapped his knees, tears running down his cheeks. "Whoo boy!" he said. "*Stole* twelve dollars and nineteen cent from myself and can't get it back! *Wait*'ll I tell Stoneman, he'll laugh for a month."

"I kind of doubt it," my father said. "He's been dead a year." He put his hand on the old man's shoulder. "I'm going up to see Mother now," he said. "I'll be down to talk to you later."

"Don't worry about Irene," the old man snapped. "She ain't never been sick a day in her life. I don't know what they had to bring that doctor down here for." Then he suddenly looked worried. "Did you come down here because of Irene?"

"I came for your birthday," my father said.

The old man glowed. He smiled and turned his face, stared out the window again. "What birthday?" he said, immensely pleased. "I'm too old for birthdays."

110

Junior and my father argued in the living room. My father, as always, had turned up the thermostat, but the old man had turned it down to sixty again and it was very cold.

"I don't like it," my father said. "In fact, I hate the whole idea. I agree completely with Tiny."

"I'm your sister," Junior said. "Tiny's the maid. And what's wrong with it?"

"Everything. It's the meanest thing I ever heard of."

"There's not any nice way to do it. Would it be nicer to have little men in white coats come drag him out of his house? Put a straitjacket on him?"

My father chewed on his fingernails.

"I'll try to talk him out of the house without it, but don't count on it," Junior said.

"I'm not going to have anything to do with it," my father said.

"You've got to at least go with me. I can't handle him by myself, you know that."

"This is terrible," my father said, shaking his head.

"I know it. I don't like it any more than you do. But any way is terrible. Can you think of a better way to do it?"

My father sighed long and sad.

"I ain't dressing up like no trick monkey," the old man said, hovering over one side of his chair, keeping it between him and the suit Junior was fluttering at him. He moved nervously from one foot to another like a crane in a marsh. "What's wrong with what I got on? I ain't going nowhere."

"I guess we'll have to tell him," Junior said. "We wanted to surprise you, Poppy."

"Tell me what?"

"We're going out. It's a birthday party for you. We're going to the cafeteria and have a birthday party for you."

The old man's body relaxed. He tried to hide his grin. "What I want a birthday party for," he grumbled, trying to sound ornery. "Who's going to be there?"

"All your old cronies," Junior said. She turned to my father. "Tell him who all's going to be there."

My father put his hands in his pockets and his head down.

"He doesn't want to spoil it for you," Junior said. "Everybody's going to be there, all your old cigar-smoking cronies from way back."

"I guess I'll have to go then," he said. "I bet they're all counting on it."

"That's right," Junior said.

"I wouldn't want to disappoint them. I bet they're waiting at the cafeteria right— Wait!" he yelled. "Wait a minute! I ain't going to that cafeteria. They let niggers in there. I ain't going to eat with a bunch of—"

"Hush, Poppy," my father said.

"You seen how they let apes sit down to eat ever'where. If I wanted to eat with apes, I'd go to Africa."

"Hush!"

"Oh, you don't have to worry about that," Junior said. "That's why we're going to the hospital cafeteria."

The old man flicked his eyes from Junior to my father. "Hospital cafeteria? How come? What hospital?"

"Memorial Hospital. Because they don't let the coloreds in there."

"They don't?"

"Of course not. They have their own hospital."

"I'll go ask Tiny if they let niggers in there," he said, wrenching out of the room and stalking down the hall like a heron in long loping strides.

My father grabbed him by the sleeve. "Wait, Poppy," he said. "Don't you go bothering Tiny."

"Everybody's waiting there for you," Junior said. "We're got to hurry."

He looked at my father. "Are you going to this party?"

"Yes."

"All right," he said. "Here, Junior quit standing around with your finger in your mouth. Give me that suit. We can't keep them waiting all afternoon."

The old man, wearing a suit several years out of fashion in which he had once looked almost dandified and which now hung loosely about his frame, sat perched in the backseat of his Cadillac; Junior hovered beside him and kept her eye on him as though she expected him to fly away out of the window. He was excited. "Who all's going to be there?" he kept asking. And in depressed silence we could give no answer beyond Junior's constant reply, "Everybody, Poppy. Everybody."

He walked serenely and slowly, with exaggerated dignity across the hospital parking lot. He refused my father's arm in mounting the steps, climbing them himself with the help of his cane.

In the elevator Junior pushed a button for the tenth floor. "I thought the cafeteria was in the basement," the old man said. "When I come to see Stoneman last year, I thought I went to the basement to eat."

"Everything is arranged differently now," Junior said. He looked suspicious, and he watched the numbers light up and go out one by one as we rose to the tenth floor.

We left the elevator and walked down a hall and turned a corner. There was a desk and Junior led us to it. "This is Mr. Jackson," she said to the nurse or receptionist who sat behind it.

"Oh, yes," she said, looking at the old man and smiling at him. "We're all ready for you."

"Where are the others?" he said.

"We need some information," the nurse said. She handed Junior a form. "If you'll just fill this out for Mr. Jackson."

"What's going on here?" the old man said.

The nurse pushed a button and a buzz sounded just beyond a door in the hallway. The door was shut and the far side of its small window was barred. The door opened and two men came out. One appeared, by the stethoscope dangling from one pocket, to be a doctor; and the other was obviously an aide or an orderly.

"That ain't no cafeteria," the old man said. He turned to my father and asked plaintively, a little scared, "Where's the cafeteria?" My father, with a sick look on his face, turned away.

Junior put the form in my father's hand. "You'll have to do this," she said. He looked up at her.

"What?"

"I don't know all the information," she said. She spoke to Poppy. "And I can't hang around while you have your party. You and all your cigar-smoking cronies, you'll just feel dampened if I'm there. You'll want to have all-man talk."

She began walking away. We all watched her as she disappeared around the corner.

"Where's she going?" the old man cried. He began backing away from the desk. "What are you doing to me?"

The two men stood beside him. The doctor laid a hand gently on his shoulder. "Just relax, now," he said gently.

My father stood in the middle of the hall, the form hanging down in his hand. He stared at the floor.

The other man took Poppy's elbow and began leading him to the door. "It's right this way." The old man looked about him in amazement, and allowed himself to be led the few feet inside the door, twisting his head around and staring over his shoulder at my father as the door began to swing closed. "Ain't you coming?" he yelled. When the door closed, there was a brief silence, and then a wild uproar. The old man cursed and raged. My father swung rapidly around and walked down the hall, his head down and his face now drawn tight and blank, as though he had let down a lead curtain over it. The old man's outraged shrieks came muffled through the door. I followed my father. I looked back. Then I saw the old man's hands, that yesterday had been around Irene's throat, gripping the bars. I could see his working, contorted, furious face, and caught flashes of the two men heaving about the old man. A great crunching and tearing noise filled the hall and the old man's infuriated outraged face and the two men suddenly disappeared from the window and then instantly the old man reappeared, his face a caricature of itself as he began pounding on the glass with both fists until the glass broke and he continued to pound, the fists growing red and blood spattering on the floor and running in small streams down the blond wood. I turned away and followed my father. We heard the old man's furious noise until the elevator closed on us and moved slowly down to the lobby.

Junior was waiting for us in the Cadillac. "I don't see why Mother won't let me have the car now," she said. "Don't you think she will, Harlan?"

My father did not reply. We drove back to the house in silence. They both stayed for a short while, talking to their mother in her bedroom, going up separately. They did not speak to each other until they mumbled quick good-byes when they left to go home.

When they were gone, Tiny asked me to help bring my grandmother downstairs. We went slowly down, step by step, Irene between us; she was stiff and sore. At the bottom of the stairs she turned into the hallway.

"I want to look in the mirror," she said.

"You stay way from that mirror," Tiny said. "Don't you go fretting with it now."

"Now is the time," Irene said. She stood before it, leaning close. It was dim in the hallway, as though light were sucked down into the basement from the cellar door behind her. She carefully touched her contusions, ran her fingertips over the face rumpled with age. "I guess he got it at last," she said.

"Got what?" I said. "Who?"

"You come in heah in this living room right now. Quit that fretting over it. You was no more'n a baby and it was just a lot of no-gumption foolery. Come in here."

"I know," she said, almost whispering. "Lives have gone by." She turned to me. "Tiny knows all about this mirror. I told her about it a couple of years ago. No one else knows, but now that Poppy is gone, I guess I can tell you too."

We helped her into the living room. "I'm all right now," she said. "The stiffness is working out." Her face looked ruined. She sat in the armchair beside the empty fireplace. "How long will they let him stay at the hospital?"

"Until a place is found at a nursing home, if it doesn't take too long to find one."

"I don't see why it's so hard to get the nursing home to take him."

"He's too violent."

"I hope he doesn't have to go in the state asylum."

"I do too."

She sighed and stared at the fireplace. "Well, some of our most prominent men have died there. Let's have a fire."

"Sure," I said. "Is the coal in the garage?"

"I mean a real fire, a big blazing fire. Doesn't it feel cold in here to you?"

"Well," I said, surprised. "But you don't have any wood, do you?"

"There were always fires at Greenfields, great roaring blazes. There was a fireplace in every room."

"But you said Captain Perrin would only allow a small coal fire. Didn't his first wife die in a fire?"

"He didn't live at Greenfields. Can't you go out and get some wood for us?"

"Didn't live at Greenfields? Captain Perrin didn't live at Greenfields?"

"No," she said. "He never did."

"But I thought you—"

"Oh, I visited there."

"I thought it was Captain Perrin's house. I remember distinctly—don't you remember, the first night I spent in this house, you came up to my room . . . you said Greenfields was the family's heritage. Your father never lived there?"

"No, an uncle of mine. A very old uncle. Can you get us some wood?"

"You can't just go out and buy some. You have to order it. You can look in the paper in the classifieds and find someone who sells wood by the truckload. But sometimes it takes a couple of days for them to get around to you."

"Oh," she said. She gazed into the fireplace as though looking distractedly into flames, dreaming. "Tiny can get us some," she said. She picked up her little bell and rang it. Tiny reappeared.

"Get us some firewood, Tiny," she said. "We want to have a fire this afternoon."

Tiny looked at me.

"I don't think we'll be able to get it by this afternoon," I said.

"Tiny will get some. Tiny will know someone."

"I'll see," Tiny said.

We had the wood within an hour. I helped the man unload and stack it in the garage next to my grandfather's almost-virgin Cadillac. The smell of wood seemed alien to the house, but it smelled of my childhood; the edges biting into my palms felt good.

"This sure is fast service," I said.

"Yessir," he said.

"Is Tiny a special friend of yours?"

"Yessir."

"Relative?"

"Nossir."

"This looks like mighty good wood. All oak and hickory. I particularly like to burn hickory. Don't you?"

"Yessir."

"I wish you wouldn't call me sir. My name's Harlan." I stuck out my hand and he removed his glove and put his hand limply against mine for a moment.

"Yessir," he said.

"Do you have any kindling?"

"Nossir."

I looked around the garage and found an old crate which I cracked into pieces with a log. I carried the kindling inside.

Some logs were already in the fireplace. My grandmother stooped over them, a pack of matches in her hand. She was striking matches and throwing them at the logs from a yard away. "Something's wrong with this wood," she said. "It won't light."

"How did you get those logs in there?"

"Tiny put them in there for me."

Tiny appeared in the doorway. "Man want his money," she said.

"I'm not paying for any wood that won't light," my grandmother said. "You tell him I said so." She was still throwing matches at it.

"There's nothing wrong with the wood," I said. "You need paper and kindling to start it. I'll get it lit for you."

She hesitated.

"Go on and pay the man," Tiny said. "He freezing half to death out there. Harlan git that thing lit for you. He grew up with fireplaces."

"My purse is upstairs."

I pulled out the logs and laid a fire and lit it. We each sat on one side of the fire in armchairs, facing each other. My grandmother laid her head back. The fire was reflected off her swollen face.

"Captain Perrin was right," she said. "It does make a terrible mess. Look at all that bark over the carpet. I hope no one comes to visit."

"Probably they'd rather have bark and fire than a clean rug and cold," I said. "I'll sweep it up in a minute."

"Thank you," she said. "Tiny needs a rest."

I could not accustom myself to her new relationship with Tiny, though it had grown slowly ever since the old man retired. Irene was silent for a long time, gazing into the fire, and I remembered Tiny sitting at the table in the kitchen, puzzling her way through her newspaper; her grandson had taught her to read. I sat beside her with a cup of coffee; I was fifteen years old and she thought it was high time I drank coffee. The gentle spring air came into the room through the window like a stream of clean water, almost drinkable. Tiny sucked at her coffee noisily, her lips puckered, not taking her eyes from the newspaper. The harder the words were for her to decipher, the closer she peered at the paper. Sometimes her eyes almost touched it; she screwed up her face and frowned and pursed her lips, turned the paper slightly sideways.

"This word here," she said. "De-ca—de-ca . . ." She jabbed at it with her forefinger, looked up.

I leaned forward to look and told her. "Decapitate."

"My, my," she said, proud of me. "Even my grandbaby don't know that word yet. And he studies all the time." She read some more and looked up again. "I can't see what it means," she said.

"It means to cut off somebody's head."

"Ah," she said. "I kin see that now." She nodded, read, nodded some more. "You right, you exactly right. That's just what they're talking about. They done it to her and then put her in little pieces in the refrigerator."

"What?"

"They did. It says so right here." She ran her angled forefinger along the lines of print, bent eagerly forward into the story. "It gives me the horribles all over," she said.

My grandmother came into the room. "Tiny."

"Yes'm." Her head stayed bent to the words, she strained forward, eyes squinting constantly.

"Have you finished the breakfast dishes?"

"Yes'm. Done everything."

"Have you done the laundry?"

"Yes'm."

"Have you ironed it?"

"Yes'm."

118

"Vacuumed?"

"Yes'm. Law! The first thing they found was her eyeballs!" She put the paper away from her eyes for a brief moment. "Lord, give me breath!"

"Dusted everywhere?"

"Yes'm, done everything."

"Would you straighten the basement for me, then. It's a terrible mess and we never have gotten around to doing anything about it."

"Done thought of it last week and took care of it."

"There must be *some*thing you can do."

"Yes'm, they is. I'm reading this paper. You go on to your meeting."

"I pay you to work. Now if you can't find something worthwhile to do, something you're supposed to get paid for, you can just go home and not get paid for the rest of the afternoon."

Tiny looked at me, laid her paper down. "I'd hate to had lost that quarter," she said sourly. "I tell you what I could do. I could go down to Woolworth's and eat lunch with them college boys at the sit-in. I could come back and tell you all about it."

"You stay away from that demonstration, Tiny!" my grandmother said. She was horrified by it; she thought an uprising had begun. Tiny's interest shocked and hurt her. "You've got no business mixing with those trash niggers."

Tiny stood. "And what am I?" She looked at the floor, a quivering angry smile on her lips, her cast-down eyes flashing and sparking.

"You're a colored person, Tiny, and don't you ever forget it."

"Ain't likely."

"You're my *favorite* nigra; why, I feel like you're family. But I can't afford to pay you if you don't work. Now find something to do." A horn honked out front and she turned away. We heard her go out the front door.

Tiny and I both rushed for the radio. She turned it on, found a local station. They were covering the sit-in live as it happened. "Like her family!" Tiny said. "Lord save me from such a fate." We both hovered over the radio; she smiled at me across it. "My grandson was on the T.V. yesterday."

119

My grandmother roused herself from silent reverie and, turning from the fire, without preamble or any apparent acknowledgment of my presence, reminisced aloud.

"Every winter we rowed across the river to Greenfields. We went before Thanksgiving and stayed until after the first of the year. My mother made Captain Perrin send us; she wanted us to know; she wanted us away from the constant grind of country work and near poverty that the Yankees gave us. She was just a baby herself when Captain Perrin was wounded; but she knew, oh, she knew, she knew. At Greenfields during the Christmas season they had balls just like in the olden times, going on day after day, and it was Simon Fairchild who rowed us across. Simon's grandfather was supposed to be a natural African, brought over on a ship, and Simon had some wonderful fairy tales about him and about Africa. You would never know he came so straight from savage blood, because he had been your great-grandfather's personal servant. He saved his life at Chancellorsville and he never left his side. He died in Captain Perrin's bed. You can't find nigras like him anymore. Once they thought he had run away across Yankee lines to be free, but Captain Perrin said, you just wait, and two days later he came back through the lines again, with four mules and a wagon loaded with enough food for a company. When the Yankees shot your great-grandfather in the leg, it got infected, and Captain Perrin wouldn't let the doctors near him; Simon chopped it off with one blow of an ax while he slept, and burned the wound until it closed. Of course the ax hitting his leg woke him up and Simon had to call in half a dozen white men to hold him down while he cauterized it. Simon nursed him and carried him home in a wagon, Captain Perrin cursing him all the way, over every bump and jar for ten days. Simon was supposed to be a hundred years old in those days he took us across the river; one hundred was a nice round number and he never got any older than that.

"I remember how the river looked and how it lashed around us. My sisters and my cousins—cousins on my mother's side—all went. My mother was a Cole, of the Warwick County Coles, and *her* mother was a Page, a second cousin twice removed to a governor of Virginia. There were five of us. In memory now it seems that every year was the same year, it was always the same, each time like every other time, they all sort of slide together; the sky and the river always gray, reflecting each other, the color of old pewter, and the river swarming waves around the boat; old Simon, his white wool bobbing up and down as he pulled and pulled to get us silly, frilly girls across before we all fell in and drowned; when we started out you could hardly see the other side of the river, all you could see was Greenfields out of the mist, grand old Greenfields, which you have never seen and I guess never will now, shining on the bluff like a dream or bright memory, all the windows glowing in the gray day.

"Such balls! *Just* like the old days; everyone said so; like before the war. In a way my mind knew those days twenty-some years before I was born better than it knew the days I lived in. Everybody I knew was old, except my sister—my half-sisters were grown and were more like aunts—and my cousins, and my mother. She didn't live long enough to get old, died when I was ten, and for a while I lived with an aunt, and then my father married for the fourth time and I moved back with them. I was twelve, then. He had another child, and I adored her, absolutely adored her. She died of scarlet fever when she was six. You know, I still miss her. Maybe that's why I was in such a hurry to get married at sixteen—to replace Mary Sullivan with a child of my own.

"Women and men and girls came from all over the state; nobody else had balls like that, so few had the money for it. We stayed for weeks! Of course we should have *lived* there if the Yankees hadn't stolen the house from Captain Perrin. They gave it to my uncle Stancil Perrin because he had refused to fight in the war—spent the war in Ohio—and he had the money to pay off the mortgage Grandfather left. Now my uncle Stancil knew Lafayette—"

"What?" I said. "How could that be?"

"Why, he was introduced when Lafayette visited Greenfields."

"An uncle? Are you sure?"

"Of course I'm sure."

"And you knew him?"

"Certainly I did. Almost as well as I know you."

"And *he* knew Lafayette? Your uncle?"

"I could not claim they were intimate. He shook hands with Lafayette on the second step of the main stairway, when he was nine years old. Lafayette was spending the night at Greenfields, or a couple of days, I think." She paused and thought. "My grandfather hadn't remarried, then."

"How many times did he marry?"

"The same as my father, four. Perrin men tended to go through a lot of wives. Each one of them outlived four. Except my father had a child by his fourth wife, and my grandfather didn't."

"You knew a man who knew Lafayette," I said.

"Yes," she said. "It seems like so long ago only because life is so short. Like birds we flit across the sky, and then we're gone." She was silent for a while, running her fingers gingerly over her bruises before she began again.

"At every ball I would squint my eyes in the candlelight and I could see them, the two of them—Lafayette and Uncle Stancil—coming down the balustrade to watch us dance; saw them both as old men, as I knew my uncle, as Lafayette actually would have been."

"Is that where you met Poppy?"

"Lord, no! At a ball, at *Greenfields?* I can't picture it. I met Jackson at a Baptist picnic in Silk Hope, way up the river under the shadow of the mountains. You could say the river brought us together, like so many people. You know the creek down there runs into the river; the river comes down from Virginia and flows into the sea."

"I know that, of course, but somehow it never occurred to me that you and Poppy lived on the same river."

She nodded. "I don't know how they have the nerve to call that little trickle in Silk Hope a river. Except it turns into the river. It's not two hundred yards wide at Silk Hope, and at Greenfields it's a mile across.

"There was an excursion by boat for the Baptist do. Jackson was teaching school, and he taught the Sunday school too. He was good with figures, but he could hardly read and write. Of course, I didn't know any of that then. He asked me if he could bring me some fried chicken and I said yes, please, and he brought it to me and sat down beside me and we ate and then he asked me to marry him."

"Just like that?"

"Just like that."

"And you said yes?"

"Well, not right then, of course. I hadn't a notion of marrying a perfect stranger, and besides, Spencer Harrison was courting me at the time."

"When did you say yes?"

"About six months later. He moved to our town just after that picnic. Said it was because I wouldn't marry a country school-teacher."

"And he clerked in a tobacco warehouse."

"He was their bookkeeper. It was four hours to Johnston, but he came back to court me several times a week. And six months later he was a partner. I thought to myself, 'This young man is going places.' And Spencer Harrison asked me to marry him; no, he *proposed;* Beau asked. It was at a ball, the last one I went to, the last year I was there, and he took me to stroll in the boxwood maze and we sat on a bench by the well, under a great live oak tree. He got down on his knees and folded his hands together and asked me to be his bride; I will never forget that moment as long as I live, it was so romantic. I was sixteen years old, and I was afraid I was going to be an old maid.

"It was late in the evening and music and firelight came from the house; I looked out over the river and felt the mist wetting me and I thought to myself, I approve of Mr. Harrison's family, and Mr. Jackson's ambition. And I said to myself I will stand up and close my eyes and spin around and around and stop and open my eyes, and if I am looking at Greenfields I will marry Mr. Harrison, and if I am looking at the river it is a sign to marry Mr. Jackson. If I'm not facing either, I will wait. I told Spencer Harrison to go inside and wait while I thought about it, I would come in and tell him my decision. And he waited and I spun and when I stopped and opened my eyes, there was the river."

She looked into the fireplace, dreaming in the flames. She was silent a long time. "I always think it was the river that brought us together, almost like an accident. It *was* an accident. Like two waves in the river flowing together to make one wave; they could have splashed into any other wave about, but they just happen to reach the same place at the same time. It could just as easily have been another wave I splashed into.

"I went inside and told Mr. Harrison I could not marry him and he was insulted; he had been courting me a year, and I must tell the truth: I encouraged him. But he was a gentleman; he didn't make a scene. The next day he brought me the mirror that is hanging in the hallway. He said, 'I give you this to keep forever, and when you are old you will look into it and you will remember the name I give it:

Harrison's Revenge.' We both knew it was a joke that came from real feelings. I took the mirror and told him I would keep it to remember him by, and would never forget him, which of course I never have. Not a day in my life has gone by without thinking of Spencer Harrison."

"And you married Poppy."

"Yes," she sighed. "Yes, I married Harlan Jackson."

"And moved to Johnston."

"Law, that was years later. To hear him tell it, he snapped his fingers and got rich. We were married years before Young Irene was even born. I lost three in stillbirth before she came—one of those was named Spencer Harrison, but don't you dare breathe a word where it came from. The name. Then two years later, your father. It was at least six years before Helen was born and then two years again, and Sully died—was born, I mean. She was a baby when we moved to Johnston. And yes, he made money, we were very comfortable, but it wasn't until the middle twenties that he made a fabulous fortune. But just as soon as he made it, the Yankees stole it from him."

"The Yankees?"

"They fooled everybody," she said. "That stock market of theirs." She leaned her head back and stared again into the fire. "Such a life I've had," she said.

Chapter 8 _____

"HARLAN," CAROLYN SAID. "Harlan, I said what do you think, don't you think it's going to be a beautiful wedding?"

"Oh, yes," I said.

"Are you coming, Aunt Sully?"

"I'm allergic to Detroit," she said. "And you know me. I might be getting married myself the same day."

"Isn't she a riot," Carolyn said. Sully walked across the room to the couch. When she walked in front of strange men, she looked like she was walking on eggs.

"Aunt Sully's always been so much *fun,*" Carolyn said. She whispered close to my ear: "What in the world did she do two years ago to make everybody so mad? Why wouldn't our grandmother let her come back again?"

"I don't know," I said.

It was two years before that Junior had held her garden club meeting at my grandmother's house, and my grandmother and Sully had both joined the polite, constrained circle in the living room, sipping coffee and eating the delicate little cakes Tiny had made. Sully had come to borrow money from Poppy, and found he was too far gone to help her. I was in the den making sure Poppy didn't burn the house down, and I could hear their exchange of gossip and gardening information. Junior was methodically teasing and embarrassing Sully, asking her to describe antiques that she knew had long ago been sold off, pretending not to know they were gone. At one point she described in detail how she had set her own dining-room table for a party; she went on and on in elaborate detail, describing each article on the table, making everything sound elegant and expensive. Much of what she described were items Sully herself had once had; and many of the women present must have recognized the articles, as I did, listening in the den.

Finally she finished and, her voice coming thick with syrupy sweetness through the door, she said, "You must have very flossy *affairs*, Sully, as we all know. Tell us, what do you like to do on your table?"

"Some very serious fucking."

I burned to see the looks on all the faces after Sully's bitter, sudden voice died away. There was no noise from the other room; no sipping, no china clinking, no stirring; the house stopped breathing. The silence went on and on; I was surprised Sully did not leave. Finally conversation resumed, beginning with a voice I did not recognize. Junior and Irene never mentioned the comment to Sully; they were too mortified. But Sully was never allowed home again until the funeral.

I circled the room once more, shaking hands again, taking leave of the visitors, saying hello to some who had entered since my first circuit. Pictures were still going around from hand to hand. Sully was sitting again beside her sisters on the couch. Hollis and Richard were standing against the wall and Carolyn was trying to engage them in conversation. I had not even noticed them at all before that. Sully's eyes were glistening, on the verge of tears as she spoke in a low voice to Miss Varina, my grandmother's cousin. She was the last Perrin in the world.

"So thin," Sully said. She did not realize other people were beginning to listen. The photographs stopped moving as people grew interested; they stopped listening to Junior talk about them. "And she looked so . . . so *dead*, Miss Varina. They have her hands crossed on her chest and her hands looked dead and so thin and her face . . ."

Junior looked at the people listening to Sully, and started sniffling.

"Her face wasn't *asleep*-looking at all. . . . It looked so dead, and then as if I hadn't know it before, I knew then that she really was dead."

Junior outcried Sully; she leaned against her as she took a handkerchief out of her sleeve and wiped her eyes. Sully drew back, startled, and Junior leaned more against her, almost lying in her lap. The harder she leaned, the farther back into the couch Sully pressed herself, looking bewildered, her eyes darting about like the eyes of a skitterish horse. She touched Carolyn with her head as she pulled back. Carolyn's tanned skin glowed against Sully's papery skin, which looked beside Carolyn's more tarnished than tan.

Helen reached around Sully and patted Junior's hand and whispered to her. Junior sat up and wiped her eyes with her handkerchief. She made a momentary smile with her mouth. "I'm sorry," she murmured. "I've caused such a stir."

"Oh, no, Junior," said Miss Varina.

"Of course not," murmured people together.

"Poor Junior," someone said.

"It was so hard," she said. She blew her nose. "I'm all right now. This next photo was taken at the beach during a family reunion. You're all going to love this one."

I left through the front door.

When I returned, Sully was in the kitchen, hanging up the telephone. "I was just calling up Peanut," she said.

"I hope you had a nice talk. How is he?"

"Uh, well, he wasn't there. Is that my beer?"

"Where in the world does he go out in the middle of a desert? What was it you said? The closest town is two states away?"

"Right. I guess he just likes to go out and commune with the desert. Oh, I know what it was. They said he was asleep. Yeah, and he's going to call back. Is that my beer?"

I handed her the paper bag and she took it and sat at the table.

"Is everyone gone?"

"Finally. Except those that are sleeping here. Junior's trying to steal Tiny's house. She started in on your father as soon as the last visitor went out the door."

Her hand was thrashing in the bag as though of its own volition; it brought out a beer. An opener lay all ready on the table. Sully took it and punched two holes in the can and drank. She tilted her head back and took a long swallow. "God, I hate beer," she said. The alcohol seemed to give her strength for a moment and she radiated energy briefly, sitting erect in the chair. Then she faded and drooped, leaning an elbow on the table. "Poor Tiny," she said. "Where's she going to live? Junior was even trying to butter me up, for Christ's sake. Harlan, you've got to do something."

"There's nothing I can do," I said. "I don't have anything to do with it."

Sully had found some perfume somewhere and the room was full of the scent.

"Mother said she was going to change the will and get the house for Tiny. She said so the last time I was here; she told Junior, she told everybody. Of course she wouldn't have bothered to have informed me, but I was there, I heard it. Junior's got my brooch, why does she have to steal Tiny's house? That goddman hovel she's making such a fuss over that Tiny's been living in for thirty years and thinks is her home probably isn't worth as much as my brooch. Why didn't Mother get his will changed?"

"Poppy wouldn't let them," I said.

"S'pose you was fat as that!" the old man yelled. We went into the restaurant. We sat down and when we had ordered, the old man leaned across the table, wrinkling his nose in a scowl as though the nose were trying to pick itself up off his face and leave. "Do you know what they're trying to do to me now?" he said. "They're trying to steal one of my houses."

"Who is?"

"Irene," he said. "Your grandmother and your daddy. I never seen anything like it," he said in disgust, looking down at his plate as the waitress put his food in front of him.

"What do you mean?" I said.

"They're trying to *give* her that house. They want to take my house away and give it to her. For nothing!" He leaned forward again, clutching a fork in one hand and a knife in the other. "And to a nigger!" he said, his face astonished and frightened.

"Your house?" I said. "Don't you mean Tiny's house?"

"That ain't her house, it's mine. Who's side are you on, anyway?"

"It's hard to believe they're trying to steal it," I said.

"I thought the same thing myself," he said. "It is, but they are. I don't know what come over 'em. I thought your daddy had more sense than to try to make me give a damn nigger a house, even if he is a liberal."

"Aren't they just trying to leave it to Tiny in your will?"

"Yes," he said, whispering but seeming to yell. "That's exactly what they're doing!" He used his knife and fork on the food, cutting long gashes across the plate, mixing everything together. He grinned. "You should have seen 'em trying to get me to sign a change in that will," he said. "I told 'em I done made it and they couldn't make me change it. Oh, I was tough. *Then* they tried to make me sign a brand-new will that would give Irene everything." He bent his face to the plate, forking the slush of food into his gaping mouth. "I seen through that in a second. They thought they could trick me," he said, looking up, vastly amused. "They thought they could trick me into giving that damn nigger that house. Why, there ain't nothing wrong with that house!" He pushed away his plate. He had eaten about half his food. "Your daddy's a bleeding-heart liberal, but I'm surprised at Irene, ain't you?"

"Yes," I said. "I am very surprised."

"Give her a house," he muttered. "My folks never owned no slaves. It ain't none of it my problem."

He pulled his plate back under his chin and picked at his food, then shoved it away again. "Just you and me," he said. "A whole house to ourselves. What do you say?"

"I don't think we could do that."

He leaned forward, his expression and tone pleading again, childlike. "You got to," he said. "I ain't going back there. If you won't do it, I'll just set right here. I ain't going home."

"You've got to go home."

"I can't. They treat me like some kind of fool ain't been weaned yet, like I was a two-year-old afflicted boy."

I was silent and for a while he watched the other customers eating.

"We've got to be getting back now," I said.

"You bring me here again?"

"Yes," I said. "Sure I will."

"I guess she's too old to leave her all alone now, nobody but Tiny to take care of her."

"That's right."

"They been poisoning my peanut butter."

"No, they haven't."

"Trying to make me give a nigger a house. I got to go back, to keep my house. Are you going to sit there all day, or wait till you get dusty?"

On the trip back he cried for a few minutes, his head turned to his window, and then he fell asleep and did not awaken until we pulled into his driveway.

Sully upended the paper bag and the other beer tumbled out and rolled across the table onto the floor. She lurched for it and almost fell on the floor herself. I picked it up and handed it to her. "What's she going to do now?" Sully said. "Her husband's gone, her children all grown up. Even her grandson has moved off to Washington and lives in a hotel." She punctured the can and the beer sprayed up in a fierce little geyser and splattered all over Sully. The foam spilled out of the can and Sully licked at it. Most of it landed in her lap. "Oh, no, half of it's *gone,*" she said. "And I don't have any more."

She grimaced with the effort of puncturing the other hole in the can. "Why do they have to make these things so *hard,*" she said. "If you invented a soft beer can you could make a million dollars." She put the can to her lips and drained what remained and dropped it on the table. "I'm not going to let them do it," she said. "I'm going in there right now. Somebody has got to show some guts around here." She put one hand on the table and stood. I followed her.

As we went through the dining room she waved her hand at the packing boxes and piled-up goods. "Would you just look at this," she said. "Listen, if I thought it would do any good, I'd tell Junior she could have my brooch. I could trade her my brooch for Tiny's house. But, God, if I said that in front of witnesses, you can bet your bottom dollar I'd never see that brooch again."

My parents were in two chairs beside the fireplace. Junior and Helen and Roy were on the couch. Junior leaned to see around Sully as we entered, and looked at me. "Dolly came," she said. "She and Carolyn went to that bar to try to find you. You must have passed them on your way back."

"I guess I'll let Richard and Hollis keep them company," I said.

"Oh, they went home to bed."

"Back kinda early, aren't you, boy?" Roy said, grinning. "It's not midnight yet, is it?"

"It's around ten."

"Mighty early," he said. "You couldn't find one, huh?"

Sully leaned against the wall, arms folded, looking down at Junior.

"What are you planning on doing?" she said, her whine loud and harsh in the room. "Moving into Tiny's house when you take it away from her?"

"Not now, Sully," my mother said.

Junior looked up, her mouth a circle. Then she closed her mouth tightly, compressing her lips into a straight line through the space of the disappeared circle. She looked at Helen and Roy and my parents. "Would you listen to this," she said.

"I know what you're trying to do," Sully said.

"I'm not trying to do anything," Junior said.

"I guess you'll nail my brooch over the mantelpiece when you move. If that shack had a mantelpiece, which it doesn't."

"I have nothing to do with any of it," Junior said. "Mother said to give your brooch to Carolyn because you would pawn it. It's not for me to decide one way or the other."

"Mother also said Tiny should have the house," Sully said. "It sounds like you're deciding about that."

"That's different," Junior said. "There's nothing we can do about it." She turned to my father. "Harlan, tell her about the will."

"The will includes the house with his others. It's a part of the estate to be divided equally among us. Poppy was afraid Irene would work some way to give Tiny the house, so he specified in a codicil that the house be shared by all four of us."

"You see?" Junior said. "There's nothing we can do about it."

"For Christ's sake!" Sully said, not quite yelling, tottering away from the wall. "We could *give* it to her. We're all of us here, we could just give it to her."

"Poppy's not dead yet," Junior said. "When he does die, you can give her your fourth of it. But I'll bet she'll never see a red cent from it. You can't keep money long enough to give her any. Before you got ink on paper you'd have a new dress on your back."

"And what about my brooch," Sully said. "My brooch was never in the will. Mother gave it to me."

"She decided to give it to Carolyn," Helen said. "I remember her exact words. She said—"

"Just wait until after the funeral," Sully said.

Roy was humming. When they stopped, I could hear him. He stared blankly over the fireplace, humming "Onward Christian Soldiers," while he drummed his fingers silently against his knee.

"Let's don't have any more fighting," my mother said. "Harlan will take care of all this after the funeral."

Junior cleared her throat. "Well," she said. "Of course *I* am trustee."

Sully smiled, walking toward Junior. "That's what you think, sweetie."

"What do you mean?" Junior said. She looked at my father.

"You're not going to be trustee any longer," Sully said. "When he dies, you won't be executrix."

"What is she talking about?" Sully had stopped right in front of her. "Oh, you smell like a distillery," Junior said, waving her hand in front of her nose. "Go away."

Sully stomped to the doorway and went up the stairs. She came back down. "I wouldn't be like this," she said. *"You're* the one that tore up my pictures." She ran up the stairs.

"What on earth is she talking about?" Junior said. "She ought to be rooming with Poppy. And Harlan, I wish you wouldn't go see him. You know what the doctor said. It stirs him up."

"I want to stir him up," my father said. "What's wrong with his remembering?"

"He keeps trying to run away."

"Well, at least he can end his life trying," my father said.

"If he tries to run away so often, maybe he should be put in another place," my mother said. "Maybe the people aren't competent."

"He's already been three places," Junior said. "And there's nothing wrong with the people."

"How do you know?" my father said. "You've never been there."

132

"Why is everybody picking on me? Whose side are you on, anyway?"

"I'm not on any side," my father said.

"Junior's had such a terrible time," Helen said.

There was silence for a while, no one looking at anyone else, the only sound Roy's subdued humming. The tune had changed and I did not recognize it. Roy looked like he would like to float away unnoticed through the window he was staring out of.

"I'll bet you didn't find any note," Junior said. "I knew I didn't remember seeing a note like that. Is that what Sully was talking about?"

"No, I certainly didn't find the note. We'll talk about it tomorrow."

"And Sully. We've got to have a very serious talk about what we're going to do with Sully."

"Do with her?"

"We've got to help her."

Everyone in the room stared at her.

"Well, we do," she said.

No one answered.

"She's my sister, isn't she?"

"Help her how?" I said.

She did not look at me; she addressed my father. "We'll talk about it tomorrow." Roy and Helen followed her upstairs

Chapter 9 _____

IN THE DIFFUSED MORNING LIGHT, I watched Sully coming down the hall toward the den. She stopped at Harrison's Revenge and examined herself. When she entered the room, she closed the door behind her. "I look like a witch," she said. "My face looks like old clothes I slept in."

"You look fine," I said.

"I don't. When Herman shows up he's going to take one look at me and turn tail. And then what am I going to do? I age about ten years every day."

"Did Peanut ever call back?"

"No. Do you know what they're doing now? Rooting around in the cellar," she said, heaving a sigh. "*Garden* tools," she droned lazily. "Rakes, old pieces of hose. Have you seen the pile of stuff they lugged out to the garage? Have you been out there this morning? God, it's gotten cold all of a sudden. They just toodled all that stuff out there without mentioning one word to anybody. Not that I know who else would want all that junk. Helen found an orange crate, for Christ's sake. Can you be*lieve* it? A beat-up old orange crate, she's going to ship it to Detroit." Sully laughed hoarsely. Then she sat up and cocked her head from side to side, listening.

The stairs to the basement ran down behind the wall and we could hear a heavy scuffling, then a bump, then the scuffling or scraping again. Sully grinned at me, screwed up her lips, and pushed them to one side of her face. "Can you *imagine?*" she said. "Maybe Junior's bringing up the basement floor to take home with her."

We heard a knocking on the door that led to the basement stairs. I opened the door of the den and reached through to let Junior out. She stood there sweating and breathing hard, pulling at a long flat sheet of cast iron. She looked up. She looked proud of herself. "Look what I found," she said happily.

134

"What is it?" Sully said, leaning forward, bent almost double to see around the corner from the sofa.

"I don't know," Junior said. "I'm going to put it in my garden."

"What on earth for?"

"Just to have it there," Junior said. "I can probably think of something to use it for. Besides, I think it'll look nice. It looks real earthy, don't you think?"

"That's an understatement," Sully said.

"Well, you don't have a garden. What do you think of it, Little Harlan?"

"It's a right fine sheet of cast iron."

"I think it'll look nice in the garden." She turned to Sully and spoke hurriedly. "There's a pile of your junk down there. A painting and some other junk."

Junior started down the hall, dragging the sheet iron with her, bent over and walking backward.

"Let me help you with that," I said.

She leaned it against the stairway. "That's all right. I've got to go down there and bring up some more stuff. I haven't been in the basement in years. I have to go through all of it. It's like a treasure hunt. Most of it's garbage, but every once in a while you run across something useful."

Sully followed her down. "I better go too, I reckon," she drawled. "I want to see what painting of mine managed to survive this house for thirty-some years." She looked back to me and muttered, "Oh, ex*cuse* me, I mean what junk." She clung to the rail and descended with faltering care. The musty odor and dank wet air of the cellar covered us like a film of sticky grime. Cobwebs hung from the ceiling and crossed all the corners of the room. The only light came from small windows set high in the wall just above the ground; they were masked with an accumulation of grit and soot and the light that came through was a weak, gray light.

"God, it's like a dungeon in here," Sully said.

"Your stuff's over there," Junior said, pointing to an old washing machine with wide-apart legs that crouched like a huge, gray insect in a corner.

"Thanks, Junior," Sully said. "You remind me of the tour guide I had in the catacombs on the Via Appia." Sully moved over to the old machine. In the soot-filtered half-light, with her white pants and white blouse, she looked like an apparition sliding over the floor. She stood for a moment before the grimy mildewed machine and then with thumb and forefinger she began gingerly removing things.

Junior rummaged loudly through boxes and piles of tools and other used necessities or luxuries now cast off in a heap against the wall. She tossed things behind her and they clattered on the cement floor: a box of screws; the head of a hammer with a jagged piece of handle poking through it; a rake; a garden trowel with no handle; the metal bowl from an electric mixer and the mixer itself, the motor housing cracked; long, endless tangles of electric wire.

"I don't believe it!" Sully exclaimed. "I found my dream."

"Your *what?*" Junior said, turning her face while she was still bent over the pile. Her face appeared from behind her dark clothes; it seemed to hang and glow unsupported in the dark, like the moon.

"You wouldn't understand," Sully said.

"I'm sure I wouldn't." Her eerie face disappeared as she picked up an armload of garden tools and lugged them to the stairs. The end of the rake bumped each stair as she mounted them. "There's not a thing wrong with this rake," she said.

Sully yanked at the painting. She almost fell when it jerked suddenly loose from the machine. "Come on, Harlan," she said, excited. "You've got to see this in the light of day."

Sully set it on the table in the hall, leaning against and covering Harrison's Revenge. She turned on the lamp and stepped to one side and stared at the painting as if in a trance. A darkly translucent layer of dust covered it and mildew spotted it, but the colors showed dimly through. It was a painting of horses. They grazed and stood and ran in a blue field under a yellow sky, and every horse was a different color. There were red horses, pink horses, green, blue, brown, yellow, black; and they came in several shades of each color. In a high corner of the field—I could not tell whether or not it was actually a hill—a white horse with wings loomed hugely.

Junior stopped fooling with her tools to look at the painting, her hands on her hips. "Well, what's it supposed to be?"

"Can't you tell? I bet Harlan can. Guess what the title of it is, Harlan."

"Uh, I'm afraid I'll have to give up," I said. Junior laughed.

"*Horse Heaven*," Sully said. "Because see"—she pointed to a number of the horses—"they all live in Horse Heaven and every horse can be any color he wants to be. If he wants to be a horse of another color, see . . ."

"That's the silliest thing I ever heard of in my life," Junior said. She disappeared into the gloom of the basement while we stood in front of the painting, with Sully watching my face.

"Well, I like it," I said. I tried to think of something to say about it. "I like the way the colors go together." I looked at it some more. "And it's very strange, the horses are all these colors, but they're very real looking. You can almost see them twitching off flies."

"Do you really think so?" She looked back to the painting, eyes shining. "I'd almost forgotten how terrific I was."

Junior snorted behind us.

"Hark," Sully said. "You can even hear them."

Junior put down a window frame without any panes. She leaned it against her sheet of iron. She looked at the painting again. "Why did you have to be so . . . realistic?"

"What do you mean? Have you ever seen a pink horse?"

Junior tapped the white horse. "I mean like on this— Are those *wings?*"

"I wanted to be realistic."

"But I mean, why did you have to show his . . . sex like that?"

"He's really hung, isn't he?"

Junior blushed to the roots of her gray hair, glancing quickly at me. She opened her mouth, closed it.

"But, why did you *exaggerate* so much?"

"I had George pose for me," Sully said. "What was I supposed to do, dress them all in bloomers?"

"But the way you've done it, you can't help but notice."

"You can't? You can't help but notice it?" Sully grinned at her sister. She looked transparent beside Junior. "Junior, I find that *very* interesting."

Junior picked up her small window and carried it toward the dining room.

Sully wiped at the painting with the palm of her hand, smearing the dust around. "It's a dream I always had when I was a little girl, I always wanted to paint it. I had it for years and years, and when I got older I tried to paint it but I never could until . . . I said George modeled for it but . . . it wasn't then. I painted it in Baltimore. Oh, God, my life began and ended when I was sixteen in Baltimore, Maryland. He was beautiful and perfect and he loved me." She had her face covered in her hands; she took them away to try to peer into Harrison's Revenge, but her dream intervened. "All those horses have everything, have exactly what they want. They're any color they want to be and no one says a word about it. There's even the Horse Angel to take care of them." She turned to me and a puzzled expression flashed across her face. "What the hell do you reckon Junior wants with that busted-up old window?"

We took the old man's car again when we went to visit him. When we stepped out into the parking lot, the sun felt bright on my skin without real warmth, the air feeling as it does in the morning by the ocean in early spring before the heat begins.

We made the same cautious approach to the building we had made the day before, both of us looking up to the glass door, expecting to see the old man there, gazing out on the world.

"Do you remember the day we put him in the hospital and he tore a grate off the door of the psychiatric ward?" my father said.

"He couldn't do anything like that now," I said.

"No," he said sadly. "He couldn't."

"Let's hope he didn't run away again," I said. It seemed shorter through the halls the second time. Even without the old man's shuffle to slow us down, we proceeded slowly, as at a funeral.

Turning suddenly into the corridor that led to his room, we saw him and he confronted us suddenly with his petulance; there he sat, glowering in a wheelchair, tied to a radiator. He pouted, his head jammed out and down into the space of the hallway as though daring anyone to pass. His lower lip poked out so that he looked like a fountain about to spew water in a stream. He would break through the walls if he could only rise up and walk. But he could not: through a loop in the rear of his pants his belt was passed, then turned twice around the back of the wheelchair, and was buckled finally, out of his reach, to the radiator. Even jammed forward he looked tall in his wheelchair. His head rested heavily on the stalk of a neck, like a chunk of polished stone, the lines cleanly sculptured, standing out under the fine white hair, which seemed to float like a haze or an aureole above his profile. Over his rumpled white shirt he wore the blue robe; it was tossed across his shoulders like a cape. One hand tightly gripped a plastic cup. His forearm hung in the air above the arm of the chair, rigid, the muscles taut like thin ropes just under his skin.

He jerked his head up on our approach. "Take me home," he ordered. "I hate this place."

My father grinned at him. "Why, hello, Harlan Jackson," he said. "Have you seen us lately?"

He wrinkled his eyebrows together in a scowl and pressed his stained teeth together, making large knots appear and disappear at his temples.

"Such bad luck ain't my fault," he said. He looked my father up and down. "I don't understand a man that wants to wear shirts look like they was made out of old blankets."

"I haven't seen you so spunk in a long time. What's my name?"

"You claim to be my boy," he said. "But you won't let me go home."

"What's his name?" my father said, pointing to me.

"I know who he is," the old man said, pointing his cup at me. Drops of orange juice ran thickly in the bottom. "What's he doing here?"

"He came all the way from Virginia to see you. He's working in Norfolk. He drove five hundred miles just to come see you."

"Well, hooray for him. Do he win a prize?"

We laughed.

"That's right," Poppy said. "I'm a catbird all right. I don't know how come they don't put me on T.V."

We laughed again and he looked from one to the other of us in quick succession and began to pout again. He was interrupted by a nurse who squeaked up on rubber soles. The old man glared at her.

"He's been naughty again today," she said. She smiled at my grandfather. "Haven't you, dear?" To my father: "He's tried to run away again."

"Almost made it too," the old man said, glowering. "Next time I will." His plastic cup split in pieces and the pieces fell to the floor.

The nurse winked at my father. She looked as though she might have been made of foam rubber or sponge; as though if she were poked with a finger, the flesh would give deeply and spring back into place. "He got into the laundry and the steam pressers

139

found him, trying to force open a door. I don't know how he knew it went to the outside. He kicked one of the pressers in the leg."

We looked at the old man; he turned his head away, a faint coy smile on his face.

"She quit," the nurse said. Then in a low voice, hesitant, "She's colored."

"I could have broke it if I'd wanted to," the old man said, still smiling. "I should have."

The nurse stooped to pick up the fragments of the cup, her face flushing as she bent over. "Do you want some more orange juice?"

"No! I hate orange juice."

"He loves orange juice," she told us. "He's just mad at me because we had to tie him up." She put her arm over the back of his chair and bent over him; he shrank away. "Don't you love orange juice?"

"I ain't saying one word to you," he said. "Not now, not ever."

She laughed and he scowled, his nose and lip wrinkling upward. "You try awful hard to be mean," she said, "but you can't fool me." She squeaked away.

"Huh!" he said. "They *call* it orange juice. That woman don't know when she's got herself in trouble."

"How are you feeling, Jackson?" my father asked as he took out his own comb and began to fix his father's hair.

"I'd feel a whole lot better if I was somewheres else," he said. "Quit messing with my head. Why can't I go home?"

"You can't go home, just yet," my father said. "The doctor says you're still sick, and have to stay a while longer."

"Sick," the old man spat out. "All I need is a little whiskey in this here orange juice, as they call it. Snookers been stealing my clothes again, why don't you do nothing about it?"

"Snookers? What are they?"

"It's only one of him."

"I don't think there's anybody here named Snookers. I've never heard of one, and I've never seen him, for sure."

"Why, you can't hardly miss him. A feller about the size of a used-car salesman. Wears shoes that look like they could tie themselves and a puce-colored flowered shirt that puts me in mind of a guided-tour vacation I took in Hawaii, spring of nineteen fifty-six."

My father held his father's hands, looking at large purple blotches on the backs of them. "Do your hands hurt?"

140

"Sometimes."

"Why did you try to run away?"

"I hate it here." He jerked his head up, stared at my father. "I already told you that when you come prancing in here leading that mustache around. Can't you remember anything?" He examined my father's mustache, running his eyes slowly from tip to tip. "Looks like a rat's nest," he said.

"They're taking pretty good care of you, aren't they? It seems to me like they take good care of you."

"No, they don't," he said petulantly. "All they ever do is come around every few minutes and pour orange juice down your throat."

"The food's good, isn't it?"

"I wouldn't give it to someone else's dog. I ain't ate nothing but a biscuit in three months. I believe I ate that about two weeks ago on a Tuesday, about ten in the morn— Hey! What are you trying to do to my feet?"

"Do they hurt?" My father was kneeling in front of him. His feet were swollen and almost blue, puffed out over his slippers.

"Sometimes," he said, looking down curiously. "More especially when some meddler comes along and starts poking at them."

He reared back in his chair, raising himself up with his hands on its arms, and glared at a reed of a man who was being pushed toward us in his wheelchair. My grandfather leaned forward, a menace, glaring malevolently. When the other man was close enough to hear, he said loudly, "They ain't nothing wrong with him. He just likes to ride." The other man returned the glare, twisting around to keep an eye on the old man as he passed us by.

"Don't you remember him, Jackson?" my father said. "You roomed with him when you first got here, until a private room opened up."

"I remember him," the old man said. "But I never roomed with him. I never lived with nobody. And if I had, it wouldn't have been him. I'd sooner live with a moccasin snake than that pussel-gutted son of a bitch."

"Do you want some apples?"

"I wouldn't mind," the old man said, relaxing back in his wheelchair, suddenly mild. "But you can't get any."

"I'll see what I can do," my father said, leaving us and walking down the hall past the nurses' station.

"You can't get any!" the old man shouted after him, turning in

141

his chair. "They ain't got nothing around here except orange juice." Then, turning back to me, his tone quiet and petulant: "Well, they call it orange juice. I don't know your opinion, but I believe it comes out of a durn jar."

We sat together in silence. He looked around him, watching the flow of people around the nurses' desk, visitors coming and going and patients walking slowly with canes or walkers. "Irene says I don't like green olives," he said. He continued watching and occasionally his mouth dropped open in astonishment at some person who appeared to me quite normal, and these people he watched with intense interest, following their every movement until they were out of sight. From time to time he turned to me and we gazed steadily at one another until he watched the activity by the station again. "I like green olives fine, but they give me the hiccups," he said. "I'd rather have the croup than hiccups."

I leaned toward him and asked, "Do you remember the time you took the calf across the river in a rowboat? And it fell in the water?"

He looked at me, puzzled. "What?" he said.

"You remember," I said. "You and some cousin of yours had to take a calf across into town to sell it, and you figured if you carried it in a rowboat instead of paying for the ferry, you could keep the ten cents."

He looked at me, his eyes straining at mine.

"And the calf fell in. Do you remember?"

"I seem to remember something about a calf," he said slowly.

"It was raining," I said. "And the river was high. Do you remember how you got the calf to shore?"

He pondered, looking down at his hands, turning them over and over.

"Do you remember? The boat turned over. What happened then?"

He looked at me, his eyes troubled. "Boat turned over," he said to himself. "Fell in."

"And you and your cousin swam the calf across. How did you do that?"

He strained with thought; then he gave his head a quick, hard shake and his eyes emptied. "You tell me," he snapped. "You seem to be the one knows all about it." He stirred uncomfortably. "What

142

are all these questions for? You and your daddy come in here, ain't been nothing but questions, questions, questions since you come in. Where'd he go?" he said, looking around in surprise.

"He went to get some apples."

He shook his head. "Can't get any," he said complacently. "They got no apples around here."

"He went out to a grocery store to get them."

He looked startled, his eyes wide with incredulity. "You mean he's out there all alone with just that mustache? Leading that mustache around the countryside, rambling around by hisself?"

I could not help laughing and he looked at me, pouting. Then he cocked his head and squinted. "You know," he said, "there's rent on that chair you're setting in. It ain't high; in fact, I would say it's very reasonable." He grinned, his eyes alight; when he had teased me with this joke as a little boy, he had scared me because I thought he had meant it, and I had no money. He leaned forward in his wheelchair and whispered. "Don't tell nobody else, we don't want a rush on the place, but as you're in the family, I'll let you pay at the end of the week. Most folks have to pay in advance, not to speak of deposit." After a period of silence, he said, "Now where'd you say your father's gone?"

"He's gone for apples. He won't be gone long."

"He won't stay long when he gets back. He won't let me go home." He put his face close to mine, his eyes looking into mine, the light making bright triangles on the faded blue discs. Intense, plaintive, he said, "Make him let me go home. I hate it here. I'm all right now. I'm not sick." He looked down at his hands folded together, gripping each other in a tight, hard variation of his spastic brushing. "Tell him I won't be no trouble to anybody. Tell him I'll do everything they tell me to do. Can't I go home? Please? I hate it here, I ain't got no friends here. Do you see why I can't go home?"

"I don't have anything to do with it," I said, looking away.

"Nobody talks to me. I sit here day after day after day, looking at the wall. He's your daddy," he said. "What sons won't do for fathers, fathers will for sons. Make him let me go home."

My father appeared at the end of the hall, a brown paper bag in one hand.

"There he is," I said.

The old man looked up, stuck out his hand as my father reached his side. He pumped my father's hand enthusiastically.

"Hello! hello!" he said, suddenly effusive. He jerked his thumb toward the people around the nurses' station. "You see all them folks stirring around in and out of here like a bunch of little rats? Listen, it's ruining business, it's ruining everything. Can't get hardly any salesmen in here, not to speak of customers." He peered at the bag, looked up from under his eyebrows at my father. "Did you bring your whole line?"

"Do you want an apple?" my father said. He cut one into sections for him. The old man nodded at me. "This feller here's been giving me some kind of story about when he went out and drownded a calf. Stupidest story you ever heard in your life. Why he was telling it, *I* don't know."

He ate the pieces of apple as my father handed them to him, chewing vigorously, totally absorbed. His temples bunched into huge knots as he chewed. When he finished, his hands began to brush themselves, sweeping each other off. He looked at them with growing alarm.

"Do you want to wash your hands?" my father asked.

The old man looked at them studiously. He turned them over and over while they moved. "I reckon they need it," he said.

Chapter 10 _____

WHEN WE RETURNED TO THE HOUSE, the sun was climbing, the columns of light angling through the hedge into our eyes as the long car
rolled to a stop behind Junior's four-year-old Chevrolet, over the top
of which we could see the porch and the three sisters sitting there.
The mockingbird fluttered up into the pin oak as we got out of the
car and cocked his head at us as we passed beneath him to walk up
the steps. A light breeze cuffed the hedge, clacking the branches
together. White clouds rose over the trees like white blossoms,
spreading out of a uniform gray bank below which, through the
trees, a hem of white sky showed. The swag-bellied clouds rolled
toward us; they would soon be overhead.

On the porch the light cut the brick wall in half. Sully sat in
one of the white metal chairs by the metal table, the sunlight making
a line across her hips, her face and torso in shadow, her crossed legs
and her red toenails shining in the light. Junior on the lounge chair
blinked against the light as she looked up at us, shading her eyes with
one hand. Helen's back was to the sun and she sat staring at the wall,
lost in thought. All of their eyes were red and they all seemed
subdued.

"Where's Tiny?" my father said.

"We thought you were going to get her," Junior said. Like
Sully, she wore pants this morning. She looked like a blue sedan, the
cloth stretched taut across her wide hips, one roll of fat cresting
above the mound of belly. Junior's face drooped and she apparently
had slept very little; the energy of earlier in the morning was gone.
The rims of her eyes were red as sores.

"I thought she would come on the bus," my father said.

My mother came out from the kitchen. "I'll go," she said.
"You stay here with your sisters."

"I appreciate it," my father said.

"I'll go with you," I said.

Sully stirred in her chair. Her face moved in a slow circle as she talked. "I want to go too."

"You need the fresh air," Junior said.

"What do you mean by that?" Sully said.

Junior tried to smile. "Really," she said. "It'll make you feel better."

"There's plenty of fresh air out here on the porch," Sully said. "It's getting cold."

She lurched from her chair and we walked out. Sully looked for the mockingbird. We went past Junior's car and my grandfather's car. Sully took my mother's arm as they walked. They sat in the front seat of my mother's car and I sat in back.

Sully watched the trees and houses as we drove, looking distractedly out the window, and I could see her turned face, her shiny melon-colored lips drooping like a mustache. "Well, today's the day," she said after a while.

"Yes," my mother said.

"Do you know what, Elizabeth?" Sully said.

"What?"

"I did last night what I told you I thought I ought to do."

"Which one did you do?"

"I called George and told him off. I told him I'm finished with him for good. I told him on the phone last night that he's a son of a bitch and he's off my list forever. I thought he was going to cry like a baby."

"Your life needs some readjustment," my mother said.

"Well, I readjusted the hell out of it last night. That's what was going on when you came into the den last night."

"It seemed that you were very angry."

"Boy, I'll say. Harlan was right there, he'll tell you how I told him off."

"What are you going to do now, though, Sully? Where are you going to live?"

"Well, Herman's coming."

"Herman?" my mother said. "Herman's coming here?"

Sully nodded. "I think he'll be here this morning."

"Herman's coming to the funeral?"

146

"I asked him to."

"And you think he will?"

"He does everything I ask him. But to tell you the truth, I'm a little nervous about it, because it *does* make things permanent with George. If he knows I've been alone in the same town with Herman for as much as five minutes, he'll never let me back in the house again."

"Maybe you should ask Herman not to come." My mother sounded hopeful.

"Well, Herman has this idea for a job. Do you think Harlan would lend us the money to move back here?"

"Sully, he just loaned you the money to move from Connecticut to California three months ago. I don't know. I don't think he'd go for it."

"I don't have that much to move. George said he had already shipped it on the bus. But just a little to get a fresh start, you know. If Herman's job pans out, it's this great idea—"

"Herman always seems to have an idea for some great job. What happened to the idea for a job in California?"

"Well, I don't know. It didn't pan out, or something. And you know I was living with George. Herman was afraid if he had any money, George wouldn't let him come around. You wouldn't believe how mean the son of a bitch is. You should have heard what he told me on the phone last night."

"But Sully—"

"I think this one would really work out. He can get a job selling used cars, anytime, but what kind of career is that? He's fifty-two years old, he's got to think in terms of a career, you know what I mean? Don't you think so? I think this one would really be great. He's going to talk to Harlan about it when he gets here."

"Herman is coming all the way across the country to talk to Harlan about a job he *might* get?"

"Well, it's this idea we had. I think Harlan will go for it. I bet we could pay you back what we owe in four, five months."

"Go for it? Go for what?"

"Well," Sully said, smiling as she drawled, her nervous grin reflected in her window. "We'll just have to see about it. Herman will talk to Harlan when he gets here. I told him as long as it was my idea, at least he could talk to Harlan about it himself."

My mother looked at me in the rearview mirror and I shrugged my shoulders.

We had gone through most of the town and we turned into the street on which Tiny lived.

"I haven't been in Death Valley in a thousand years," Sully said, looking out the window at the desolate, crumbling section of the city she had named years before.

Some of the houses we passed were unpainted and sagged in the middle of the roof line; they looked like piles of scrap lumber dumped onto bare weeded lots not much exceeding in linear dimension the houses themselves. Others were owned by their inhabitants and were in good repair, painted white or sometimes in bright colors, their porches solid and even, their yards growing grass and shrubbery and an occasional tree. Tiny's house stood out among them, despite the fact that she, in effect, rented it from my grandfather as part of her pay. It was small and old, but it always looked as though it had just been painted. The tiny house had a little porch, with a railing around it painted green, bright lines across the face of the house. The shutters were also dark green. A flower bed stretched in front of the porch, and flower beds lined the short walkway to the steps. The beds were covered with pine needles now; in spring the house looked like an afterthought to the garden surrounding it, or merely a place to hold the profusion of porch plants.

I walked onto the porch and Tiny called out before I knocked on the door.

"Who?" she yelled.

"Harlan," I yelled through the door.

"Why, ain't you nice," she said. "Come on in."

The house was dark and warm and full of smells. The smell of kerosene like heavy musk mingled with odors of cooking, the odors going rancid as always but never quite stinking before they faded and were replaced by fresher smells of the same origin from the kitchen. From just inside the door where I stood, I could see into the kitchen. There was a door in front of me that led to the bedroom; there were no other rooms. I could hear Tiny walking in the portion of the kitchen beyond my view.

"I got to fix my hair," Tiny said. "I be out in a minute."

I could hear a metal top being unscrewed and a moment later a thump as she put the whiskey down and then the tin sound of the top turning back on. "Here I come!" she called.

She wore a long dress, dark purple with lighter purple flowers printed on it. The dress fell midway between her knees and ankles, the bottom half of her calf muscles showing, squeezing into tight hard knots as she walked, rolling from side to side. Her wig was on straight but already starting to slide before she reached me at the door. As she passed out the door, she turned her face away from me, but the smell of alcohol billowed all around her, mixing with the kerosene and odors of cooking. Tiny's eyes were red, like those of Sully and Junior and Helen. Her eyes around the deep walnut irises were the color of tobacco.

"They're trying to steal your house, Tiny," Sully said as Tiny climbed into the backseat. I sat beside her.

"Who is?"

"Junior."

"Junior got no use for my house," Tiny said. "She never been out here in her life. Junior wouldn't venture out here for no reason."

"She could sell your house. She wants to get one fourth of whatever it's worth."

"Ain't worth nothing much to nobody but me. Who gone buy that house? And Junior got nothing to do with it no way. Miss Irene told me she was gone leave me that house in her paper."

"Well, something happened," Sully said. "Poppy wasn't dead yet, or something."

"Junior wouldn't take that house from me," Tiny said. "She might try to order me around like she's the mistress of Greenfields and I'm her house nigger, but she ain't mean enough to take the roof from over my head."

"Ha!" Sully said. "What about my brooch?"

"I ain't going to say nothing about that brooch. But she's trying to give that to Carolyn, she ain't even trying to get even that for herself."

"Well, it's a good thing she can't put your house in a pocket or a suitcase. You wouldn't have it five minutes."

Tiny leaned over me and reached into the front seat to pat Sully on the shoulder. I opened the window. "Don't you worry about it, honey," she said. "Miss Irene's paper and Mist' Harlan gone take care of everything."

"I got the impression Junior and Helen made a truce with you this morning," my mother said.

"Me too," Sully said. "I wonder what the bitch is up to."

"Don't you think the funeral coming up has a lot to do with it?"

"I don't know, Elizabeth," Sully said with sad reluctance. She sighed. "Sometimes it's hard to remember that Junior is an actual person."

They were all on the porch when we arrived. My father was leaning in a corner with his arms folded, looking out over the woods and beyond the creek. Roy was talking to Hollis and Richard, and Carolyn and Dolly were talking at each other in low voices across the table. Dolly had red hair as bright as a carrot and she was already plump.

"I never would have gotten anywhere in the business world if I hadn't played football," Roy was saying. Richard sat beside his brother. Hollis, like a pillow in the chair, was staring blankly at the lawn. I looked past the woods and saw that the thunderheads were moving closer. "You ought to go out for one of these city leagues while you're looking for a job. You might not be as lucky as Hollis here. I think forty percent of my success in the business world—I might not be rolling in it, but let me tell you, being a tire salesman for the second largest tire company in the world right in Detroit isn't too bad—is due to having played ball." While he talked, Richard looked from Hollis to his fingernails. Occasionally he mumbled, "Yes sir."

"All these men out here are getting might hungry, Tiny," said Junior. She was trying to smile and her voice sounded as though it required effort for her to use it.

"Well, whyn't you fix something, Junior?" said Tiny.

"I know you don't like anyone else in your kitchen."

Tiny went inside, mumbling on her way. "I don't know," she said. "I never had much chance to find out."

One of Helen's shoes was off and she stared at her foot, turning it to the side and then flat and back again, curling her toes up and down. "I have the prettiest feet," she murmured. She sighed and looked at her daughter, her face momentarily alive and thoughtful with admiration and envy.

Sully stood in the middle of the porch, looking around her. Hollis and Richard did not move. "One of you get up and let your Aunt Sully sit down," Junior said.

They both turned their round faces to their mother, and both slowly rose. "Oh, that's all right," Sully said. "Don't put yourselves out. Sitting's your hobby." They sat down.

"Richard! Get out of that chair."

"But, Mother, she said—"

"Oh, sit here, Sully," Junior said, moving her legs off the lounge chair, slanting them to the floor. She patted the empty space. "Sit here."

Sully sat down. "What time do we have to leave?" she asked my father. He was still leaning, his hands behind his back.

"It's at one," he said.

"I don't think Herman will make it in time for the funeral."

"Herman?" Junior said. "Herman? Isn't he one of your husbands? He's coming here?"

"Y'all have never met Herman, have you?" Sully asked. "He sure wanted to come and I thought this would be a good time for all of you to meet him."

"I feel like I know him well enough," my father said. "I talk to him on the phone about a loan every month or two."

"He's coming *here?*" Junior said. "Now?"

"Like I said, I don't think he'll make it in time for the funeral."

"But he's actually coming? Today?"

"I think so," Sully said. "I think he'll get here today."

"Where's he going to stay?" Junior said. "He can't stay here."

Sully looked at Junior. "Why not?" she said, her voice edged, the nasal tone rising.

"There's not enough room."

"I guess everybody would curl up and die if I mentioned the parlor," Sully said. "Can't he stay at your house? Since you're staying over here?"

"I don't want some *sales*man loose in my house," Junior said. "Besides, Carolyn and Dolly are staying there. I don't think it would be a very good idea for him to stay there with them."

"Oh, for Christ's sake, Junior, he's my *hus*band." Junior looked at her and my mother and father looked up. Sully looked around. "Well, he was. And we're going to get married again."

"He can stay in a hotel," Junior said.

"Richard and Hollis are staying there, too," Sully said. "It's not like—"

"You're right, so there wouldn't be room there, either. Tiny!"

Through the window I could see Tiny. She wore her uniform and she was washing the dishes they had left from breakfast. "You better take a head count," Junior called. "I know I can't eat today." She asked each person in turn about their appetite and reported each answer to Tiny, yelling through the window. She turned to Sully last.

"I'm sure you'll want to eat," she said.

"I don't feel like it," Sully said. "I never eat lunch anyway."

"You've got to eat," Junior said. "You ought to put on weight. People are going to think my sister can't afford to eat. I don't want people thinking my sister can't afford to eat."

"I don't see why he can't stay in the parlor," Sully said.

Let's just wait until after the funeral," Junior said. "Just wait until he gets here." She patted Sully's hand, which Sully quickly removed from her reach.

Tiny stood in the doorway. "It's too cold and too crowded to eat out here," she said. "Y'all can come get your food in the dining room when it's ready. I'm gone clear off that table."

"Wait!" Junior said, popping from the lounge chair. "Wait, we'll do it." She walked quickly around Sully's long, outstretched legs. "Come on, Helen."

Sully pushed herself to the head of the chair, heaving herself around until she could fall against the back. "Carolyn," she said, "have you heard anything about my . . . um, jewelry?"

Carolyn looked up from her conversation with Dolly. She seemed to be going over her wedding dress thread by thread. "About what, Aunt Sully?"

Sully pulled out a crumpled pack of cigarettes and took one out, bent and twisted. She scratched the match across the lighting surface of its pack, pulling with both hands, and the end of the match crumbled into little pieces that sprayed over her white pants. Roy stepped over and lit her cigarette with a lighter.

"About what, Aunt Sully?"

"Um, jewelry."

"Jewelry?" Carolyn looked bored and innocent. "Have you got some nice jewelry?"

"Oh, God, loads. Like this wonderful brooch, worth absolutely millions. You've seen my brooch, haven't you?"

"No, I never have."

"Never seen it?"

"No, I'd love to see it."

"Well, it's lost. And loads of furniture. I've got loads and loads of antiques, you wouldn't believe it. Oh, you ought to come see all this stuff sometime," she said, speaking very hurriedly, running her words together so fast I could barely understand her. "Y'all ought to come out to California— Oh. Well, wherever. I've got gobs and gobs of stuff you would absolutely go nuts over. You, too, Dolly."

"I'd like to see them sometime," Carolyn said. "Aren't you lucky, to have all those nice things."

Sully looked at me and then at my mother. "Yeah, honey," she said. "I was just born lucky."

Chapter 11 _____

AFTER LUNCH, DRESSED IN BLACK, the three sisters looked serene, each enclosed within herself with her own grief, each personality for the moment blurred, the edges of their differences dulled; they were made for the moment harmonious and composite by the one accord of their grief.

Stepping down from the back porch, Junior and Helen helped down by Roy, and Sully by my father, they formed a black cameo against the sunlit house, framed together for an instant as in a photograph, Sully behind and above Junior and Helen. Sully's tan glowed in the midday light and the tinted hair acquired a sort of dignity. Her sisters, with their veils and dresses, their faces still and pensive, set against the event, looked portly and matronly rather than gross and absurd.

Tiny followed behind, her long purple dress swirling around her calves as she managed the steps alone, holding to the rail, putting the same foot forward on each succeeding step like a child until she reached the bottom. From inside the car, Sully held the door for her. The whiskey reeked and her forehead glistened with beads of sweat. She had been crying and she carried a white handkerchief with which she occasionally dabbed at her eyes.

Helen and Junior entered Junior's car, squeezing in against my cousins. They looked like shrubbery in the backseat. The mockingbird shrieked at us from the pin oak as we pulled out; we had all forgotten to feed him. There were no limousines and no procession, merely my father leading the way in the old man's car. We drove to a portion of the cemetery as yet only slightly used. The site sloped in a gentle swell up from the cemetery road and then down again to the woods. My grandmother had bought it just after the old man went away.

We were sitting at her dining-room table, drinking tea. She had asked me to take her to the cemetery to look at the plot and I did not want to go. "What do you need a grave for?" I said.

"Everyone has to have a grave," she said. "I don't want someone else to pick it out for me after I'm dead. Since I can't be buried at Greenfields, it's not in the family anymore."

"You've never been sick a day in your life. You might outlive us all."

"I'm an old woman and my time will come. I'm ready for it in my heart and I want to have a place to rest. I think I should settle it now so your father won't have to worry about it."

"It's like going out to look at a house or something," I said. "I didn't know graves were advertised in the classifieds."

"It's a private party," my grandmother said. "They're selling the plot themselves, they already bought it from the Rose Hill Perpetual Care Society."

"They decided they won't be needing it after all, I guess."

"Now don't you tease me about this. Folks move, and so on. People advertise them all the time. I tried to get two plots from Rose Hill, but when I went out there, all they had were six plot groupings. Can you imagine anybody wanting six graves together? I can't see what on earth for, myself. Anyway, the man said he did have one two-plot situation left, and he drove me over to see it, but it was in that section where the gravestones are about this high." She held her hand above the floor to show me the height. "And I said are they the same price as the others? Because it was hard to believe they would be. And he said yes and naturally I told him this looks like the poor section, I don't want to be here."

"Well, naturally."

"So I found these in the paper and they're in a *very* good section. They could be gone tomorrow, it's such a good price for the neighborhood. Only two thousand dollars."

"Two thousand dollars? For a little plot of grass? Good Lord! Give me the money, I'll bury you out in the backyard."

"Hush," she said. "They're expensive. This one's five hundred dollars less than most of them."

"It's outrageous."

"You don't want me buried in the city cemetery," she said. "Like a pauper. You don't know what kind of riffraff you might be in with. I'm telling you, the plot's in a very exclusive section, all the best people go there. And it's hardly been used at all."

"Why don't you use the money and go to Florida or somewhere?"

"Why, Harlan, I've got to have a place to rest."

"You could take a long vacation, go anywhere you want. I thought World Travel was your hobby."

She blushed. Several years before, she had gone to London to seek out her forebears in various registers; she was trying to prove connections with Sir Walter Raleigh. When she returned she revised her biography in *Distinguished Persons of North Carolina,* an exclusive book open only to those with fifty dollars for a subscription and a desire to be included in its pages. She crossed out Gardening as her hobby and replaced it with World Travel.

"I can't go running all over everywhere at my age," she said.

"Why not? Poppy's not at home, you could take Tiny with you if you need a traveling companion and help on the way; you've got plenty of money. All these years to make and save all that money, now it's time for you to enjoy it."

"I'm not about to spend it."

"Why not? Your children have plenty of money, except Sully."

"Well, you know what they do. I saw the paragraph about Stella Mixon, I was shocked. I was embarrassed for her."

"What? What are you talking about?"

"The newspaper puts in the financial section how much money is in your estate when it's settled. If I spend all my money, people will think we were poor. Stella's estate was thirty-two thousand dollars, can you imagine?"

"Everybody already knows you're rich," I said.

"Wealth depends on how much you keep during your life, how much you've got left."

So I gave up and we went. She had directions to the plot written on a piece of paper. There were marks on the side of the road that I had never noticed before during my occasional exercise jogs through the cemetery. She stopped me at number 132. "Aisle thirty-two, row eight," she said. "Plot fourteen."

"At least if you decide to leave, it will be easy to find your way out," I said.

"Hush." We walked up the hill. The markers were in the grass too. There were only a few stones marking graves. We reached the top of the hill and stopped. "This is it," she said.

We stood for a moment and looked around. In the direction from which we had come, we could see the creek, a winding gleam through its green wandering valley, and we could see the woods that masked Clifton Park and her house. Away from town were woods and beyond the woods were hills. She looked at and beyond the hazy woods of the hills at the creek going through them out of the town, stared past the hills humped together and fading into the horizon, rising and falling and repeating themselves into the hazy distance. She stood stock still; her chin lifted to the distance, she looked like her own grave marker. "I think I'll like it here," she murmured. "Don't you?"

Across the bright grass a crowd of people waited. They all looked at us as the two cars parked at the end of the line of cars and we crossed on foot toward them. Their eyes on us made our progress seem slow, dreamlike. A green tent hung like a poisonous cloud above the hill, and to one side of the tent humped a pile of clay, raw and red. There were folding chairs in two rows.

The crowd parted in the middle as we approached, and as they absorbed us it felt warmer. I could distinguish among them people who had visited the night before, and here and there saw a face vaguely remembered from years past; the majority were strangers to me. Suddenly the coffin lay before us at eye level, looking very large, looming out of proportion to the frail body of my grandmother in the last weak days of her life. Such a monstrous metal thing seemed entirely unnecessary for the sparse remains it held. I averted my eyes, looking at Sully, and saw her turning her face away too, looking at the ground. My father led us along the line of chairs; there were not enough spaces in the front row, and Tiny and I sat in the second row. When we had taken our places, the waiting crowd filled in the remaining seats. Each chair squeaked as it was sat on; the noise embarrassed everyone. The squeaking stopped and there was a rustling; then a complete stillness until the edge of the tent over the grave began to slap in the wind.

A tall, thin man with freckles and hair the color of the clay behind him stepped forward and intoned a beginning. The hole in the ground was covered with a piece of green canvas, matching the tent above our heads; two bars of steel protruded on the near side. As soon as the preacher began speaking, thunder began to rumble, mingling with his chanting voice; this reality was so melodramatic and absurd as to be almost unbearable. I looked at the clouds, higher on the horizon but still not above us, darker now and unfolding toward us as I watched. The preacher called sonorously on the Lord to witness His faithful servant's joining Him, listing and extolling precisely those virtues she had lacked. He recalled and lingered over the piano she had given the church, bringing to ninety-nine the total number at its disposal; he spoke of her career and success as a wife and mother, while the thunder rolled as though on cue in a bad film, and the clay behind the man, almost the color of blood, made the funeral like a dream, distant and not quite tangible, less real than a dream. Except: I could not look at the coffin; the side of Tiny's face shone, a constant flowing stream; Sully and her sisters and Tiny made a chorus of wailing, their conclamant cries ascending into the sky and spreading across the afternoon, as circles from a stone thrown in water push further and further out in waves, their grief and noise of grief spreading across the clean grass, mingling with the thunder, the preacher's morbid tone, the clay the color of blood.

It was over very quickly. As they arose, Junior took Sully's face between her palms. "Don't cry, baby," she said. "Don't cry." Junior was crying still. Sully stared in blank surprise.

They filed out one by one. My father took Sully on one arm and my mother on the other; I escorted Tiny. The heavy odor of chrysanthemums flooded us as we passed the coffin; Sully ran her fingertips along its length. A blade-faced man with slick hair stood at the end of the coffin, looking both proprietary and bored; he nodded to each of us as we passed.

The grass was still wet from the dew, not evaporating, I supposed, in the chilling air; I thought by nightfall the morning's dew might be ice. That sort of weather happens in our country; when I was six we had a day in January with the thermometer racing upward to a summery seventy degrees, and the next day there were three inches of snow on the ground. Our shoes were covered with the dew and with freshly cut blades of grass. Sully stumbled in front of us, hanging onto my father's arm. We reached the car. My father joined his other sisters at Junior's car, and together in a line they gravely shook hands, accepting condolences like little gifts.

"Should I go over there and be with them, Elizabeth?" Sully asked. "Do I have to?"

"Not if you don't feel like it," my mother said gently. "I'm sure they'd all understand."

"I'd rather not," Sully said, wiping her eyes. She raised one gloved hand, showing us a white chrysanthemum. She smiled faintly and said, "Look, I got one of the flowers."

"Ain't that nice," Tiny said. "My, my."

"Did you want one, Tiny?" my mother said.

My father opened the door and started the engine. His face was a mask.

"Yessum," Tiny said, the car pulling away. "I sho' wish I had me one, I never thought to get one. I thought the funeral parlor would want to use 'em again. It must be hard to find mums in wintertime." She looked at the flower. The brown streaks in the corneas made her eyes look like the eyes of an old poodle. "I could keep it on my dresser to remember her by. I would keep it until the day I die."

Sully fondled the petals of the flower with her fingertips, looking at it with the same longing expression as Tiny. Suddenly she thrust the flower at Tiny. "Here, you take it," she said.

"Oh, Law, chile," Tiny said, her eyes wide, lurching against me away from the extended hand. "I couldn't take that flower from you. You *needs* that flower."

"I want you to have it, Tiny," Sully said. "Please take it. I've got my brooch."

"Not yet you ain't."

"I will. That's all I need to remember her by. When we get back to the house, I'm going to get a lawyer over there and raise a ruckus about Junior taking everything until she coughs up that brooch. Here, take it."

"Don't you go fussing with them," Tiny said. She looked at the flower; Sully pressed it on her. Tiny reached out gingerly and took hold of the flower and when Sully released it into her hand, she held it steadily in front of her breast, gazing down at it. "Thank you, Sully," she said very quietly. "If you ain't the sweetest thing. You always were the sweetest thing."

My mother was jabbing my father in the front seat. Finally he sighed and nodded his head.

Sully beamed through her sorrow, which had been steadily

wearing out. "I'm glad you like it," she said. She seemed happier than at any moment since we had met her at the airport. She turned to look out the window, watching the scenery flash by. "There's the old folks' home over there," she said. "I wonder what Poppy's thinking about in there."

My mother fumbled in her pocketbook. "Sully," she said.

"Yes, honey." She still stared vacantly out the window.

"I found your brooch."

"You did?" she asked, turning to her. "Where?" she said, excitement growing as belief took hold. "Where is it?" She perched forward on the seat.

"Never mind where I found it. It's here now." She reached over the back of the front seat, holding out the brooch.

Sully gazed in wonder, childlike, gingerly plucking the brooch away. It glittered on the palm of her glove. Delight spread across her face and her eyes danced with light; she looked for a moment as she had in my childhood.

"My brooch!" she shrieked, exploding, bouncing up and down on the seat, springing Tiny into the air each time she landed. "My brooch, my brooch!"

Tiny beamed with her, holding her wig with one hand. Sully stopped bouncing and Tiny said, "Ain't that the nicest thing. I knowed Miss Elizabeth was gone get you that pin somehow." Tiny patted Sully on the shoulder as Sully leaned forward to embrace my mother, squeezing her around the neck with both arms, pinning her to the back of the front seat.

"Thank you, Elizabeth," she said. "You always were more like a sister than either one of those bitches. How did you get it away from them?"

"They didn't know I was going to give it to you."

"The bitches," Sully said, grinning down at her brooch.

"Just don't pawn it," my father said.

"Ain't it nice," Tiny said. "I got me a flower, and now you got your brooch."

We pulled into the driveway, Roy and Junior and Helen and my cousins behind us. "Are you sure they don't know, Elizabeth?"

"I'm positive they don't," my mother said. "Junior's going to faint when she sees it."

Sully giggled with delight.

160

"Don't you cause no trouble you can't finish, girl," Tiny said. "You got your brooch, now you behave yourself."

Sully hopped out of the car and skipped down the driveway to Junior's car. Roy and my cousins were already going toward the steps and Junior and Helen were consoling one another in the backseat. Sully stood on Junior's side, waiting for her, grinning, unable to stand still. She clasped her hands behind her back, hiding the brooch. All sluggishness had vanished. She bobbed from side to side and then up and down, as though making short bows in quick succession.

Junior got out of the car and Sully danced in front of her. Junior saw the smile as she left the car and tried to force one on her own face. Sully shoved her hand into Junior's face, laughing, tinkling and musical. "Look what I got!" she shouted.

Junior stopped, stared, her expression of grief and her attempted smile melting together into a frieze of bewilderment. She stared at the diamonds sparkling in Sully's hand and glared at my mother. She grabbed at Sully's hand. "Mother said—" she began to shout.

Sully twisted violently out of her grasp and ran backward against the privet hedge, scaring the mockingbird from underneath it up into the pin oak. "Leave me alone!" she screamed. "It's mine!"

My father turned on the steps. "Junior," he said.

Tiny jumped in front of Junior as she started after Sully. "You leave that little girl alone," she said. "That brooch of hers is none of your bidness." She stood glaring up into Junior's red face, one huge black hand on a hip, the other in a fist in front of her midriff, holding the chrysanthemum.

In silent fury Junior started to stomp away. But she turned and looked Tiny up and down. "What are you doing with that flower?" she demanded viciously, her voice rasping. She snatched the flower with a roundhouse sweep of her arm and tore it and threw it into the air with one motion. "I paid for those flowers," she said. "Those were *my* flowers on that coffin."

Tiny stood transfixed, her mouth open, watching the pieces and petals float down around her. She watched them float to the ground and then stood rigid, staring down at the pieces. Junior towered fatly over her, her lip curled in contempt and small bitter triumph. Behind Tiny, sinking into the hedge, Sully shook with rage or fear.

Tiny pounced in a flash, her dress flowing around her calves,

161

her hand squeezed into a fist just like a man's. She held her hand behind her ear and swung at Junior, now immobile in her turn, her eyes going wide. The blow sounded like a gunshot, snapping back Junior's head. She staggered heavily backward, her eyes rolled up, and she fell into a sitting position, her legs sprawled in front of her.

"Golly," Sully said. "Junior, you shouldn't have done that."

Junior sat in the driveway, her mouth open, her eyes unfocused, seeing neither my father nor Helen as they hurried toward her. Roy had come to the back door and stood on the step above my mother, speechless and frozen into place. Blood trickled from Junior's mouth onto her dress. The red glowed against the black like ceramic jewelry. As her eyes began to focus, they opened wide and surprised at Tiny, and her jaw dropped as though she were yawning.

Tiny stooped in the driveway, her legs wide apart, her dress spread like a tent between them. She cried and mumbled, picking up the petals of the flower. She found one piece larger than the rest, examined it, and held it up for Sully to see as Sully kneeled beside her to help, and then continued searching for and picking up the petals, silent and earnest and absorbed.

Junior looked on dazedly, sounds beginning to emerge from her mouth, the stream of blood still trickling as my father helped her to her feet, while Helen fluttered around with nervous hands. "I still think Carolyn ought to have it," Helen said, her voice timid and shaking. "Don't you, Harlan?"

Sully looked briefly up. "You can't steal something that's been mine for fifty years," she said. "It's my family heirloom; I got it when I was born."

"Aren't you going to do something?" Junior said, her voice thick. "Aren't you even going to call the police?"

My father pushed her gently toward the house. My mother took her by the elbow to help her up the steps. Junior turned and said, "You, Tiny!" Tiny continued looking for her petals. Some of them were stuck to her wrist and the back of her hands, gleaming white against the black. "You're fired!" Junior yelled.

Sully looked closely at Tiny.

Tiny looked up at me, her face grave, utterly calm now. "Didn't I tell you I don't work for that strange woman?" she said.

She licked her forefinger and pressed it against the last petals, brushed them into her other palm. She and Sully stood. The mockingbird was shrieking from its favorite limb in the pin oak. "I better feed my bird before I go," Tiny said. "It gone be one freezing night tonight."

"I'll feed him again," I said.

"You won't forget?"

"No, I won't forget."

"Course you won't."

We stood for a moment, casting looks at the darkened sky.

"Fixing to rain," Tiny said. She held her fist, clutching the petals, straight out from her hip.

Sully took Tiny's arm in her hand. "Come downtown with me. I have some things to do. I've got to buy some clothes before I meet Herman at the depot."

"Got to git home before this rain falls."

"It's on the way."

"I got to get my things."

"You can get them later," I said.

"Come on," Sully said. She pulled at Tiny's arm.

"I told you I don't work for that strange woman," she said again. She began walking with Sully toward the bus stop on the corner.

I watched them for a moment and then listened for the mockingbird, but he was gone. The rain began, falling in large spattering drops, and I went inside the house.

Chapter 12 _____

W<small>E SAT IN SILENT INSULARITY</small> in the living room. As time passed, the sense of waiting grew more and more oppressive, although we had no notion of what we waited for. Junior's children had driven Roy and Carolyn to the airport, and then gone home themselves. After they had left, Junior went into the den and, speaking loudly so that we could hear, made an appointment with a lawyer on an urgent matter. Then she fell again onto the sofa. She had been holding a washrag to her cheek for more than an hour, occasionally taking the cloth away to look minutely for spots of blood.

I went into the kitchen and came back with an apple. The crunching seemed to fill the room. I remembered my grandmother giving me an apple when I was twelve years old, telling me not to waste any of it, sternly watching me to be sure I ate enough of it, then growing concerned as I chewed away at seeds, core, and stem.

Once Junior rose and went into the hall, examined herself in the mirror. We heard her gasp as she saw the swollen cheek. "I look like a frog!" she yelped. She pounded back into the living room and lay down again.

Finally I went around and turned on the lights. Because of the heavy clouds and the rain, it was as dark as night. The air was growing colder and colder. Already the rain was mixed with sleet.

"You'll be all right, dear," Helen said gently. Junior started at the sound of her voice and glared at her. She glared at my father, and at me, and last and longest at my mother.

She spoke to the back of the sofa. "Attacked by a half-wild nigger servant and nobody lifted a finger. Nobody said now, Tiny, that's not right. Like it was *my* fault. Even if I can't understand why my mother's dying wish concerning a valuable heirloom should be denied on the very day of her funeral, I guess I can live with it because I couldn't have expected otherwise. But why somebody couldn't even call the police is beyond me. As if she was the sister and I was the maid. I suppose that's what I get for having acted like a maid in this house for twenty years. And who knows but what she might get likkered up and come back here to finish me off. At least then somebody would probably call the po—"

"Here she is," my mother said. We all stirred at once as the door opened and we could hear the sudden loud drumming of the rain in the gutter.

"If she has that black witch with her . . ." Junior muttered.

Sully hummed, a wavering, thin melody; the sound preceded her into the house. There was rustle of paper bags being stacked in the hall. Then Sully made her entrance. At first glance she appeared to be a new woman, newly arrayed; she posed in the doorway, hips thrown out, arms spread, her hands dripping from her wrists, a big smile on her face as she trumpeted, "Da-da daddaaa!"

Junior looked her up and down. Junior's face bore a look of astonished dismay which turned to puzzlement, and finally, as the truth struck her, to triumph.

"Where's your brooch, Sully?" she said.

Sully flicked her eyes at my father, twice, and then around the room, as though she were looking for it. Suddenly she slapped and snatched at the dress. She looked down at the cloth above her breast and opened her mouth wide. She clasped her hands dramatically in front of her. "My God! I've been robbed."

"Didn't I say she'd pawn it! What did I tell you! Did I say she would, or didn't I!" Junior said, almost yelling, her voice strident with fierce, bitter triumph. She raised herself on the sofa to one elbow, twisted her neck to Helen, the washcloth still against her cheek. "Helen, what did I say she would do with the *heirloom?*"

Helen looked at Sully with an expression so nakedly hateful that Sully turned away. "Pawn it," Helen said.

"You see," Junior said, falling back into the sofa.

"I tell you, I've been robbed." Sully looked again at the floor, in front of her new shoes and behind her in the hall, as though she might find the brooch without moving from her spot, as though it might have followed her home. "Or it's lost."

"Pawned it," Junior said.

Sully seemed to shrink inside her new clothes. Suddenly she

whirled out of the room, gathered her paper bags, and headed for the kitchen.

"We have a responsibility here, Harlan," Junior said.

"What do you mean?" my father said.

"I told you she'd pawn that thing. She's going to throw away the rest of Poppy's money if we don't do something about it."

"She can't touch his money," my mother said.

"Her inheritance."

"She doesn't get it yet," my mother said. "Nobody gets anything yet. Your father's still alive."

"Golly, that's right," said Helen.

Junior answered my father as though he had spoken. "She's fifty years old and Poppy's not going to be around much longer, painful though it is to think of. She hasn't grown up at fifty, she won't be grown up when he dies. She never will. I know people don't see any reason to care about my feelings—why should they? But at least we can protect Sully from herself and the inheritance for all our descendants. We've got to do something about her."

My father sighed deeply. "I've got to go see Poppy," he said. "Find out if they untied him yet."

"I've got it all worked out."

"There's nothing we can do about it."

"I think there is; I'll be executrix of the will, and if you'll help me with it, I think we can put her share of the inheritance in trust, and I'll take care of it for her. I could handle that too, as long as I've gone without pay for everything else from grocery shopping to handling rents, and getting beat up for my troubles, why I might as well—"

"Your face is looking much better," my mother said.

"And she needs a long rest. A *very* long rest, where people can take care of her."

"It's her money," my father said. "When it comes."

"Isn't it her child's money too? If she gets all that money at once, she'll blow it in a week. It only took her two hours to convert that brooch into clothes and whiskey." Junior snorted, remembered her washrag, and put it again to her cheek. "On the day of her mother's funeral!"

"It's disgusting," Helen said.

"Helen's with me. Are you?"

My father stood. He looked out at the gray light. It looked later than it was. "I don't see what I can do about it," he mumbled.

"Don't you want to protect her? Don't you know she'll blow every nickel that comes her way?"

"She probably will."

Junior pointed to the portrait of her father hanging on the wall above my father's head. The man in the picture and in the chair were the same age; if someone had drawn a mustache on the portrait, they would have looked like brothers. "Do you think he would have let her get away with it?"

"He's the one wrote the will. I've got to go see him. It's past three o'clock."

"Well, I'm trustee and I'm going to have a thing or two to say about it."

"No," my father said, forcibly gentle; his nose almost against the windowpane. It occurred to me suddenly that his reluctance to confront Junior was not merely the family habit of reticence, but his state of mind as well; he was the only one grieving, and they would not let him alone to grieve in peace. "You won't be executing the will." He was very quiet and very sure. "I'm going to be executor, and if I can do anything to save some money for Sully in her old age, I will, but you won't have anything to do with it."

"What? What do you mean, I'm not going to be executrix?" Junior forgot about her wounds and sat bolt upright, cradling her stomach in her lap. "What are you talking about?"

"I've got to go see Poppy." Little beads of ice clicked against the glass. He turned around, but did not look at anyone. "We'll talk about it when I get back."

Sully came into the room with a drink in her hand. "I called the police," she said. "They said they didn't think there was much chance of catching anybody."

"Ha!" Junior said. "You can say that again."

"I guess I'm going to have to talk to you about that brooch," my father said.

"I called Tiny, too, to see if she had noticed any suspicious characters lurking around downtown and *she* didn't see how on *earth* it could have been stolen, it's probably just lost, she said." Sully looked nervously at the edges of all the faces in the room.

"I bet," my father said sourly. "I've got to go."

167

"Somebody tell Sully she better find it," Junior said. "I've decided as trustee of the estate that unless she gets that brooch back and gives it to Carolyn, she's not getting anything from her inheritance. Not a penny. Tell her I said that."

"You can't do that!" Sully whirled to my father, her new dress swirling around her thin legs, looking out of place on her. "Can she do that?"

"I'm going to see Poppy."

"Listen," Sully said. She twisted her fingers together, shifted weight from one leg to the other. They were standing in the middle of the living room like strangers to the house, unsure of where to sit. "Herman's in town."

Junior popped up, the washrag clamped to her cheek. "He can't stay here."

"I saw him downtown. I met him down there, took Tiny with me. And he asked me to talk to you."

"I can't lend you two any more money," my father said. "I understand you've left George."

"Oh, we won't need any money, it's this idea we had. An idea for a job. Herman's waiting at the bus station for me to call him back. I bet we could pay you back what we owe you in a year or two. I bet we could pay you back sooner than that, because this is a *golden* opportunity, and Herman's just perfect for it. We'd have enough money from this to invest and God knows what would happen if I could just get started with some capital."

"She could dream up a whole string of chicken farms out of one egg," Junior muttered.

"I don't care about what you owe me," my father said. "It's just that I can't do any more. What kind of job has Herman found?"

"Well, it sort of depends on you. Since Junior's not going to be trustee anymore."

Junior muttered to the sofa, "Sneaking around *eaves*dropping. A certain person around here I won't mention, even if I could keep her last name straight from year to year, not that I need to mention who—"

"Depends on me? Depends on me how? Does he need a recommendation, or what?"

"Well, I don't know all the reasons for what's going on."

168

Sully's sleepy drawl came in staccato bursts with odd effect, like an uneven pulse. Her hands in front of her dress seemed to be washing themselves. "But she's *not* going to be trustee, is she, and so— Wait. This will just take a minute. . . . So what I've thought out is this: you'll be out of state and who around here can handle the estate and Poppy's bills and stuff like that? Nobody. And you don't want to drive all the way down here all the time. All those stocks and bonds, and things . . ."

"I'm going to sell his houses right away. I'm going to list them with an agent in the morning, before I leave. The other things I can handle from up there, but what—"

"All these things to look after," Sully said, making her hands go alternately white and red with the twisting pressure. She cleared her throat, sat down suddenly on a Queen Anne sidechair. It creaked and she jumped up.

"That's Junior's chair," Helen said. "Mother gave it to her four Easters ago. I was here with Carolyn. I remember exactly what—"

"And you need somebody to look after them, since you won't be here, and Junior, for reasons we need not go into—" Sully's voice grew elaborately careful and she fluttered her blue eyelids at her, then continued. "So, there it is."

My father waited. He looked as gray and cold and tired as the day outside. "There what is?"

"Herman's *job!* He could do all these estate things for the family. The estate needs a manager. . . ."

Junior looked like she did not know whether to laugh or scream.

My father looked at her blankly and coughed and looked away. "Sully, this is the craziest idea you've come up with yet," he said. "The man can't even manage his own salary, when he has one. It's so absurd I don't know what to say. It's ridiculous."

"He only wants fifteen thousand a year," Sully said. "He's going to take the bus to Memphis at five if he can't do it."

"Fifteen thousand? Dollars?" Junior exclaimed. "There's nothing to do! It doesn't take half an hour a month, clipping some little coupons, making rent deposits."

"Ha!" Sully said. "You're the one who's complained about how hard you've been working at their affairs since Mother got sick."

169

Junior addressed the empty fireplace. "Tell Mrs. Whatever-her-name-is-today that her extreme stupidity made me forget for one moment that I'm not speaking to her." She stood, the limp wash-cloth to her face. "Come on, Helen. I've got to dress for my appointment with the lawyer. *He'll* straighten things out around here in a hurry, I can tell you that." As they heaved together up the stairs her disembodied, angry voice came like an echo. "Stealing heir-looms, stealing . . ."

"It's out of the question, Sully," my father said. "Junior's right, there's not much to be done. Not enough for a full-time person. Even if we did need to hire someone, it wouldn't be Herman. Tell him to forget it. It's absolutely impossible."

"He needs a job," Sully said faintly, looking at the floor. I could barely hear her. "He needs it to support me."

"He'll have to find another one. After Poppy's expenses in the home, there's not much cash left anyway."

Sully sat in the sidechair again. "I told George I'm not coming back," she droned. "I told him I'm going to stay with Herman, and George is ready to kill me, good riddance, he said." She put her head in her hands and tugged her hair. "What am I going to do?"

"I'm going to see our father," my father said. "You said you wanted to see him sometime while you're here. Do you want to go now?"

Sully raised her head and stared out the window at the rain. "No," she whispered.

"I'll be out in a minute," I said as my parents left.

I sat and watched Sully watch the rain. "There's ice out there now," she said. "It's amazing, how hot it was yesterday, how cold today."

"You've lost them both now, haven't you?"

"Yes." She was sitting perfectly still, her face empty, chewing her lower lip to ribbons.

"What are you going to do?"

Drops of water on the windowpanes traced broken lines. The drops grew large and heavy and rolled down, strewing fragments of themselves. When almost nothing was left they stopped flowing, filled and spilled again until they reached the bottom.

She turned her face from the window and looked directly into my eyes, shaking her head sadly as though not for herself but for me. "More things happen to people in this world than you ever dreamed of," she said. She looked out the window again. "I don't know what I'm going to do," she said. "I always wanted to do something shining and wonderful and I've never done anything at all, except one time. I've only lived two weeks out of my entire fifty years. If you knew how much I loved him!" she said. I thought she was going to cry, but she did not.

"Herman?"

"No, no," Sully said. "Good God, Herman. *Him.* I know you know about it. I know it's no secret. When I was sixteen. If you knew how much I loved him you would sink down on your knees and thank the Lord that He allowed someone somewhere to love so much. Oh God, oh God, I loved him more than breath! And Mother took my breath, my breath of life, she came and snatched me one of those few times he was gone, pulled me out practically screaming and kicking, grabbed me by the hair and slapped my face and called me names I never knew she knew and drug me down the hall like a goddamned runaway dog. If your mother hadn't been there I know I would have died. My breath! She knew Mother would take the only beauty in my life—the only love I ever knew, the only purity I ever had—and twist it into something hideous and filthy and dark and terrible and she wouldn't let her do that. I would have died maybe I shouldn't thank her for that, I think I would have been better off dead—and when I do die, and if I go to Heaven, I'll wake up in a hotel room in Baltimore with him by my side and it will be dawn and the sun's red light will shine on his face and I'll watch his whole body bloom like a rose in the growing light and I'll lie there and the smell of his body will fill me and then I will touch him and his body will fill me and fill me with joy and I'll live that moment over and over forever and ever and if you were to ask me did I then, during those two weeks out of my fifty years, did I delight in daylight so begun, I would say I would die, *let* me die a death each day backwards to sixteen to have one more instant of that impossible joy."

She pressed her nose and forehead against the window, rolling her forehead on the pane, back and forth.

"In that room was like floating in silky clouds the earth a million miles away; all storm outside and cold, and fluffy and warm together inside our room, the room around us like a tight closet but at the same time the walls moved out and out, like a bank of cloud taking over the sky, and sky and sea and everything that was, was part of us; cozy and warm, and the whole universe, all at once. The little room that was my world, is where I live still, my only home."

She turned to me again. "Except for those two weeks, those few other times I was ever happy—and there were damn few times— it was a pale glittery thing, a feeling I could never touch or really understand, it was like it was all outside me, like a dream that never touched me but sort of filmed me over; it was—it was this feeling high and sharp, like bubbles almost invisible rising in champagne: you never can see for sure what happened to them. And when the happiness was gone, what little there was never lasted long, there was nothing but a foul taste in my mouth and a hammering in my head and I wanted to die. And now there is nothing, now I hold back the fading crescent of eclipse, turn my eyes inward to the bitter dark: I'm going to die a grim terrible lingering death. I know I am. I'm too tired to even hold it back anymore. I might as well have cancer too. Or be locked up with Poppy, foaming at the mouth and prancing around the nut house like a monkey in a cage."

She heaved out a sigh.

"What about Peanut? You could live with your son, couldn't you?"

She spoke in a dry precise voice I had never heard her use before, as though she were measuring in centimeters the length of her sentence. "My son has been a great disappointment to me. He won't speak to me."

"But—the letter . . . and—"

"Oh, I know what I said. I just wanted to brag. I wanted him to be what I never was. I haven't seen or even heard from Peanut— George—in years. And do you think Georgie really quit because of that germ warfare, or whatever? Hell, no! He's just too damn lazy to work for a living." She threw back her head and screeched her high metallic laugh. "Just like his goddamn mother! Isn't that rich? Is that perfect?"

"But at least you could live with him. You've got to have some- where to live, some way to live."

"He won't even *speak* to me." She bent forward, face in her hands, eyes covered. "When I tried to call him last night. He was there, he wasn't even asleep. He wouldn't come to the phone, won't call back. He wasn't communing with the desert. His mother just isn't good enough for him to talk to. Who can blame him?"

"I don't understand. The letters he sends . . ."

"He wrote that stupid letter five years ago, when he was still in college. I think he was asking for money. Now he's a worse junkie than I am. He can't stand it in his mother. He thinks I'm the worst trash he ever heard of. He kicked me out of his pad. Some misunderstanding. . . . He just completely *mis*understood the entire situation. I mean the boy was a *child,* eighteen, or something. It wasn't what he thought at all, nothing going on. . . ."

The horn honked outside. Through the rain it sounded far away.

"Are you going to be all right?"

"I look out the window on the world, I see no colors; I go outside, I can't feel breezes anymore, can't smell anything, everything's gone all still and gray on me. I'm like a blind little speck, a little eyeless maggot, munching shit from day to day—and *why?* Why, why? What have I done? Why do I have to take all the blame? Why can't I blame my mother? Can I blame my mother? *How* can I blame my mother, the creepy bitch, the insect egg-laying bitch: because she was raised by a dying race already ancient and cold as stone statuary the day she was born. *Her* fault? She suffered as much in her way as I have in mine. And my wonderful sisters? Aren't they the same? *Exactly* the same as me, only killing themselves with different drugs?

"I thank God *you* have escaped. I wonder if the *way* you have— No, I musn't tell you that, I don't care how, as long as you have. Well, I do care, because—I guess I *do* have to tell you: in your own way, your kind, gentle, retiring, sweet-spoken way, uninvolved and uncommitted, you are just as cold as she was. I don't want to hurt you, I want to save you from it. Because sometimes for all you say and do you might as well be deaf and dumb. What do you think of that?"

"I don't know."

"He doesn't know. The boy, this man now, the *brilliant* young graduate with the super-duper job in Norfolk, Virginia, he doesn't know. Let me tell you, honey, you better find out, and you better find out quick, or one day soon you'll die in your steps while you're walking along minding your own business and you will shrivel into a maggot like me—another kind of a bug, maybe, but no less a bug you surely will be, dried out, nearly invisible, your little plug of a soul feeding on its own cowpile. You can take that straight from the maggot's mouth."

"But Sully, I care—"

"Oh, of course you do. You care terribly, deeply, who else do I know who cares so much for so many people. And does so little about it. In this way you've got your own strain of the family disease; you refuse the responsibility of blood to blood and generation to generation, and if you don't want to be like the rest of us, you better learn to take it on."

"Sully," I said. "I know people need people, I know—"

"Oh, Jesus, you're so young. So very young. You know I can't talk, I'm not articulate, so how can I explain it to you? You have to learn it anyway, nobody can tell it to you. It's not that people need people, it's how, it's what they need each other *for*—forget it. Go now, go to your grandfather, my father."

"Sully—"

"Go. Leave me with my little soul, my silver drop of grief, my lovely life. Leave me be."

"Are you going to be all right?"

"Terrific," she said. "You go on with your father to see Poppy. I'll be fine." She sucked in a great breath and steadied her body and her voice. She traced letters on the windowpane with one of her long curved nails. "I'll be absolutely splendiferous."

174

Chapter 13 _____

THE NOISE OF THE THUNDERSTORM had rolled away and the rain had settled into a steady, slow pour that fell colder and colder, beginning already to freeze on the trees, as winter at last declared itself. The wind slashed like a knife, cuffed the trees, their branches clacking together. As we fought across the parking lot, the wind searched through our clothes and we were wet and chilled before we reached the door.

The old man was not waiting at the door. We rambled through the halls toward his room; he was no longer tied to the radiator.

"Well, I guess he calmed down, anyway," I said. "I guess he hasn't tried to run away since this morning."

He was not in his room. The bed was made, the green spread slightly wrinkled, as though it had been sat upon by a visitor. On the flimsy chest lay a brush and comb. They belonged to the nursing home. The closet door was open; there was nothing within except one coat hanger. It was as though no one lived in the room at all.

We stood for a moment in the middle of the room. My father poked his head inside the bathroom.

"Where is he?" I asked, as though my father would know.

There was no one at the nurses' station in the hall. We went toward the lobby and the main desk. We heard a hurried squeak behind us; the foam rubber nurse of yesterday trotted up breathlessly.

"Mr. Jackson!" she said. "Mr. Jackson has disappeared."

My father looked immediately out the front door at the end of the corridor. It was like looking down a long tunnel. A newspaper tumbled across the parking lot like a kite out of control, whipped savagely by the wind.

"We've called the police," she said. "They have three units out looking for him." She spoke excitedly, breathlessly. She seemed to be having a good time, the way people do at wrecks and fires. She looked from one to the other of us. "They said they never have much to do when it rains in the afternoons."

We drove along a wide boulevard, the windows down because the heat of our breath was glazing them over. A mile up the road was the house my grandfather thought he still owned. I doubted he could even find it, a house like most of the other houses, expensive, ungainly boxes, his perhaps the barest and harshest of all, a perfectly square building on a perfectly square lot.

In the median of the boulevard, elm trees grew, saved by some committee my grandmother had served on; their vase shapes bucked and swayed in the wind, their branches thrashing like arms in the air. The drizzle hissed above the hum of the engine and the thump and screech of the windshield wipers. I looked out my window and my father searched from his side, the car swerving back and forth across the painted line of the double-lane road. He looked forsaken.

"You look like you've had about enough of this day," I said. "And it's only half over."

He merely shook his head. Through the gray mist I saw a figure walking slowly alongside the road, a dark garment swirling in the wind, head bent down against the rain.

"There he is!" I said.

My father looked back and slowed down. "Hold on," he said, and we jolted over the raised median strip, the tires spinning for a moment in the wet dead grass. He drove back to the old man and we bumped once more over across the median; this time the car skidded on the pavement and spun around in a full circle; then my father got control of it, letting the car slide sideways into its spin. The tires held and we reached the figure in the rain and stopped. I jumped out and as I approached, the man turned his face and I saw it was not my grandfather. He stopped, surprised and fearful. "Excuse me," I said, walking backward to the door of the car.

"It's not him," I said as I climbed in. The man watched us as we drove away. "He must think we're crazy."

We went a few blocks farther; we were more than halfway back to Poppy's house. I saw another figure, off to our right on a

176

parallel road, the fast thruway through the town. It was a raw new road through the wooded fringes of Clifton Park, where my grandparents' house was located. Between the two roads lay the creek. The stream wandered through the town, patched along its length with city parks. The land was too low for building; it flooded in every heavy rain. In places the lowlands were wide and open and the cool wind or breeze that flowed always above the course of the creek seemed to gather itself to strength in those open stretches, and poured and roared like a gale when it funneled through the narrow gully the creek passed through at the edge of the thruway.

The figure was like a stalk pushing against the wind, moving slowly up the hill, appearing to slide over the ground, the long form leaning to an acute angle with the slope.

"Look," I said. "Do you think that's him?"

As we slowed down to watch, a police car approached the figure from the opposite direction. My father accelerated rapidly and we traveled several blocks to the ramp that carried us onto the thruway. The road went down and then up as we reached the crest of the hill.

My grandfather was surrounded.

There were already two police cars. Policemen swarmed around him. He reared and bellowed like a bear cornered by a pack of hounds. Then the old man broke loose, twisting away, his body shaped for flight. His hair strung out in the wind, his robe flowed behind him. We stopped and I saw that the policemen were fewer than they had seemed at the first sight. I ran toward them, my father behind me. A policeman grabbed the old man's arm with both hands and tried to twist it behind his back. He bellowed and it sounded like my own blood raging.

The old man turned as the policeman turned his arm, ducked under and behind and they were caught in a whirling, careful dance in the slippery mud. He twisted away again; the others caught up to him and they all groped for him. He was raging wordlessly. One policeman dropped to his knees and threw his arms around the old man's legs. My grandfather beat at the top of his head, flailing furiously with both fists, the three other policemen all trying to catch his hands. His hands were a blur. The one on the bottom squeezed tighter and tighter, closing the old man's legs together, then he picked him up. My father was shouting something behind me. As they groped and tugged at him the whole group slid slowly in the red mud, slid as if in slow motion down the embankment and for a moment out of sight. We reached the edge and saw them tumbling to the bottom and saw the old man rise up, taller than their tallest; he reared, pulling his head as far away from them as he could, splashing backward in the few inches of flood covering the grass. As I was almost on them, more falling than running down the slope on my heels, my father yelling behind, I saw the broken chunk of concrete that he held high above his head: it flashed down, smacked loudly into one face. The face turned almost instantly red, the blood flowing freely down the man's chest and into the water, pausing for a moment before it curled and thinned toward the hidden channel of the creek.

One of the policemen lunged at the old man as another hit him in the back with his fist. The first caught him with his shoulder in the chest, and the old man sat with a sudden gasp and a splash beside his bloody victim. They grabbed him under his arms and started dragging him up the embankment. We scrambled behind, the policeman who had been hurt beside us, helped by one of his partners to the top.

A third car with two more policemen standing beside it was at the top of the hill. One of them was grinning. He had bars on his shoulder. "I thought I was going to have to call the Marines in," he said, shaking his head, still grinning. "My, but you boys is four tough cookies, ain't you?"

"He's my father," my father said from behind me. "Let me—let me—"

The old man was shaking all over, his chest heaving. There was still a policeman attached to each arm. "I was only going home," he shouted in a rage. "I was only minding my own bidness, going home!"

His feet were blue, one slipper gone down the bank. I turned and looked down into the flood for it. My father's mouth trembled and he swallowed very hard.

"My father—" he began again.

My grandfather saw us for the first time and struggled against the policemen, fluttering his arms against their hold. "A son!" he screamed. He gasped, drool slid from the corners of his mouth. "I raised you and fed you and now you treat me like this! Locked me up! Won't let me go home!" And then, his voice rising high, full of venom and heat and fury, beating back the wind, winter, everything, he shrieked, "I took you to the circus in nineteen thirty-two when there won't no circus money!"

He spent himself and went slack. The policemen moved him without struggle. Meekly, mournfully, as they led him to their car, he whispered, "I only want to go home."

"We'll take him back," my father said.

"I'm sorry, sir," the one with the bars said. He moved toward us and stood next to my father. "We have to turn him over to the custody of the home."

"Will there be any charges against him?"

The officer shook his head. "No, no charges. I'm just sorry the boys had to rough him up a little. But I don't think they hurt him much, do you? He gave out more than he took."

The damaged policeman was lying on the backseat of one of the cars. His friend held a cloth to his nose with one hand and wiped blood from his face with another.

The old man balked again when they put him in the car, but his resistance was momentary. He was panting heavily.

The officer standing with us chuckled. I half expected him to dig my father in the ribs with his elbow. "Spunky old devil, ain't he?" He rubbed the toe of his boot around in the mud, grinning. The rain dripped from the beak of his cap and splattered on the end of his nose. "I hope I got half that much in me when I'm his age," he said.

Chapter 14 _____

My father parked in the driveway and let the engine run while he stared blankly at the back of the house, a dark shape rising in the gray. The wipers screeched and thumped and the drizzle needled down, mixed with fine bits of ice which accumulated in the corner of the windshield. He looked at the upstairs windows, stony-faced. There were tears in the corners of his eyes. He switched off the ignition and we sat a while longer, he resting his chin on his fist, touching the tip of his mustache with his thumb. He sighed and shook his head. There was a flash under the privet hedge against the porch; it was the mockingbird, out of place and out of season.

"It's too cold," I said. "He ought to be somewhere else."

"And the rest of us too."

In the distance the sky was opening, a small rift in the sheet of cloud, and the late afternoon began to brighten a little, though the misty rain still fell.

"It's going to clear off in a while," I said.

"It might," he said. "Don't count on it. Are you going back with me tonight?"

"Yes."

He took a deep breath, cleared his eyes with the back of his hand. "Now I've got to deal with Junior. And Sully." He shook his head again and we left the car and walked through the chilling rain. Pellets of ice rolled underfoot on the steps.

Sully sat in the kitchen drinking straight whiskey out of a water glass. The bottle was in a brown bag under her chair, beside her new shoes. Her dress looked rumpled now, ill-fitting, and no longer new. She had obviously been lying down in it.

"They're packing Poppy's things now," she said. She did not

180

look up. She talked into the glass. "What the hell are Helen and Junior going to do with an old man's suits?"

"Is Junior upstairs?"

"Yes."

"I want to talk to you in a little while," my father said. He went upstairs.

"Where's my mother?"

"Hiding."

"Are you all right?"

"I'm wondering where Tiny's going to live."

"What about you?"

She shrugged her shoulders.

"Did you call Herman?"

"Gone," she said. Her words were more slurred than usual. "Checked right on out of town. Gone to mooch off his sister. Are you mad at me?"

"No."

I stood and she sat in uncomfortable silence for a short time, and then I went down the hall and into the bathroom between the den and parlor. The odor of my grandfather's cigars lingered there still. After he set the carpet on fire and they tried to keep cigars from him, he would hide in the bathroom, sucking away at his last forbidden pleasure. The stale smoky smell clung to the room, to the wall, the curtains, to everything, even to the clothes of anyone who entered for a short time. I remembered when I used to have to pass by the old man in his chair at work to use the bathroom. And every time he would say, "What? You've got to go *again?* They ought to use you for a fountain in front of the museum. You wouldn't never run dry." And he would take his stare from me and shuffle his papers. "Well, don't flush it. You flushed it yesterday." When his water bill for one quarter was over six dollars he threatened to remove the downstairs bathroom.

I could hear my father talking to Junior. "There's no one in here in the den. Let's sit in here and talk."

"What's this all about?" Junior said, her voice shaky. "Is this about that note you can't find? I thought we had that all straightened out. I told you I never saw a note in there."

"Sit down."

I heard the cushions fold under them. I could not decide whether to cough and stir around and make noise or whether to stay perfectly still.

"Tell me about that note," my father said after a long silence.

"You know, I really don't know what *note* this is you've been asking me about."

"Just tell me about any note."

"Well, I can't think of one," Junior said, her brashness muffled by the door and by her nervousness.

"Can't remember any note you might have signed that Poppy kept in his lockbox?"

"No, I can't."

"About your house," my father prompted. "A note for the amount of your house, which Poppy bought for you. You don't remember anything about that?"

"I remember some kind of papers we had to go through, years ago. . . ."

"You don't remember seeing a note in the lockbox about your house?"

"No."

"Well, fine," my father said. "That's settled, then."

I could hear Junior releasing her breath. Her voice relaxed as she spoke. "Is that all?" She sounded a little surprised.

"Yes."

"Well, I can't imagine what you kept hammering on about it for. I *knew* there was nothing to it, but you just kept on. Well, I've got a little more packing to do. Did I tell you what the lawyer said about Sully and her obvious—"

"I just wonder where you're going to live," my father said.

Junior did not try to continue about Sully. There was another long silence, and I wished I could see their faces.

"What are you talking about?"

"I'm going to be putting all of Poppy's houses on the market, including the one you live in. It will be sold. You'll probably have a month or so to get out." He spoke wearily but calmly, without expression or intonation, as though he were discussing the weather with a stranger.

Junior exploded. "What!" she yelled. "That's *my* house! You can't put my house on the market!"

"Oh, no," he said. "It's Poppy's house. The deed is in the lockbox. Also, there's a provision in the will for thirty thousand dollars to be deducted from your share of the estate. I tell you this incidentally, so you won't be surprised when he finally passes on, and the estate is settled."

"What—what are you—?"

"I was hoping," my father went on, "that you had signed some sort of note for your house, so we could prove that the thirty thousand was being deducted for the house. But since there isn't any such note, obviously the thirty thousand was for something else. It's too bad, because if there had been a note, you'd only have thirty thousand taken out of your share of the estate. This way, you lose the house along with the money."

"It's *my* house!"

"The deed, as I told you. The deed is there, it's in his name."

"You can't do this to me!"

"Maybe there *was* a note, and you sort of forgot about it, until now?"

Another silence. Then, speaking low, almost whispering, "I guess there could have been."

"You guess?"

"Yes."

"You have to be *sure* of it, I'm afraid. You have to be positive."

"I *know* I signed a bunch of papers. . . ."

"And lifted the note out of the lockbox?"

"Well, I *never!*" I could hear her stand. "If you think I'm going to sit here and listen to this— It's Sully, isn't it? This is something Sully dreamed up. Are you going to believe her instead of me?"

"Sully has nothing to do with it."

"I wish they had never saved her from that sailor in Baltimore," Junior said. She spoke in a low voice but she seemed to be shrieking. "She'd still be in some sleazy hotel room not bothering any of us, not poisoning her own family."

"Now calm down," my father said. "Sully has nothing to do with this at all."

"Calm down? Calm down? You're accusing me of being a thief, and you ask me to calm down?"

"I can't understand why you did it."

"Do it? I didn't do it. And you can't tell me Sully's not behind this. You wouldn't have come up with anything like this."

"The lawyer came up with it," my father said. "That note was in the box, and now it's gone. The deed is still there. The deed is in Poppy's name."

"That's *my* house," Junior said. "I don't care whose name it's in." I could hear her sitting down again. I tried not to move; I controlled my breathing but every breath seemed to ring in my ears in the narrow space. I remembered the old man telling me not to fidget.

"You're going to have to sign another note for it, or you're not going to get that house," my father said.

"How can you do this to me?" Junior wailed. I heard sniffles. "To me, your sister, your own flesh and blood."

"How could you try to steal thirty thousand dollars from your own family?"

"I didn't steal anything from anybody. That house is mine. You know it is. You know Poppy said I never had to pay for it. He said I could have it. He said—" She faltered. "He said—I could have that house."

"I know what he said. He explained it to all of us. He said that the cost to him of the house would be taken from your share of the estate if you didn't pay the note off."

"Well, that was not my understanding of it," Junior said. "Harlan, there's been a mistake somewhere."

"That's for sure."

"Maybe I didn't understand exactly right, but . . ."

She sounded like she was trying to be reasonable, but he would not let her off the hook. "You understood perfectly. That's why you took the note. You thought you would get the house *and* another thirty thousand dollars, you thought it wouldn't be deducted from your share with the note gone. Now you're not going to get either one." My father's tone was even and calm.

"Why—why—" Junior said. I could barely hear her.

"And, as I said, you'll have to move from the house as soon as possible."

"No," she said. "No, this isn't happening."

"Because as trustee of his estate, I'm going to convert all his real estate into bonds."

"I'm trustee!" Junior shouted. "You can't do this."

"You won't be, tomorrow. I'll take it to court, and we will prove that you took that note and that you are unreliable and you won't qualify. The lawyer has a list of everything in the lockbox, quite aside from what the will says."

"You can't do this to me. You wouldn't. You would never do this to your own flesh and blood."

"I never would have believed you would steal from your own family."

"What family? There is no family." Junior uttered the words as though she had suddenly confronted something horrible and unspeakable.

"But I don't want to do it, and we don't have to. If you will cooperate."

Again Junior did not speak. Finally, her voice strained, her tone careful, she said, "Cooperate?"

"You'll have to sign a new note. You'll have to voluntarily give up your charge as trustee and executrix. Will you do that?"

"I don't see that I have any choice. Since you're on their side."

"Whose side?"

"Tiny's and Sully's."

"They don't know anything about it," my father said, irritated at last. "I told you that. There's one other thing."

"One other thing? What?"

"You'll have to pay Dick Stanley back the five thousand dollars you embezzled from the jewelry store."

Junior bubbled. She sounded as though she were drowning. When she finished she gasped, "I don't know what you're talking about."

"I'll loan you the money," my father said. "I know you don't have it. But you'll have to sign a note to me, and I'll take the money out of your share of the estate. If you do all these things—and I hope for your sake and everyone else's that you will—then no one else will have to know anything about it. Of course you'll be forced to sell your house to have enough to live on."

Silence flowed like a cold substance through the crack under the door.

"Will you do it? Will you sign these?" I heard him shuffle papers together; he must have shaken them under her face.

185

"Sully doesn't know about this?"

"No."

"Don't tell Helen," she said. "Please don't tell Helen."

"I'm not going to tell anyone."

"I'll sign them," she said. "But I don't see that I've done anything wrong."

"Nothing wrong?" My father's voice raised for the first time, incredulous, verging finally on anger.

"That house is mine!" Junior said violently. "I paid for it a hundred times over, a thousand times, a hundred thousand times. Everyone else moved away and I stayed here and took care of Mother and Poppy, and listened to them every day, put up with them day after day, week after week, every day every minute, interfering with my life, complaining about everything in their life and mine. And what about all the money he threw away on that *slut?*" Junior was shouting now. "Are you trying to tell me he didn't pour more than thirty thousand dollars down her drain in the last twenty years? And for what? For what?"

"He gave you a thousand dollars a month."

"I didn't have a half-dozen men keeping me," she said. "The bitch. I don't see what they saw in her."

"Are you going to sign these?"

"Yes," she sighed. "Yes. You've forced me into a corner. Your own sister. I'll have to talk to the welfare people tomorrow," she said heavily. "I don't know what this business of Stanley's is all about. That was just a *loan*. I had three children to support. I still do. What's going to happen to my poor children?"

"If it was a loan, it's time to repay it," my father said. "And your children are grown up now. Hollis is working, Richard's looking for a job, and all Dolly's expenses are paid by the education fund our father set up for them."

"What's she going to do when she gets out?" Junior wailed. "I can't support her or Richard either. I'll be sewing on buttons at the Salvation Army."

"People work," my father said. "They'll get jobs, just like everybody else. Now sign here."

The papers rustled and Junior began to cry, a bubbling whimper.

"Don't blur the ink," my father said.

"I took care of Mother this year. It was terrible, terrible. That ought to count for something, even if being your sister doesn't. And your *older* sister too."

"If you weren't my sister you would be in jail."

"If I only had a man to take care of me," Junior whimpered, "none of this would be happening."

"Let me see these," my father said.

"I used to read to you, before you could read," Junior said.

"They look all right," my father said.

I could hear the sofa springing back into place as Junior stood. "You'll keep your promise not to tell Helen?"

"I won't tell anybody anything," he said.

She opened the door and left without another word, her heavy thud retreating down the hallway. I could hear my father sighing deeply, and twice a little groan or grunt. The papers tapped against his knee or the table beside him; then he rose and the bathroom door opened and he looked down at me in surprise.

"I thought you'd never finish in there," I said.

"Well," he said. "Well, I guess you heard it all."

"Yes."

"I figured I'd have to tell you anyway. You'll have to oversee all this mess if anything ever happens to me."

"Count me out," I said. "I don't think I have the Perrin blood."

"I'm serious," he said.

I looked down at the toilet. "I guess it's all right to flush it now."

"He'll never know."

"What about Tiny? What about her house? If you're going to sell all his houses, where's she going to live?"

"It's out of my hands."

"Whose hands is it in?"

"I don't know," he said, looking around.

We moved out of the bathroom. "What are you going to tell her? How are you going to look Tiny in the face and say, 'I'm sorry, you've got to get out by sundown'?"

"There's nothing I can do," he said. "I feel sorry for her, but I'm not going to have a fight with Junior over the business, not after I just threatened to throw her out of *her* house, which she'll certainly have to sell anyway."

"Why not?"

"She's my sister, and I've done enough to her."

"I don't understand," I said.

He ran his hand back through his silver hair. "I'm not sure I understand it myself."

"It seems like you could do *some*thing."

"I don't know. I don't know what else to do. The fact is, I don't know what would've happened if Junior had stood up and said, 'All right, I'll go to court to keep being trustee.' She's so mad at Tiny, she might do just that if I try to give her the house. I'll do anything to avoid a fight with her, in court."

"Couldn't you buy the house for Tiny?"

"I couldn't afford it. I don't know where I'm going to get the five thousand to pay back Dick Stanley."

"Sully would give up her part of it."

"She needs money so badly, she might not do that."

"I'm sure she would."

"I still couldn't do it anyway, there's two more shares."

"What's Tiny going to do?"

"What's anybody going to do?"

Sully entered, smiling and holding her glass of whiskey. "Boy, you must of really laid it on Junior," she said. She made for the sofa, clutching her way from one piece of furniture to another like a blind person feeling her way. "She's curled up on the sofa in the living room like a dead slug."

My father sat down in the chair where his father used to sit. "I want to talk to you now," he said.

Sully drank. The glass rattled against her teeth. "I needed to talk to you too," she said. She stood, rising with effort. She paced.

"Excuse me," I said, walking to the door.

"No," Sully said. She held my arm. Her hand was dry and brittle and cold. "Please stay," she said. She moved beside my father's chair and looked away from him. "Harlan, do you suppose . . ." Sully stopped, nervous. She squirmed, turned her toes together, looked at the floor. She blushed. "Do you suppose I could borrow some money?" Her words rushed out, slurred together.

"Not much, I don't need much, just enough for a bus ticket, maybe a sandwich on the way or something, twenty or thirty dollars would do. . . ."

"I thought you had plenty of money," my father said, his tone and expression slipped out of the tight mask.

"Are you kidding? Me? Money?"

"How much did you get for it?"

Sully stared at the floor. Her eyes kept floating sideways and she kept snatching them back to a spot in front of her feet. She twisted her chain necklace around her fingers. "What do you mean?"

"The brooch. How much did you sell it for?"

She looked up at him, her eyes filled as though a light had been turned on, a gleam of hope. "Oh, I didn't sell it. I swear to you I never sold it."

He was silent. They looked at one another: Sully's intense look faded and she looked down again.

"You did pawn it," he said. "You let it go for nothing. You know you'll never get it back."

"You're not going to give me any money, are you?" Sully said, her voice sounding weak and far away, lost, as though she spoke last words before fainting.

"You tell me how much you got for it," he said. "I'm just about fed up. You tell me how much you pawned it for, then I'll see about lending you the money."

"I was robbed," Sully whispered.

"She *was* robbed," I said. "That's exactly the whole thing. Robbed." They both looked at me in surprise. "Never mind," I said.

"Maybe I lost it," she whispered, trying not to cry, blinking her eyes at the floor.

My father stood and started toward the door.

"Wait," she said.

He stopped.

"Two hundred dollars," she said. I could see her wilt. She closed her eyes for a moment, then looked up at my father, then looked down to the floor, and then he looked at the floor. I could not help looking down there too.

"Pawned it," he said. "I never subscribed to Junior's theory that you would pawn it. I thought you would sell it, but I never thought you would *give* it away. What the hell did you do with the two hundred dollars?" he said, his voice full of irritation. He sounded personally affronted. "You're fifty years old, are you ever going to grow up? How the hell could you take a brooch worth thousands and get two hundred for it, and then blow that last money to your name in an hour on a rainy afternoon?"

"It wasn't hard," she said. "I couldn't help it. I don't have anything, never have, I'm just an old hag with nothing and nobody. It seems like at least I could have some decent clothes."

"Where's the pawn ticket?" my father said.

"I don't have it," she said.

"Get it and give it to me."

"I can't, I don't have it."

"Don't have it all? You don't even have the ticket to get it back with? What did you do with it?"

"I gave it to Tiny to keep for me."

"To Tiny! Who's so drunk she can't see past her nose today."

"I thought Junior might go through my things looking for it."

"Get the ticket back from her and give it to me."

"No. No, I'll never do that. That brooch is mine."

"Right now it's the loan shark's." My father sighed and shook his head, looked down at his feet. "Gave it to Tiny," he said, his tone less icy now, less disgusted, but still edged with an outraged wonder and disapproval. "I wish you luck."

"I'll never get any," Sully said. "I guess I'm not going to get any money either."

"What would you do with it? Buy more clothes and another bottle of whiskey?"

"I told you. Buy a bus ticket."

"Where are you going?"

"Hell, *I* don't know. How much are you going to give me?"

"So whenever you get wherever you wind up, you'll call me collect and ask for some more."

"I won't, I promise I won't."

"I promise you won't get any. This has been going on for too long. I've had it. I've had it with everything, with Junior, with . . ." He heaved another sigh. The flesh of his face seemed to drag earthward, tugged by forces worse than gravity and age. He handed two bills to Sully. "That's all the cash I've got," he said. "And I mean what I say, it's the last I can ever give you. Ever."

She took it and looked away from it, stuffed it quickly up her sleeve. "Thank you," she whispered.

He was on his way out of the room.

"Harlan," she said.

"Yes?"

"Do you think—do you think. . . ? Listen, is there any way for me to use my inheritance before Poppy—"

"No," he said. "It's impossible. It's against the law."

"I thought so. I just thought I better ask. How long—how long do you think he'll . . . hold on?"

"You're going to have to get a job, Sully."

"God, with all the junk I take? Have you seen me shake? Have you heard me try to talk?"

"Stop taking all those pills."

"I'd kill myself the next day. The doctors all say so. They all completely agree. I'm suicidal." She seemed to have a sort of quiet pride about it.

"Well, I don't know what you're going to do," he said.

"I don't either," she said. She laughed her long, wavering, metallic laugh, desperate and humorless. "I could ask Junior if she wants to find an apartment together." She stepped backward and sank onto the sofa when the backs of her calves touched it. "Boy, we'd have some kind of time."

"You'd better be serious about it, Sully," my father said. "I'm telling you, I can't take care of you anymore. I've got my own family to think about."

"I've never been so serious in all my life," Sully said. "I'm going to take a bus out of here as far as seventy dollars will go."

My father left the room, head down and moving heavily, as though he were plowing.

She crossed her legs and swung her foot rapidly to and fro. "Isn't it interesting that he has his own family, of which I am not a part, and I have no family? Do you know what I think, Little Harlan?"

"What?"

"I think life is a crock of shit," she said. "That's what I think."

Chapter 15 _____

SULLY TURNED THE GLASS AROUND and around in her hands, then finished the whiskey in a gulp. "You're sure you're not mad at me?" she said. "About earlier?"

"I'm not mad."

"You know I was going to redeem that damn thing, didn't you?"

"Yes."

"Your father doesn't seem to know that."

"I think it's a question of where you'd get the money to redeem it."

She waved her hand in the air. "Oh, I don't know," she said. "I took it to Stanley's first, to see how much they'd give me for it. They said they'd give me three thousand. To tell you the truth, I wanted to sell it. I can be honest with you, can't I? That's what I really wanted to do. Not just for the money. It's mine, I didn't want them to have it. I don't know, when I walked in there to sell it I thought . . . I felt like I was getting free. . . . But then I thought what a ruckus would happen if anybody found out I'd sold it. Jesus, you'd think now I *gave* it away. I need another drink."

We passed through the hall on the way to the kitchen; Sully stopped in front of Harrison's Revenge. She looked into it, her face close, and studiously, almost with grief, she watched her fingertips caress the lines and hollows of her face, the shadows of her sad ruined beauty, her luminous agitation bouncing out of the mirror. She sighed and turned away.

In the kitchen Junior was directing Helen. Junior sat at the table, holding a fresh washcloth to her swollen face. Helen fluttered around the cupboards, tentative and unsure, as though she might have been in a stranger's house. She kept bumping into my mother, who had not been in view all afternoon, and who—while she prepared a supper before my father and I went to check on Poppy—was obviously in no mood to listen to the sisters anymore; Helen skittered away from her at each moment of contact, snatching herself out of my mother's way and bumping into my father.

"Right above the sink, Helen," Junior said. Helen wedged between my parents, opened the cupboard. "Behind the waffle iron," Junior said. "Get the waffle iron, too."

Sully sat beside Junior. Junior leaned ostentatiously away from her. Sully knocked over the whiskey in the bag as she reached under the chair for it.

"Mother just laid to rest," Junior muttered. "It's tragic."

"Would you like a drink?" Sully said sweetly to her. "Just one itsy-bitty little drink? You couldn't *possibly* be worried about your figure."

Junior's expression of mournful weariness and martydom did not change; she ignored Sully completely. "Put it in the box labeled MISC. APPS.," she said. "Oh, good Lord, here comes that black witch. Aren't we ever going to get rid of her?"

Tiny heaved herself slowly up the steps. We watched her through the glass as she came painfully across the porch. She opened the door and leaned against the jamb a moment, catching her breath.

Junior glared from under her washcloth, raised off her head with one hand. "What's she doing here?" she whispered harshly. Tiny looked down blankly at her. I knew she was trying not to smile.

Tiny looked at Sully. "I said where you just only los' that brooch," she said.

"*What?*" Sully said.

"What do you mean? We know all about that brooch. She took one of our family's precious heirlooms and—"

Tiny fumbled in her bag. Everyone watched her and she grew a little embarrassed; it reminded me of when we used to try to help her clear off the table. Her wig hung from the back of her head, leaving the bald front dome exposed and dully gleaming. "Heah hit is," she said. The diamonds shone in her brown palm. "It won't stolen. It was just all the time lost."

Sully looked for a moment as though she had been set in position in concrete, staring with fixed eyes. Then she jumped out of her chair, and froze again. "How—how—how—?"

"I jes' thought where to look, is all," Tiny said. She took Sully's hand and placed the brooch in it. "Heah, honey," she said. "Now maybe they won't give you no more trouble about it." She looked around the room at each of us. "You take it away wid you and don' bring it roun' heah no mo'." I wondered whether her natural idiom was from drink or because she no longer worked in this house.

"No," Sully said. "You take it. I want you to have it."

"What!" screamed Helen. "What!"

Tiny backed away from Sully's outstretched hand. "Law, chile, I got no use fo' it. I got my house, en' my gahden, what else I need?"

"Where are you going? What are you going to do?" Sully said.

"Home," Tiny said. She turned slowly and walked to the door. It was almost dark. "Got to go. Got to catch that las' bust."

"Ha," Junior said. Her eyes threw sparks at Tiny's back and she spoke to Helen. "She'll have to manage outside that house. I'm going to give her exactly one week to vacate."

"En' whut bidness is it of yours, I like to know. I tell you what bidness, it ain't none of you' bidness. Miss Irene, she gimme dat house in her paper."

"Tiny," Sully said. "Tiny, Tiny."

Tiny turned back to her and hugged her, patting her on the back. "There, there, baby," she said. "You gone be jes' fine."

I looked at my father and he looked at my mother; but she was giving him the same look I was, and he left the room.

"Come on, Helen," Junior said. "Before we get drunk on the fumes in here and we *all* get committed." She shuffled backward out of the room, dragging the box marked MISC. APP. with one hand, the other hand still squeezing the cloth to her injured cheek and mouth.

Tiny leaned away from Sully and held the reedy arms in her huge hands, as though holding out a doll to admire. "You write me now, you heah," Tiny said.

"Of course I will," Sully said, still crying. "You write me too."

Tiny nodded. She went toward the door, rocking sideways.

"Is there anything we can do for you, Tiny?" my mother said.

"No'm," Tiny said. "I be fine." She went out the door and down the steps, holding the rail, moving over the slick ice, melting into the gray.

As she disappeared completely I jumped up and ran to the steps. "Tiny!" I called. "Can I drive you home?" It was much lighter outside than it had appeared to be from inside, and I could see her quite clearly as she turned at the end of the drive.

"I took that bust ever'day for thirty-five years," she said. "I reckon I kin ride it one mo' time." She waved. "You come see me," she said. "You know where I'll be."

"I'll come in the morning," I said. "Will you be home tomorrow morning?"

"Can't think where else I'd go."

"I'll stop and say good-bye."

She smiled and waved and turned the corner around the hedge.

I went back inside. Sully was sitting at the table, perched on the edge of her chair, rocking back and forth. My mother had gone out of the kitchen and carried the dinner plates with her. Sully's knees were drawn close together and she held them in both hands, pulled them under her chin. She chewed the knuckles of both thumbs. Her eyes were closed and tears hung in her lashes. "What am I going to do?"

"Don't yell," I said. "They'll hear you."

"I'm not yelling. Don't you think they *know*. You know your father knows, and Junior must know too. She guessed, she knew right away. Tell me, Harlan," she said, looking at me with intense hope, "what was it Junior did? What did she do?"

"Junior probably thinks Tiny stole it," I said.

"Can't you tell me what she did?"

"Or that it really was lost. She can't imagine Tiny, or anyone, having the desire to do something like that for someone else."

"I wish you would tell me."

"Not to speak of the money. She can't imagine Tiny having the money to do it, any more than the desire."

"I can't imagine where Tiny got the money, myself," Sully said. She held the brooch in front of her face and examined it with distaste. "I hate this goddamn thing," she said. "It's been hanging over me for thirty years. I only wanted it so I could get rid of the damn thing. What am I going to do? Poor Tiny, Tiny. I bet she spent every nickel she ever *made*, I'll bet you anything. And now she's not only got no house, which she doesn't even know yet, she's got no money because of me." Sully weaved as she poured herself

195

another drink. The whiskey splashed in the glass and all around it on the table.

"I'm fifty years old at the end of my life and look at what I've got, look!" Sully jammed her open hand forward as though she were striking out and the brooch were a weapon. It scattered highlights in the dim room. "A goddamn handful of rocks."

She tossed it onto the table and bent over it, elbows on the table. It seemed to take a great effort for her to hold up her own weight. The skin of her arms was dry and blotched. She turned the brooch over and over on the table, her orange lips pursed roseate, pushing together the wrinkles around her mouth, making herself look like an old woman. "Memories," she said. "Nightmares. I told your parents I couldn't eat yet, I don't like to eat until it gets dark. So I'll have something to keep my mind off it being dark, for a little while." She started suddenly, as though she had heard something, sat up and faced me. "I can mail it back to Tiny," she said. She laughed, almost hysterical, squeaking like a ranting bird. "Oh, God, can you see the look on Helen and Junior's faces? Can't you just see it?"

"Tiny won't keep it," I said. "She'll just send it back to you."

"How's she going to know where to send it? Even *I* don't know where I'll be."

"She might send it to your husband."

"Which one? Oh, George. God forbid. She might. I'd rather Junior get it, that son of a bitch. I don't know, I don't care what she does with it, it's hers isn't it? She paid for it. I know! I could sell it! Why am I so stupid? Stanley said he'd give me three thousand for it. I could sell it, and send her the money." She looked at me with hope.

"Then she'd just send the money back," I said. "And again, to George. You know she'd know exactly where it came from. Who else would send it to her, especially two hundred dollars."

"Three thousand."

"What? The whole thing? She definitely wouldn't take it, and—"

"I don't know," Sully said. "She thinks I still have a lot of antiques. I could tell her I sold my antiques for oodles of money."

"She doesn't believe that any more than I do. And what about you. You need the money as much as she does, *more* than she does."

196

"I don't care. I've always wanted to do something shining and wonderful, right? Well, here's my chance."

"She won't take it."

"All I can do is try. Will you try to make her keep it?"

"I can't make Tiny do anything," I said. "Not even your mother could make her do something she didn't want to do."

Sully splashed more whiskey into her glass.

"You better slow down on that," I said.

"I've got to do something," she said. The whiskey slopped out of her glass as she drank. She was weaving in her seat. "I've got to figure everything out."

"I think I have an idea," I said. "I think it would work."

My father entered the kitchen. "Are you ready?" he said. "We've got to be getting on. I don't want to drive in this ice after dark any more than I have to." He turned to Sully. "Do you want to go? This might be your last chance to see him."

"Last chance," Sully muttered. "I got to figure out what to do."

"That's for sure," my father said.

"Maybe if I kill myself there'll be an investigation and Tiny will get her house."

"Good God," he said. "Sully, put that whiskey away."

"I guess I have to, if I'm going with you to see Poppy."

Chapter 16 _____

WHEN WE ARRIVED, the day was almost gone and the sun nearly spent; an unsettling deep yellow light glowed in the air, seeming to emanate from the air itself under the thick dome of cloud cover, imparting a sense of both impermanence and foreboding.

Sully looked around nervously as we walked through the scattering of sleet to the door of the building. "I wish I hadn't come," she whispered.

We entered and looked for him. Sully shied away from the people in wheelchairs, from the nurses and orderlies, from every noise and every shadow. We found him wandering with painful slowness through the halls, lost.

As we came up behind him, my father took him by the arm and he turned around, looking at us with his flat faded eyes. Sully turned her face away.

"Have you seen us before?" my father asked.

He regarded my father briefly, without interest. He did not look at us. "Can't say as I have," the old man said. His voice sounded distant, or as though it were filtered.

"I'm your son."

The old man blinked. "If you say so."

"Harlan Junior," my father said.

He did not appear to have heard; he looked around at the walls, at us, at the coming and going of other people, all without interest, apparently without even seeing us. It was as though he were not there at all, his body merely a symbol and reminder of his vanished self.

Sully looked at him, and looked away, and tried to look again. She could neither keep from looking at him nor keep from trying to look. She tried not to cry.

Suddenly the old man was amused. He was staring off into nothing. "I never seen anything like it," he said. "Have you?"

"Do you want to go to your room?"

"I don't care."

My father took him by his arm and we moved toward his room, walking slowly. I took Sully by her arm. She was trembling. "I'm scared," she whispered.

"Scared of what?"

"They're all like this. Is this where they'll try to put me?"

"They won't put you anywhere."

"Oh, God, I can't take this." She tried to stop and I pulled her on. "I've got to get out of this place. It smells like everybody's dying."

My grandfather walked with careful delicate steps, pushing his feet across the floor without lifting them. The flesh above his new hospital slippers oozed out like a dark blue fungus. He said nothing on the way to his room. He did not look about him. He noticed Sully when we filed through the door. "Painted women," he said calmly, "Jezebels and demons." Then he appeared to immediately forget her.

"Do you want to sit on your bed?"

"All right."

My father helped him down onto the bed, one hand holding him by the elbow, one hand behind his back.

"Don't let me fall," he said; his voice lacked any quality of enthusiasm or care: he stated out of habit a proposition, emotionless.

"Sully's here," my father said as he sat down. "Sully's come to see you."

His hands began to brush themselves, faster and weaker now. His face was as blank as the wall he stared at.

"Sully's your daughter," my father said. After a while he said, "I'm your son, Poppy, Harlan Junior."

The four of us sat silently in the darkening room. I could hear Sully's ragged breathing next to me. As the room darkened, it grew deeper, and we faded apart from one another, receding into our places in the dark and into ourselves.

"I never seen anything like it," the old man said again. And in a moment, turning to my father, like a child asking his first question: "Have you?"

My father rose and put his hand on his father's head, stroking the fine white hairs into place, and I could see myself repeating that motion years hence, with a sensation so intensely immediate that it were as if my father's hand were my own, seen in a mirror that reflected not the present but the future. "No," my father said. "I never have."

"Me neither," my grandfather said. "I ain't never seen anything like it in all my life."

We drove back toward the house, in silence most of the way, until my father said, "Well, he's gone now."

"Don't say that," Sully said.

"It's true."

"I don't care! I don't care if it's true, anybody can see it's true. Don't say it!"

"He's the living dead, you can't avoid—"

"Shut up. Just shut up." She was shaking and she covered her face. "That's where they're going to try to put me."

"Nobody's going to put you anywhere," I said.

"They'll decide to put me in that place so I'll be in there with him, punishment for their vision of my sins."

Their faces went visible and invisible in the dark broken by streetlights and car lights. We listened to each other breathe. It seemed like years before we reached the house and we all sat when the engine stopped, as if by a signaled agreement, looking up at the dark shadow looming over us in the night, larger than itself. A dim glow spread around the corner, a diffusion of light from the living-room windows on the far side of the house. No one seemed more inclined than me to enter it, and I thought how strange it was that a family house of such a length of memories should give so little comfort. At last my father moved, and opened his door, and we trailed behind him soundlessly inside.

Chapter 17 _____

LATE IN THE NIGHT Junior and Helen had virtually finished caching their load of goods. They collapsed together on the living-room couch, recovering from the long trying day. I sat in the room with them and my parents—my mother had reappeared, ironic and tentative—wondering what Sully, drinking again in the kitchen and foundering into a stupor, was going to do. She had been by turns fearful and belligerent.

She stumbled into the room. She carried a glass of whiskey in her left hand and her right hand was closed in a tight, worn-out fist. Junior and Helen, stirring with elephantine wariness, watched her, as though ready to lumber away at the first sudden move.

Sully could barely stand. "I just wanted y'all to know what you've done to me all these years," she droned. She drank from her glass and swayed, steadied herself. She looked from Helen to Junior, back and forth, and the movement made her totter again. "Just like you did to Poppy," she said, and she began to cry. "No heart so stony," she muttered. She pointed her glass at Junior and whiskey sloshed on the carpet. "You bitch!"

My mother opened her mouth to speak.

Sully stepped closer; Junior pulled back into the sofa. "You—" Sully said. "You—you—" She starting sobbing then as she stood there, rocking dangerously, trying to think of words to match her hatred, gulping in great breaths. She swallowed more whiskey as my mother walked toward her. Sully tried to control her breathing. "I'm all right now," she said. "I know what I'm doing." She stepped back and waved my mother away with her glass. She opened her fist and shoved it toward Junior. Junior was looking at the blank wall. "Look!" Sully shouted. "This is what you've done to me. This is what you made my life." Junior looked up. I looked in Sully's hand. Her palm was piled full of pills, yellow and red and white capsules. The red on the pills was the same color as her fingernails. I jumped up and grabbed at her wrist and she stepped backward and I almost fell past her. I turned and her hand was at her mouth and then she took her hand away empty, her eyes rolling wild, crossing, sparkling with fear like a mare rolling her eyes. She held the whiskey in both hands and gulped at the glass, the whiskey pouring down from both sides of her mouth. She choked and sputtered before my mother and I grabbed her, coughing and heaving, and the pills sprayed out of her mouth all over the floor.

She sank between us to her knees and her limp body fell into an attitude of prayer. Both of us knelt beside her. She clutched at her temples, tearing away small clumps of the metallic almost-white hair and she moaned; a high, fierce, throaty wail as though someone were beating her, or holding a gun to her face and she could see the finger on the trigger slowly squeeze. We tried to restrain her hands as she yanked at her hair. Her carotid artery swelled against her neck, jumping up and down. Her noise ended in a grating sound like a death rattle and she fell sideways into my mother, apparently asleep, breathing slowly and deeply and easily.

"Good Lord," Junior said. "What a sideshow."

"Call a doctor, Junior," my mother said.

Junior sat staring down at Sully and looking puzzled. Slowly she shifted her bulk out of the couch and walked toward the den. "A dear friend of mine is an extremely fine physician," she said.

We held Sully in our laps. My father came up beside us. "What the hell?" he said.

Sully stirred. My father and I put her on the sofa. Helen stood, looking down with wide eyes. "I'll go help Junior," she said.

Sully's eyelids shone like polished metal under the lamp. They fluttered open. Then she covered her eyes and cried quietly.

"Junior's calling a doctor," my mother said. She talked loudly into Sully's ear. "How many did you swallow?"

Sully shook her head and opened her mouth. She moved her mouth but no words came out. She swallowed and breathed deeply and rapidly.

"Get on your feet," my mother said. "Pick her up," she told us. My father pulled on one elbow and I on the other.

"Walk her," my mother said. "Don't let her stop moving."

"No," Sully said, her voice weak. She closed her eyes again. "I just want to sleep. I want to curl up under something in a closet and be left alone and never wake up." Though her words slid together she no longer seemed drunk.

"How many did you take?" my mother shouted in her ear.

Junior came back. "The doctor's on his way," she said. She put her hands on her hips and glared at Sully as she walked between us and the front of the fireplace. "Honestly," Junior said. "There's no excuse for this. What if someone had come calling?"

"How many did you take?" my mother shouted again.

"It's just a play for sympathy," Junior said.

Sully shook her head, said, "I didn't take any." She cried again, her eyes closed, her tears through her lashes streaming little flakes of black onto her cheeks. "I couldn't get any down." She clutched at her temples again. "I can't even kill myself. I can't do anything." She tried to turn away from us, twisting her head around and down, her hair falling around her face in bands stuck together. "Leave me alone," she said.

"What did I tell you?" Junior said. "Didn't even swallow one."

"Let's give her some coffee, just in case," my mother said. "Take her into the kitchen."

"They told me not to drink coffee," Sully said. "They said I was going to kill myself, all the coffee I drink." She laughed. She threw back her head and laughed harshly, her eyes closed. Then she hiccuped and stopped laughing. She hiccuped rapidly and hard, each hiccup shaking her body. She stumbled between us as we led her through the piles of boxes in the dining room and into the kitchen.

We eased her onto one of the chairs by the table. She leaned her elbows on it and held her face in her hands. My mother banged through the cupboards. She went to the door. "Junior!" she called. "Junior!"

Junior came in. She did not look at Sully.

"Where the hell is the coffeepot?" my mother said.

"Oh," Junior said. "I packed it."

Sully giggled. "Jesus Christ, can you believe it?"

"Go get it," my mother said.

Sully tried to control her spurts of hysterical giggles and she began to hiccup again.

Junior turned on the light in the dining room. "Helen, do you remember where we put the coffeepot?"

Helen entered the dining room. Sully's quick hiccups shook her body. "Whose was it?" Helen said.

"I don't remember."

Sully's hiccups slowed down. Her face was very pale. My mother had water on to boil. Helen and Junior rummaged in the dining room, muttering in low voices. I heard Junior say "sideshow" again.

My father shoved himself away from the wall, where he had been trying not to hear or see anything. He stood over Sully. "Are you all right?" he said at last.

"No," Sully said. She hiccuped. She seemed better. "But I didn't take any pills, if that's what you mean. Except the ones I'm supposed to take, about an hour ago."

"That could still kill you," my mother said. "Drinking whiskey on top of them."

Sully waved her hand. "I do it all the time," she said. "I just want to go to bed. I don't want to see anybody anymore. I'm going to get up in the morning before breakfast and be gone before I have to see those slugs in there again."

"Well, I think I'll go back to bed," my father said. "Get me up if the doctor says there's any problem at all." He put his hand on Sully's shoulder. She looked like she was trying to hide. "Don't you understand, I want to help you," he said. "But there's nothing I can do, nothing. I can't support you. I can't keep giving you money. It's like pouring money in a hole. It never fills up."

Her face still in her hands, she nodded. "I know," she said. "You've been very generous. This had nothing to do with you. I'm terrible. I'm sorry I couldn't do it and get out of y'all's way."

"No, no," my father said, groaning. "I'm going to bed," he said. And he walked out of the room.

Junior came in. "I found it," she said. She handed it to my mother. My mother reached for the coffee can on the refrigerator and poured birdseed into the pot.

"Poor Elizabeth," Sully said. "I don't need any coffee anyway.

I just need to go to sleep. I think I got a little drunk. I swear to you I didn't get any of those pills down. I just want to curl up in a ball in a dark place and be left alone." She had the quick shaky motions of someone with a hangover.

My mother looked at the birdseed. "We all need to go to bed," she said. She looked carefully at Sully. "You're looking a little better. Are you sure you didn't swallow any? Maybe by accident."

"It wouldn't have been any damn accident," Sully said. "I'm *def*initely suicidal. But I didn't get any down."

"She's not quite as pale as she was," my mother said.

"No."

"All right," she said. "But you have to stay up until the doctor comes."

Sully almost fell asleep on the table while we waited. "Poor Tiny," she muttered as her eyelids fell closed. Her speech awakened her. She looked around. "Who said that?"

Then we heard the doctor at the front door. Junior towed him into the kitchen like a prize she had won and wanted to show off. I had seen him but never met him; his name was Dr. Gurney. He had a reputation of being the best anywhere around in his field, internal medicine; and of being a good man except that he chased nurses. He was short and slightly balding, and seemed to be piqued at being called out so late. His manner was brusque. He looked at the bottle of pills, and then at Sully. He echoed my mother almost exactly. "One of these days you're going to get a couple of these down while you're drinking, and not wake up."

Sully weaved over the table and shrugged her shoulders. The doctor looked a little more compassionate. Junior was making a sort of face at him, but he did not see her. He examined Sully quickly with competent motions. "Do I need to go somewhere and undress?" she asked. And somehow, incredibly, despite the depth of her depression and her debilitated condition, despite being slumped over the table, she managed to arrange her body in a flirtatious pose.

"Just to get some sleep," he said. He tucked his stethoscope away and addressed everyone in the room but his patient. "She'll be fine," he said. "All she needs is a good night's rest. Don't let her have any pills, after this drinking." He patted Sully on the shoulder, as he might have patted a little girl. "Off to bed, now," he said. He tried to leave, but Junior took him into the dining room and shut the door.

Sully tried to rise. My mother and I helped her. "I'm all right," she said.

"I'll take her up," my mother said. She half-dragged Sully toward the hallway. "I'll see you if you stop by on your way to Norfolk."

"You're leaving now?"

"In the morning. Very early. I've had all of this I intend to take."

"Me too," Sully murmured as she clung to my mother on the way to the stairs.

I took an apple from the refrigerator. From the dining room I heard Junior's voice rise stridently. "Why does he have to examine her? We'll never get her to go down there, can't you just tell him what you saw?" I stopped chewing my apple. I could not make out the doctor's low even drone. Then Junior's voice came again. "To protect her." After a few moments I could hear them go out the other door; the front door opened and closed. I put my unfinished apple down on the counter and went out and up the stairs to my room and as I shut the door I could hear them rustling around again, dragging their boxes and piles closer to the front door, ready for the morning.

Chapter 18 _____

SOMETHING WOKE ME in the middle of the night. I felt a presence in the room.

"Who is it?"

"It's me," Sully whispered.

I could see her ghostly outline by the bed.

"What do you want?" I said. I found myself whispering too.

I could hear her breathing. "I'm looking for my brooch," she said.

"Sully, you've already got it back."

"Oh, yeah," she said. "Of course."

She did not move. Then she said, "Harlan?"

"Yes?"

"I'm lonely."

I could not think what to say. Most of my mind was still heavy with sleep and I tried to think.

"I can't sleep," she said.

"You better try to, Sully. Today was a hard day, and tomorrow might be worse."

"That's the goddamn truth. Tomorrow's always worse."

Still she did not move and I listened to her rapid, shallow breathing. She said, "Harlan?"

"Yes?"

"Good night." Her silhouette disappeared; I heard her bare feet going quickly away. She closed the door.

She was back in a few moments. She whispered again. "Harlan, are you asleep yet?" The shades were drawn and it was very dark.

"No."

"I think I can go to sleep now."

"That's great," I said, still whispering too.

"Harlan?" I could barely hear her.

"What?"

"Would you kiss me good night?"

"Well," I said. "Well, all right."

"I think that's my problem." She sat on the bed. "I'm not used to going to sleep without somebody kissing me good night. Who'll ever kiss me good night again?"

She put her hands on my shoulders and leaned over my face. I felt her fingers trembling on my skin and felt her hair brush my cheek. She kissed me on the mouth and I could not breathe. Then she fell on top of me and turned her face away and cried on my shoulder.

I patted her on the back. "There, there," I said. "There, there."

"Everything is so wretched," she said. "I don't think I can live."

"Of course you can," I said.

"I can't. I can't."

"Things will look better in the morning."

"No they won't. Every morning is like every other morning. There's one horrible empty day after another." Her voice squeaked as she cried and talked at once. "Nobody loves me. Everybody hates me. Everybody always hated me all of my life. Not even my own son loves me anymore, they stole him from me. I'm just an old wrinkled-up hag with nobody, with nothing, with nobody in the world. If just somebody would let me love them, they wouldn't even have to love me back."

She put her hands on my cheeks and kissed me again, still crying; I could feel her tears run down my face. She rubbed a hand over my shoulder and parted her lips and I turned my face away and she sat up. She took a deep breath and sniffed and stopped crying.

Her voice was shaky. "I guess you think it's pretty silly, me needing to kiss somebody good night so I can sleep."

"No," I said. "I understand."

"I knew you would," she said. She sat silently for a while. "Well, good night."

208

"Good night," I said. "Are you all right?"

"I'll see you tomorrow," she said. "I hope."

She stood and faded to shadow again and moved away. She closed the door and did not return. I tried to sleep.

Chapter 19 _____

In the morning my father and I ate breakfast alone and in silence, watching the gray dawn spread. I went outside to bring in wood from the garage. The icy grass crunched under my feet. It was barely light. The mockingbird, with puffed-out feathers, lay on its side under the hedge. I took a shovel from the garage and buried him at the edge of the lawn next to the woods. I carried in a load of wood and built a fire in the living room and we ate there in front of it.

Through the branches of the old huge dogwood I could see the pale rising sun, a watery orange disc slipping up from behind the trees and roofs, the weak morning sun of winter breaking through a rift in the clouds, still not too bright to look at. On the wall opposite the window the shadow of the branches swayed, the shadow more beautiful than the tree itself, a pattern of intricate lace, twisting and turning, feathery in the wall, each line intersected with every other line. The fire hissed. Sap boiled out of one end of a log and dripped into the coals, spattering and sizzling. My father, finished with his breakfast, gazed into the fire, his thumb running across his upper lip. I watched the flames dancing in his eyes. Over his shoulder hung the photograph of the old man, the life-sized portrait. More than ever before I noticed the resemblance between the two: the same age, the same hair, the same lines of face. They looked alike. My father in life had caught up to the grandfather of my memory, the one who seemed most real to me. I suddenly realized that over the years my image of myself had fused imperceptibly with my image of them. Both of them stared into the fire, my father wistfully, as though aware of the presence looking over his shoulder, and his father, stern but with a hint of a smile in the corners of his lips.

"Someday you'll have to put me away," he said.

"Never," I said.

He smiled briefly and then shut his eyes and leaned his head back against the chair. Then he stirred and sighed and looked again to the fire. Shadows moved in the corners of the room, presences almost with substance. Toward the wall away from the window the room filled with bright light.

In my mind were shadows and lights. I could not tell if the room and its patterns filled my mind, or if my mind spread through the room and put there its own visions. Every event and memory of the past two days seemed to live side by side in my mind at once, past and present jumbled together: the old man in my childhood, stern and teasing by turns, his wit failing into senility, his senility now his spiritless life; Irene, cold as ice, bitter as winter in my childhood, querulous and mean, thawing toward death and losing even before that her frightening aspect, becoming to me slightly silly, and then vanishing suddenly into a bundle of twigs now laid in the earth and covered over; Sully, like a wheel of fire, spinning and spinning, violently joyful, her dance now spent into tired lethargy; Tiny, still warm, still angular with bone and wiry bunches of muscle, her voice still a polished melody on a wood flute, her face full of generations; all of them, alive then, and each now wasted in his own way.

I remembered the trip down the day after my grandmother died. It seemed a fitting remembrance to visit Greenfields on the way, a place which, despite its importance to her, I had never seen. As soon as she died, I felt suddenly the belated need to connect myself with her origins; and Greenfields, despite the recently discovered fact that she had never lived there, seemed the place to go.

I knew the house the instant I saw its ruins. When I crested the middle of the bridge that rose in a high parabola above the vast sheet of water, I got my first unhindered view of the opposite shore. Two columns poked out of the trees upriver, gleaming faintly; and these I knew must be the remaining chimneys of Greenfields.

A couple of miles after the bridge there was a sign on the shoulder of the road, giving information about Greenfields in the peculiarly abbreviated style of highway historical markers. Although the place, or at least the idea of the place, was thronged with family myths and memories, neither my great-grandfather nor my great-great-grandfather was mentioned in the text.

The road hooked backward toward the river. It wandered

through hills and past a couple of small farms, and ended abruptly in a graveled, mostly dirt road. The woods closed in tighter, and it was almost dark driving along the track. It opened into a pasture and there before me was a graveyard enclosed by a chain-link fence. The stones were small and weathered, filmed with a thin sheet of green moss. Across the pasture the woods began again, and out of them, towering into the gray sky, were the two blank chimneys.

I climbed the fence and looked among the gravestones. I found it. It read: "Captain Thomas Coles Perrin. 1822–1914. He Served." I stood in front of it a long time. I wondered if my grandchildren would stand so before the grave of the woman I was on my way to bury. I read the inscription over and over. I rubbed the moss or algae from the flat, smooth face of the stone, but left the gray tongues of lichen growing up the sides, because I liked them, and then climbed out of the graveyard. I walked toward the chimneys. In the screen of mist everything looked one color.

I came upon the house from the rear. The walls of the back and half the sides were rubble. The interior walls stood in various stages of decay. I walked over the house, a jumble of brick and dirt and weeds, everything open to the sky. The lower fireplace of one of the chimneys was enormous and I stood inside it and looked out the straight chute to the gap of gray sky. I climbed down a rubbled wall into the cellar, which like the entire house, was completely open at the top. It was a square in one corner of the remains. I tried to imagine my grandmother going from one part of the house to another, tried to envision her at a ball. From the pit I looked up at the parts of walls and although I could not place my grandmother there, I imagined the place itself when it was whole; probably I had as clear a picture of its design as its inhabitants had had, because it was laid bare and skeletal for me, everything stripped away but a few brick walls and lines of foundations, which together showed the dimensions of all the rooms.

I went up to the front wall and looked out the door. I saw below the boxwood maze, and tall rounded cedar trees hunched over from the wind of the river. I walked out the door and down the circular steps and to the end of the completely overgrown front lawn, now grassless and weedy, a clutter of underbrush.

I turned and looked back at the house my grandmother had never lived in. As I stood directly in front of it, the entire and undamaged front wall threw forward the illusion of a whole house. But through the door and windows there appeared, like framed paintings, sky and field and woods. This illusion stayed with me during the funeral visit, and played in my mind as I watched my father watching the fire.

After I turned from the house, I had sought in the boxwood garden the place where Harrison had proposed and been rejected and felt insulted.

I felt the rubble of the walkways under the weeds. In a few bald patches the bricks gleamed slick and mossy. Through the angular spaces between the cedar trunks I could see the river like a hammered sheet of pewter, the dull reflection of a dull gray sky. The drizzle began, chilling the back of my neck, the chill running like electricity down my back and to my feet and all through inside me. But I stood to listen to it rattle through the boxweed and whisper in the grass and weeds.

I found the well—the exact spot by which my grandmother, sitting in a bench, had received and rejected the invitation to wed; the rejection an accident of thought, a girlish whim, without which I would not exist to seek the spot upon which the decision had been made. I almost fell through a thick bramble of dead blackberry canes into the well. I lurched backward and kicked the canes and weeds and undergrowth away and knelt, peering into the dark well as the rain fell on my back. As far down as I could reach, the bricks were gone. One side had caved in. I could not see the bottom. A black coolness rose from it. I tossed in a rock and it sounded a loud echoing clink when it landed in the invisible ruined bricks below.

I walked through the boxwood maze, shivering, and under the cedar trees out to the open edge of the bluff. I squinted to try to see the far shore through the drizzle. The river blended with the gray mist, and the mist met the sky up and down the river. The sky and the river and the mist had no clear beginning or end, but faded in and out of one another. It was as though the hill I stood upon were floating on a cloud; or as though I stood at the last jutting point of a flat silent earth, watching in the water at earth's end the whitecaps like gleams of life between dark and dark glisten and disappear.

And I had turned and come to her funeral; sitting in her living room, remembering the house that was not hers, I felt as though I were still standing on that shore, seeing it through the window. I felt nostalgia for times I had never known, felt myself connected by repeated extensions from child to parent to parent back into the dimness of history and forward to the dimness of the future; feeling these things and watching my father, and considering his future and then mine, all times merged into one continuous flow with one demarcation: the world my grandparents were born into and outlived in early adulthood but never forgot; and the world I knew. They were the last rememberers of another age, and my father, my link, sat across from me, an embodiment of my origins, a boding of my future.

I looked at him. "Something is passing away," I said.

He looked old and sad and reflective. "It's gone, boy," he said. "The very end of it has disappeared forever."

In the lightening room, Junior's face, pasty and puffy, contorted by its bruise, appeared at the doorway. Helen entered with her and my father rose to leave. "I'm sorry I can't fix you any breakfast," Junior said. "Maybe Elizabeth can fix us all some when she gets up. We've got to get cracking. The movers are due at ten."

"I've got to go see the lawyer," my father said. He did not look at them.

Junior dragged out a pile of torn and flattened cardboard boxes from behind the sofa and took them to the television set. She and Helen kneeled in front of it as though praying to it, wrapping the cardboard around it. They taped the pieces together. The set was still plugged in. Junior looked up. "The T.V. is mine, but I've got one. Do you have a T.V., Little Harlan?"

"I don't watch T.V.," I said. "I bet Tiny . . ."

Junior turned red as she bent over, taping more cardboard in place. Her lips squeezed into a flat ugly line. "Tiny has talked herself out of any thing at all," she said. She stood and touched the swollen corner of her mouth. "I'll guarantee you one thing. She'll get kicked out of her house before I get kicked out of mine. That's one thing I'll make sure of."

"What?" Helen said.

"If I'd known she had a nickel to her name I would have sued her for this." Junior tapped her bruise again and winced. She looked at me. "I know none of this is your doing, but please don't mention Tiny to me. The mere mention of her name makes me feel faint."

She patted the top of the television set. "That's that," she said. She looked around. "I don't see anything else but the mirror."

Harrison's Revenge had been removed from the hall and leaned against the wall behind Junior. "Helen, I wish you could have seen Mother looking in it this last year after Poppy beat her up. It was pitiful. She spent hours looking in it."

"Poor Mother," Helen murmured. She helped Junior lay the mirror on its face on top of a box marked HELEN'S KNICKS. "Why, this has my name on it!" Helen cried. "Why, Junior, I thought we remembered that Mother gave this to you."

Junior waved a dimpled generous hand. "Oh, I want you to have it. I can look at it when I come visit you. I've looked in it more than I care to."

The name was written on a scrap of paper taped to the back of the mirror. I looked around in the dim gray light and noticed for the first time that there were name tags on everything, including the carpet, written in Junior's round huge letters. I walked around the room and looked at the tags, inspecting each one closely. I could feel Junior watching me look. A few articles had no tags; all those that did were marked either HELEN or JUNIOR. The carpet was labeled HELEN/JUNIOR SPLIT/THROW. I sat down to puzzle over that.

Helen shoved her boxes to the other side of the door. "How much do you think you'll get for your house?"

"About eighty thousand."

Helen moved her lips as though counting the dollars one by one. "Golly," she said. "That's a lot of money."

"Taxes," Junior said bitterly. "Agent's fee. Twenty percent taxes. When I sell my house and furniture and some of this"—she waved her hand at the boxes and furniture and then toward the dining room—"and invest the money I'll be living on eight thousand a year. After Poppy dies, and God knows when that will be."

"Can't you live on that?" I said.

"Of course I can *live* on it," she said, looking up at me in surprise, as though she had forgotten about me. "But who in the world wants to? What are my friends going to think? An *apart*ment," she moaned. "I won't have any friends. Can you see me having my garden club turn in an apartment?"

"Life is hard," I said.

Junior looked at me in surprise again. "Don't you want to

see if your mother is up? Maybe she could fix you some breakfast."

"She's gone," I said.

"My, she was in a hurry."

"Yes," I said. "She was."

"At least you're not as bad off as Sully," Helen said. "There's always a ray of sunshine somewhere."

"Sully?" Junior said. "Sully's used to it. She doesn't care what people think. At least she's too old to throw herself on some man now. It's about time. I got so sick of hearing how beautiful she was, I could scream. It started the minute she was born, oh, how *beautiful* your little sister is, what huge *darl*ing blue eyes, and that hair blah, blah, blah. Didn't you get sick of it?"

We could hear Sully coming down the stairs. "Oh, Lord," Helen said. "Speak of the devil." They both froze in their postures, as if to remain camouflaged among the heirlooms, a matching pair of ottomans.

"I hope she doesn't come in here," Junior said. "She's been trying to borrow money from people. Tell her I don't have any, Helen."

Sully walked into the room, picked her way through the piles, and fell into the sofa. Her face was puffy, her eyes red and wandering; age settled around her like a shadow. She plucked at the name tag on the arm of the sofa, pulled it off, and held it close in front of her eyes. If she had blinked, her lashes would have brushed against the paper.

"Why, I had no idea this was your couch, Junior," she said, hoarse and slurring, her tone ironic. She glanced around the room. "What is this, nursery school or camp, or something? Everybody's got to have little tags on all their things?"

Junior and Helen bent together over Harrison's Revenge. "Tell this woman I'm not talking to her," Junior said. "Try to explain to her that the movers are coming and there's a lot to be moved and it's very confusing."

"Confusing! Ha, I'll say its confusing."

"Sully," Helen said. "Junior has to move from her house. Let's be nice to her."

Sully smirked. "Poor, poor Junior," she said. She was sprawled like a length of rope on the sofa, leaning in a corner, too tired to sit up.

I felt as if my head had dreamed my body into being, into this

216

time and place and situation. Junior had given me a notion. "Junior says Tiny will get kicked out of her house before she leaves her own," I said to Sully. Sully looked at me, trying to keep her eyes from going away. "She's going to make sure somebody buys Tiny's house *right away.*" I could feel Junior looking at me while I stared into Sully's bleared eyes, which began to clear as they filled with thought. "I think she'd like it sold today, if possible."

I glanced quickly at Junior, whose gaze beat at me like a fog lamp; she hadn't quite got the picture but she knew I was up to something.

Sully raised herself into a sitting position and lit a cigarette, coughed. "It will be for sale as of today, too," I said. "My father left just a few minutes ago to talk to Mr. Grissom, get all the houses on the market." She looked at me in mute conspiracy, a smile growing across her face. She lurched out of the sofa. Her body perked up with her sudden enthusiasm. She faced Junior and Helen; the latter had noticed nothing and was still scrambling around moving boxes. Sully cleared her throat as if she were about to make a few after-dinner remarks. She was as nearly gleeful as a person in her state could be. "I was thinking about mailing my brooch to Tiny," she announced. "What do you think of that?" I thought, No, wait, wait, that's not it; but she was leading them on.

Helen stood up, head rearing back like an alert animal at a watering hole. "What?" she said. Her voice rose up in a wail. "What did you say?"

"I figured to wrap it up and mail it to her, but I'm not going to do that."

Helen relaxed; but Junior was still silent and darting her eyes at us.

"There's no way you would give up your brooch to a colored woman," Helen said. "I mean, it ought to be Carolyn's anyway and I know if you were going to give it away you would give to her and not to a—"

"What I'm going to do is sell it and buy Tiny's house with the money and then give her the house," Sully said. She weaved out of the room and left Helen sputtering. I remained in the chair, my eyes on the dying embers of the fire, so I did not see Junior, but I heard her grunt as she viciously kicked a box of drapery toward the front door.

"Young Irene," Helen cried. "Do something!"

She stopped kicking the box and I could hear her breathing. I looked up at her. Her face was red and she worked her jaws a little, trying to keep herself calm. "I was mad at Sully," she said. "I admit it." She held out her palm against Helen, as though expecting some sort of contradiction. "I shouldn't have been, and I was, and I admit it. But we've got to overcome our feelings about all this business and help her. After all is said and done, Helen, she's still our sister."

"I don't see why we should help her," Helen said, as petulant as a five-year-old child, actually wringing her fingers. "I don't see that she needs any help. She's got Carolyn's brooch, hasn't she? And she seems to know how to get rid of it faster than any of us expected, without any help. Not once, but twice. And to Tiny!"

"That's exactly what I'm talking about," Junior said. "She's our sister and we've got to be kind. We've got to protect her from herself."

"Protect her?"

"I don't see how any one could afford to keep her in a private institution, though. She'll have to go to the state hospital."

"The state hospital?"

"Helen, what do you think I've been talking about these last three days?"

Helen ducked her head under Junior's exasperation. "I don't think she'll go," Helen said. "She said she almost went crazy in that other place, and she was only there a week."

"Of course she won't go, we've got to have her committed."

"Oh, Junior! We can't do that. She's not crazy. Is she?"

"She's a raving lunatic. Giving away her last penny to buy a *colored* woman a house—if that's not proof of insanity, I'd like to know what is. And you saw her dancing in front of me like a drunk monkey with that brooch yesterday, inciting that woman to commit assault and battery. And last night, she tried to kill herself! Foaming at the mouth! Screaming like a banshee."

"But you said yourself that was only a play for—"

"Don't be so stupid, Helen," Junior snapped. "She'll blow every penny we're supposed to inherit when Poppy dies if we don't put her away where she belongs. For her own good," she added quickly.

"But how could she get Poppy's money?"

"How could she get Carolyn's brooch? But she got it, didn't she?"

"You said how embarrassed you were when she went into that place in California, and when you had to take Poppy. Junior, I wouldn't want you to have to go through all that kind of thing again, only worse this time. Right here in town, everyone would know about it."

"I'll have to bear my burdens. I won't see anybody anyway. I'll be living in some apartment over somebody's garage," Junior said mournfully. "I'll just have to take on the shame of my sister the best I can." Her face was illuminated with sudden zest. "But it won't be nearly as embarrassing as it would be to see her catting around trying to find some other man to keep her, would it?" ·

"You know I always know you know best. And I don't approve of anything she does. But I just don't know if I could see her going into the state institution with all those slobbering people, and rapists, and . . . and . . ."

"You'll be in Detroit, Helen. You won't see a thing. It is hard, believe me, it's very hard." Junior put her hand to her heart in a fluttering motion. "I had to go through it with Poppy, too. But I don't mind; I'm used to doing all the dirty work. Somebody has to, I guess. I do it so you won't have to, poor Helen." Tears came to the corners of her eyes at the thought of her sacrifices for Helen. "I had to be there when Poppy all of a sudden saw what was happening to him."

"Oh, Junior," Helen whispered.

"All you have to do is sign this paper a lawyer had drawn up for me," Junior said briskly. She walked out of the room into the hall and came back with her pocketbook. She took out some folded sheets of paper. "Look at this," she whispered. "Do you see right there, where Dr. Gurney signed? Do you think he would sign it if she didn't really need this, for treatment, for her own sake?"

"I guess not," Helen said. "But it seems like such a great big thing to be doing."

"It's not such a big deal; people get sick in the head all the time. She might get out; Helen, think of our sister. Think of poor Sully."

"But like you said, she's used to it. Isn't that what you said?" Helen asked timidly.

"Helen, how can an intelligent, grown-up woman like you be so blockheaded? Listen, where does Sully have to go? Where?"

"I don't know."

"Nowhere."

"Nowhere?"

"No one will support her anymore. Can you support her, Helen?"

"No."

"And Harlan said he won't, and who could blame him? And I certainly can't, not with the pocket money I'll be reduced to trying to live on. And can she support herself? Has she ever had a job? Has she got any money?"

Helen looked blankly at the piece of paper.

"She can't possibly get a job. She'll pawn the brooch again, or sell it, and the money will be gone in a month. What will happen to her?"

"But she's going to give the money to Tiny."

"So she won't have the money any time at all, if she goes through with it, and what is going to happen to her? What will she do?"

Helen was silent.

"What?" Junior said, bearing down, moving her bulk against Helen, pushing her swollen face close to Helen's.

"I don't know," Helen said at last.

"I don't either, but I know it won't be good. Maybe the Salvation Army will put her on one of their cots and let her earn her keep sweeping up after drunks and bums."

"Can't she get alimony from one of her husbands?"

"Helen, she's not married to either of them. How could you forget *that*? And who else is going to marry her, either, with her looks gone. I guess even at fifty she'll still try to get passed around from man to man like some kind of . . . I can't say it. I can't say the word about my own sister. Helen, we simply do not have any choice," she said, her tone tragic, a heavy emphasis on each word.

"Is Harlan going to sign?"

"Oh, yes," Junior said fiercely. "He'll sign. He had me sign something, he can sign something for me. When he gets back from the lawyer's office, he's going to sign. He's half-convinced already."

"He won't sign it," I said. "I won't let him." They sprang apart, startled at the sound of my voice. Both of them stared at me.

"Lordy," Junior said. "You gave me a start. Where did you come from?"

I said nothing.

"I thought you left with Sully," she said. "Harlan, you ought to be more interested than anybody in getting your father to sign. You've always been so devoted to her. You saw what happened last night. Just think how you would feel if she were left running around loose, and decided to really kill herself."

"At least it would be her own decision."

They both looked at me with horror.

"You can't mean that!" Junior said. "Nobody could mean such a cruel thing."

"I'm not sure exactly what I mean," I said. I stood up. "But I mean this: I'm going to tell Sully your plans, and I'm going to keep my father from signing anything. If he would even consider it in the first place, which I don't think he will."

"You can't do that." She turned to Helen, and thrust the paper at her. She took a pen from her pocketbook. "Quick, Helen, sign it before she gets away."

Helen bent down to the wrapped television and wrote on the paper, hand trembling. I turned and walked out of the room.

"You can't do this to your own flesh and blood," Junior called, her moonlike face disfigured by its bruise and subdued fury. "I won't be stopped! I won't!"

Sully's bag was crammed full and she was trying to push it closed. She looked up as I came in. "What's all the hoo-fer-all down there? Are they about to die over Tiny's house?"

"They're signing things to get you committed to the state hospital," I said. "We better hurry." I closed the suitcase for her.

She stared at me with wide eyes, and I was surprised at her surprise. "I knew it," she said. "Didn't I tell you? I just knew it. Do you think they can really get away with it? Last night kind of did me in, didn't it?"

"Yes," I said. I picked up the bag. "Let's go."

I carried Sully's suitcase and a box containing the rest of her new clothes to my car and put them in the trunk. I put her painting in the backseat. A sheet of ice glazed the windshield and both hands hurt by the time I had all of it scraped off. The car had been parked on the street overnight and was hard to start. I let the engine run for a while. As we waited in the slowly warming interior, a huge moving van came to a stop in front of the house. "The Denver Express,"

Sully said. We pulled away. The square house—that cold geometrical space which years of habitation could not transcend, which remained therefore less a dwelling place than an inert box—and the yawning van with strangers emerging from it grew smaller and smaller in the rearview mirror and then vanished from sight as we turned the corner.

Sully's nervous excitement and an expensive, invigorating perfume both filled the car and contradicted in a startling way her tired person. She leaned forward, grew tired and dropped back, hitched herself forward again, as though by her exhausted motions she might lurch the car along faster. "I can't believe them," she said. "I knew she would try it, and I still can't believe it. I can hardly believe even Junior would really do it."

She spoke softly to the window, staring out at the world beyond which looked cold and miserable. The fine drizzle and sleet swirled over the metal with a sibilant scratching. Trees and shrubs, branches and evergreen needles and leaves were encased in glittering shrouds of ice. Some branches were cracked already and we heard an occasional pop over the hum of the engine and heater. We went across the bridge over the creek, iced at the edges, moving sluggishly as though thickened and slowed by the cold. Soon we were beyond the homes settled in the mist. Glazed trees gave way to lightposts and traffic signs hung with daggers of ice. The buildings of the town floated in the fog and sleet and freezing rain, their foundations blurred and nearly invisible, and they all took on the same dull gray color in mist packed close to earth, stark and bare and ugly, looking vacant and abandoned except for some of the newest and tallest buildings scattered about at random, from the windows of which bright sterile lights glowed without warmth.

We parked in front of Stanley's Jewel Box. "Now, are you sure about this?" I said.

"I'm sure."

I took Sully's brooch inside and talked to Rose and came back to the car a few minutes later with a check made out to my grandfather's estate. The ice in my hair melted in the car and cold water trickled down my neck. The car was steamed with Sully's breath. "Can I see it?" she said. "I want to see what three thousand dollars look like in cold cash."

"Sure, it's yours," I said. "But it's not cash, it's a check."

She waved her hand and looked out the window. "Never mind, then," she said. "A check's a check. I've seen checks written for five, ten thousand dollars. Wrote some of them myself."

As we drifted to the curb beside the bank building, a car in front of us skidded and swayed on the icy pavement. The building, the tallest in the town and the second highest in the state, disappeared in the sky. Sully looked up at the glass and steel as we walked to the revolving door. "All that glass," she murmured.

On the elevator attached to the side of the building we rose smoothly and quickly as though in a cloud, the street below fading and then disappearing before we reached the tenth floor, so that we were hung in the sky with no world around us, no substance, nothing above and nothing below but formless gray.

Sully whimpered and clutched my arm. "I feel like I'm dying," she whispered.

"Don't look."

"I can't help it."

I had to pull her away and lead her out of the elevator. We walked silently through the newly carpeted hallway to the lawyer's office. The heat was oppressive. The secretary told us after a moment to pass through to the inner sanctum. My father sat in a leather-covered chair at one side of the lawyer's huge, elegant, polished desk.

Without preamble or introduction, in a voice slurred with excitement, Sully blurted out as she entered, "I have a plan!"

My father sighed and set himself back deep in his chair. "I know. I've just been talking to Junior on the phone. You remember my sister Sully," he said. "This is Mr. Grissom."

Sully plopped into the matching armchair opposite my father and looked at him across the deserted expanse of desk. She did not even bother to fix her legs gracefully for the lawyer. Looking at her legs, I noticed that she already had a run in her new stockings.

"This is so great, you're not going to believe it!" She spoke to my father, and I could not tell whether she had heard about the phone call from Junior. She did not even give Mr. Grissom a glance. "How much do you want for Tiny's house?"

"I don't know, we're not sure yet," my father said. He looked at Sully.

"I want to buy it," she said triumphantly, almost shouting. She looked then at Grissom. She gave him a quick artificial smile that disappeared as soon as she turned back to my father, the lines of her face deepened with anxiety and fervor.

"Buy it?" my father said. "With what?"

"That's her problem," I said. He looked at me in surprise, then looked to the lawyer, who sat silently and calmly, his hands folded in front of him on the desk.

"I was just arranging with Mr. Grissom to handle the sale of all the houses, among other matters," my father said. "Appraisals have to be made, deals with a real estate man . . ."

"I have three thousand dollars," Sully said, clutching and shaking once the pocketboot in her lap. Her knuckles went white around it.

"That's not enough. They would fight that in court, and who could blame them?" He turned to the lawyer. "They'd win too, wouldn't they?"

Mr. Grissom nodded once, slowly, as though with this movement he signaled not only agreement, but understanding of everything that could possibly be asked, of everything that could occur, in his office.

Sully looked through the tall window behind my father at the gray nothingness, her eyes going wide with each occasional pip of brightness and sound as pieces of sleet plinked against the glass. "But look," Sully said, moving to the edge of her chair, "you see, I give up my share, I pay for their shares, don't you *see?*"

My father regarded her steadily and sadly, and a little coldly. "This money," he said. "I don't need to ask where you got it. You've got to protect what little you've got. I told you, I can't keep on—"

"Six thousand," I said.

"What?" He looked at me, surprised again.

"You're asking six thousand for the house. Six thousand is a nice round figure."

He turned back to Mr. Grissom. "They could still fight that. The house is worth more."

In answer, Grissom turned his palms out, and inclined his head very slightly, a modest and discreet but very definite motion of disagreement.

"It couldn't be worth much more," I said. "A four-room house, or three, in the cheapest section of town. It's close enough. Just do it."

"I've got to protect the inheritance for my own heirs," he said to Sully. "And I don't want to let you throw away—"

"She's not throwing anything away! It's hers to do what she wants to with! Do it! Give up your share—forget about your heirs. We don't need it. Protect Tiny, not us. Sully will give up her share of the property, you're going to give up your fourth, and she'll buy the remainder with her three thousand dollars." I was surprised by my loudness but I could not stop. "Give Mr. Grissom the check," I said.

Sully fumbled quickly in her purse with shaky hands, and put the check on the flat shiny desk.

"There has to be a title search, a survey, all kinds of things," my father said. "There's all kinds of paperwork. It takes time."

"Just give her some kind of piece of paper to give Tiny for now."

"A sales contract," said Mr. Grissom.

"Can't it be a deed?" I said. "We don't want her to see the sales contract. Title search, survey, that's for the buyer's protection, right? Tiny doesn't care. She doesn't even need it."

"I still don't know that I go along with it," my father said.

"Just do it."

He sighed and shrugged his shoulders, running his hand through his whitening hair. Grissom looked at him, mutely questioning. My father jerked his thumb at me. "Ask him," he said. "I wash my hands of it."

The lawyer cleared his throat. "I presume," he said, "that your purpose is not to allow Tiny to know the source of this generosity?"

"That's right."

He moved one of his plump white hands with very neat fingernails to the middle of the table and picked up the check. "I can arrange that. She need know nothing at all. We will prepare a sort of bill of sale. There will be no price, and our dear little lady here will not be mentioned."

"This is fabulous," Sully said, and although she seemed still nervous, she sank back in her chair. I wondered if I would manage to get her back to the car before she burned out.

"I want to talk to my son," my father said.

Mr. Grissom rose and walked toward Sully. He was much shorter than he had appeared sitting behind his desk. "Let's go arrange the details," he said cheerfully. He helped Sully to her feet and they went to the outer office. Sully looked back over her shoulder as the door closed on them.

"Junior has a very good point," my father said. "A *very* good point." He moved in his chair as though he could not find comfort in any position. His hands waved in the air, flopped onto the arms of the chair, went to his lap, waved again in the air. "What is she going to do? What the *hell* is she going to do?" He looked at me with a shade of bewilderment in his aging face.

"As you and Junior would say, she'd just blow her money anyway. I don't understand why you'll listen to Junior after all that's happened. You understand her motives. Junior might have covered them up to hide them from herself, maybe she's aware of them, but you know her motives better than she does."

"Sully's situation is almost impossible, now," he said.

"Where did that form come from? She had Helen sign a form, I don't know if you've seen it. She must have had it ready for days. All this business about no one to look after her now, buying Tiny's house, that's just one more piece of ammunition for what Junior already had planned. She said as much to Helen."

"I don't know," he said.

"For God's sake, let the woman alone, let her make her own choices! If anyone had let her do it before, she wouldn't be in this fix now. Her money's going to be gone soon, even if she doesn't blow it in the month you think it will take."

He sighed and shook his head. "It's crazy," he said.

"And what about Tiny? She wants to help Tiny, and why shouldn't she? What will happen to Tiny if she has no house to live in? If you want to look at it as an investment, invest in Tiny's house. The house will stay there as long as Tiny lives. Let Sully make the decision what to do with her own money, let her at least have this one thing, the satisfaction of providing for Tiny."

"That doesn't answer what Sully will do."

"That's for her to figure out."

"I can't help but think she might be better off. . . . Let Junior and Helen . . . let Sully give Tiny the house and then . . ."

"Think of Poppy last night. You already locked one up and

watched him wither away to nothing. Do you want to do it again to somebody thirty or forty years younger?"

That shook him visibly. He lifted his hand to his forehead and looked into his lap. At last he said, almost whispering, as though he were afraid of his question or my answer, "Do you think she'll make it?" He looked up at me, his eyes still uncertain and touched now with fear.

We looked at each other and I did not answer. We looked away. "Go on," he said. "Go on and get her out of here before I change my mind."

"Now I have to go to the drugstore," Sully said as we left the elevator. The manila envelope with Tiny's sales contract was tucked beneath her arm. The bottom of the revolving door screeched against little pebbles of ice as we pushed through it.

"What for?"

"To fill a prescription." She spoke and moved listlessly. Now that she had almost achieved her purpose, her energy was draining. And now that I had insisted to my father, and taken part on Sully's behalf, I felt uneasy, even queasy.

"Let's go to Tiny's house first," I said.

"It's a very important prescription."

"But we've got to hurry," I said.

"I've got to get it right now."

"What kind of medicine is it?"

"Some pills."

"What kind of pills?"

"Just some pills." She stopped and fumbled in her pocketbook. Ice fell into it. The sleet melting in her hair was like a diamond net. She handed me a creased, soiled piece of paper. "Here," she said. "If you can figure it out, let me know."

I couldn't read it. "I think you know what it is," I said. I handed it back to her.

The edges of her mouth turned up in the slightest of smiles; her fatigue seemed to keep her from a full smile. She shrugged her shoulders and turned away from me, looking up and down the street. "I guess you know too," she said. "Can't see anything in this mess. Where the hell is a drugstore?"

I led the way up the street.

"I can't walk any farther," she said after a while. "Can we take the car?" She stopped.

"Come on," I said, taking her by the elbow and guiding her around to retrace our steps to my car. "Let's go on to Tiny's first, then come back and get the bus ticket, and you can fill the prescription while we wait for the bus."

"Will there be a wait?"

"Probably." We finally made it back to my car, Sully slipping and sliding in the ice. We started for Tiny's house. I tried to think. I tried to be sure of what I was doing.

"Where are you going?" I said.

"I don't know." She looked absently out of the window. "Somewhere."

"What you should do is this: you should go somewhere you've got friends—maybe California—and tell me their names. I'll call ahead for you, and someone will meet your bus."

"I don't know . . ." she said.

"Where do you have some friends you could stay with for a while?"

She smirked a little, then faded back into her distracted unseeing gaze. "I don't want to talk about it right now," she said.

"Maybe you should wait until you get wherever it is, before you buy your pills."

She did not look at me but she laid her hand on my leg. "Don't worry, you've been great," she said. "I think maybe you'll be all right after all."

"Me?" I said.

"I don't know where I'm going," she said. "I don't want to talk about it right now. Let's just get to Tiny's house."

We were almost there. When we reached it Sully waited in the car.

I knocked at the door and peered through the panes of glass and saw her standing in the middle of the room, bent over to one side, as though she could see or hear better in that position. I called to her and she shuffled closer, still bent, and looked some more; then hobbled yet closer and looked again. I was reminded of the mockingbird hopping about, turning an eye to the ground to look for his food. Tiny turned her head to the other side and then slowly walked toward the door, a look of angry suspicion on her face until she recognized me. It was very cold on the porch. My feet were beginning to hurt and my hands were numb. She opened the door and said, "Bless your heart, child, come in out of the cold this minute. You'll catch your death."

"Not for a long time yet," I said. "I can't come in. We've got to go."

"I couldn't figure who would be out in this weather. Who that in yo' car?"

"Sully. We came to say good-bye, and to give you this."

"Sully," she said. "In this weather?"

She took the bill of sale from me and looked down at it and turned it over and over in her hands, regarding it as though it were a strange amulet or talisman she did not know how to use. It seemed to me that she suspected what it was. She did not try to read it. "What this?" she said.

"It's like the deed to your house. You should keep it somewhere safe."

She smiled all over. "Law," she said. "I knowed it was in Miss Irene's paper." She looked up to me. "They found it in Miss Irene's paper, to give it to me, didn't they?"

"The lawyer just gave it to me a few minutes ago."

"And y'all come all the way out here just for that, when you could of just dropped it in the mail. My, my." She looked up into my eyes, her stained corneas and the richer, deeper brown irises gleaming. All the lines in her mahogany face were crinkled into a smile. "Aint y'all sweet," she said. "Go get Sully and come in here before you both catch your death of cold."

"We've got to go," I said.

She came out onto the porch. "Well then, I'll come tell Sully good-bye, if she won't come in. Is that child all right? Is she going off to California now?"

"She's fine."

I held her arm as she climbed laboriously down the icy steps and walked the short distance to the car. Sully rolled her window down.

"I would have come in," she said. "I was too tired."

"And no wonder, all the goings-on," Tiny said. They held hands through the window. "It wear out any soul. They never got that brooch away from you again?"

"No."

"And you ain't gone back to that place with it? You ain't gone and pawned it again?"

"No. I'll never pawn it again."

"I knew you wouldn't." She patted Sully's frail arm with her huge hand. "I bet you had something to do with keeping my house for me. I know Junior would have tried something after yesterday." She looked from one to the other of us, rocking slightly as she did so.

"It's the law," I said. "They can't break the law unless everybody helps them."

"Kiss me good-bye, Tiny," Sully said.

Tiny kissed her on the cheek. "You go get all warm out there in California," she said. "You write me now, you hear?"

Sully could not answer; she nodded her head. Tiny turned toward the little neat house and I took her arm again. We moved carefully up the steps. "Ever'thing suffering in this weather," she said, looking around. "The trees and the birds, and us too. I knew she wouldn't pawn it again."

"Not after you got it out of hock for her."

She turned her head away in embarrassment. "I won't worried about that. Just Junior getting aholt of it again somehow if she did."

"Well, Junior will never see it again."

"Good." We reached the door.

"Tiny, I wanted to ask you . . ."

"Yes?"

"Well, how did you get the money to do it?"

She grinned widely, her gold tooth shining in her dark face and stained teeth. "I budgets," she said. She hugged me. "You drive that little car careful, you hear me? Like driving in a eggshell."

"Yes'm," I said. "I will."

When I reached the car I turned around. She was standing in the door, waving at us. "Tiny," I called. She had the paper in the hand she was waving at us. "I love you."

She grinned some more. She pushed her wig off her ear. "And you know you're like one of mine to me," she said.

I got in the car. Sully was sniffling. She looked back at Tiny's house until it was out of view.

"I've never been so happy and scared and sad and tired in my life," she said.

We drove slowly to the bus station, the slush on the pavement splashing and drumming against the undercarriage. The wipers

230

bumped and screeched and Sully stared vacantly through the mist. We parked in front of the squat colorless structure and stepped across the tobacco spit and patches of mashed old chewing gum and slush and on inside across the squares of linoleum, past a news counter displaying papers from cities far away, and magazines, ranging from *The Atlantic* to *True Confessions,* and some especially lurid ones tucked low behind the counter.

Sully went to the ticket counter and waited in line behind a whiskered, weaving man in baggy trousers that were tied at the waist with a length of clothesline. He faced us and grinned drunkenly, showing a mouth of bad teeth. The ticket agent came up, gray-haired and bored and wearing an expression of tired insolence that appeared to be permanently molded onto his face.

"Much it cost?" the man said. "Dollah 'n' somthin'?"

"Where are you going?"

"Going?"

"Where are you going?"

"Why I'm goin' Charlotte," the drunk cried, as if everyone knew not only the city of his destination, but the street address.

"Four fifty."

"Four fifty?"

"That's right."

"Uh. How 'bout Rowan. How much to Rowan?"

"That's not on the way to Charlotte."

"Nemmine that."

"Two eighty-five."

"Uh. Where can I git to for dollah 'n' somethin'?"

"Burlington."

"Burlington?"

"Burlington."

The man was silent for a moment, rubbed his whiskers. "Don't know nobody in Burlington," he said. He backed off. He looked at us, shaking his head. "I never did like Burlington," he said.

Sully hesitated. "Why don't we figure out where you're best off first," I said.

"How much does a ticket cost on the next bus that's going a long ways off?" she said. "I can't spend but forty dollars."

The man regarded her a moment, took a toothpick out of his mouth. He looked insolently at her chest and passed his other hand over his bulging stomach. "What did you say, lady?"

231

"Where's the next bus that's not going on just a short trip?"

He looked at her, looked at me. He looked us both up and down with close scrutiny, squinting, and gave up, turning his eyes down to the counter, bored again. "Bus to Cincinnati in a hour. Thirty-seven fifty."

She handed him a fifty-dollar bill. "I've never been to Cincinnati," she said. "Give me a one-way ticket to Cincinnati."

He sold her the ticket and watched us walk away a few paces. Then he picked up his comic book and resumed reading.

"Now I've got to go to the drugstore," she said. She pawed through her pocketbook as we walked out. "If I can find that goddamned prescription." She rummaged through it on the sidewalk, the pellets of ice beating on us, some of them bounding again into her open purse. A look of terror seized her; her body flexed rigid. "Where is it? Where is it?" She flailed her hand inside. "I've lost it," she wailed. A solitary figure glanced curiously at us as he carried his suitcase inside. "Oh, God, here it is." She clutched the paper in her fist and began walking briskly in the wrong direction.

"There's one up this way," I said.

We walked in silence a couple of blocks, heads bent forward to keep the cold and rain and sleet out of our faces.

"This idea of going to Cincinnati," I said.

"What about it?" she said, her nasal whine dull and soft. "Where else could I go?"

"Someplace you're familiar with. Someplace you have friends."

"Don't have any."

"Acquaintances, at least."

"Screw them."

"You could try Peanut again. He doesn't know how bad things are."

"He knows."

"What are you going to do in Cincinnati?"

She shrugged her shoulders. She looked around while she shivered, as though she were in a strange town and were seeing everything for the first time.

"Maybe—maybe you could commit your*self,* which would be a much different thing than letting them put you away somewhere, your own decision, you could get . . . a rest, get yourself upright, get out whenever you want. . . ."

232

"No. You can't get out. They keep you there as long as they feel like it."

"You could get some kind of . . . treatment," I mumbled.

"Treatment! Ha!" Energy returned for a moment. "They don't give you treatment at those places. Those places are sewers. The only treatment is, the guards rape you."

"They do not."

"They do. I heard it from any number of patients in the sanitorium who had been in state institutions. They stick these little things all on you—"

"What little things?"

"I don't know, these *things*. They stick these little gizmos all over you, and also they rape you. And worse."

"Worse?"

"You wouldn't believe it."

"I don't believe it."

"You don't have to. But I do, and I sure as hell am not going to commit myself, after escaping from Junior. I'd rather die. It wouldn't do any good even if they did give me treatment, because I'm not crazy." Her eyes blinked away tears and her metallic nasal drone broke as she spoke. "I would wind up a vegetable like Poppy," she said. "Inside of three weeks."

We walked in silence for a time. The wind whipped at us and she shivered violently as we walked. She stepped and grabbed my sleeve and stopped me. She looked with desperate searching into my eyes. Her bloodshot eyes looked big and wild and full of fear. "Don't you think I'm right?" she said over the wind. She shook my arm with her bony hands. "Don't you?"

"Yes."

We went on.

After a while she said, "But you wonder what's going to happen to me."

"Yes."

"So do I."

We reached the drugstore and went in. It was warm and brightly lit.

"Look at the normal people," Sully said. "Where did they come from?"

A few customers were scattered in the huge space. It seemed

233

strange to see them, with the sidewalks almost deserted. Sully went
to the pharmacist's counter in the back of the store. From where I
waited, near the front door, I could see the man in his white coat take
the beat-up piece of paper and look at it and then at Sully, and then
back to the paper. He leaned on the counter while she spoke to him,
and he appeared to answer. They spoke back and forth for some
time, and finally he retreated into his shelves of medicines while
Sully drooped over the counter. He came out after a few moments
with a package and Sully paid and came up to the door. We went
back into the gelid air and pelting, whispering sleet.

Sully turned the wrong way.

"The bus station is over here," I said.

"I've got to go to the whiskey store," she said.

"You really shouldn't," I said.

"I've got to. I've done all that I can do. I've got to have something to drink. It's a long trip."

"Sully."

"I can't help it."

"Listen."

"I've made up my mind."

I sighed and crunched over the ice by her side. "It's your mind,
I guess."

"Yes. What's left of it."

At least the wind pushed from behind. I stood in front of the
glass-fronted store when we reached it. After a time Sully emerged
with a paper bag, and held it up in the air and tried to grin. We
faced the wind and walked toward the bus station.

After a few blocks, we were both shivering, Sully trembling
violently in her lovely but useless coat. "I wish I had a place," I said.
"I would let you come live with me."

She reached out and squeezed my hand. Her cold skin shocked
mine like ice. "I know, honey," she said. Her face bore no expression at all.

At last we reached the bus station and walked again across the
grimy linoleum of indeterminate color to sit on one of the benches in
the waiting room. In her exhaustion she seemed to settle into a kind
of vacant complacency as she arranged her body to fit the hard
contours of the bench with the meticulous and fragile caution of the

234

very old. She put her head back and her eyes fluttered. She watched the sparse coming and going of the few people who had braved the weather, the people slouched in benches napping, or sitting talking. A few wandered around and there were a couple of readers. She watched the shoeshine man, who had no business and who puttered about his stand restlessly, shaking his head and humming.

"I don't think I've ever been in a bus station since I was an adult," she said. "Imagine that."

I wanted to talk to her some more about where she was going. It seemed useless. I excused myself and went to the bathroom and put a dime in the slot on a stall and vomited in the toilet. When I returned her eyes were closed and for a while she seemed to be asleep. Then she opened them and stared at the high ceiling. Large circulating fans hung down, stilled.

"What are you thinking?"

"Honey," she said. "You don't want to know. If you knew what I was thinking you would shrivel up and die."

"I wondered if you were thinking about Peanut."

"Forget Peanut. No help. Hell, he's forgotten me. Do you remember when we all danced and the firelight was shining and we couldn't stop, just around and around we whirled, like we would dance forever?"

"Yes."

"What fun it was. And then of course the room caught on fire. Do you remember how much it cost to fix it?"

"Yes."

"Isn't it funny, the things we remember."

They announced the bus for Cincinnati. A recorded voice with machine-like intonation, clarity, and accuracy ticked off all the towns and cities along the route. "I'm passing through some strange places," Sully said. She struggled to her feet. We went out into the frigid air and burning fumes and stood in line beside the humming bus. Soon she was shivering again. "I'm glad it caught on fire," she said. "Serves them right. Her and her wise hearts in the house of mourning. I wish the whole outfit had gone to ashes."

The line moved and she moved with it. She gave her ticket to the driver and mounted the steps into the bus. She carried her whiskey in one hand and clasped her other hand over her pocketbook. I watched her sway down the aisle until she found an empty seat by a window. She shoved up the window and leaned her head out. "Well . . . good-bye," she said. She looked around at her fellow travelers. "I'm not used to traveling by bus, you know " Her voice croaked harshly and she sounded indecisive. "I usually fly, you know. First class."

She squeezed against the side when a large round man in overalls dumped himself into the seat beside her. She took the bottle of pills from her pocketbook and popped two of them into her mouth, closed her eyes and swallowed. She squeezed the bottle of pills tightly in one fist. Her other hand still held the paper bag.

"What are you going to do?"

"I don't know." Her eyes threw back the world as shards of light and dark, reflecting the gray light bouncing off the ice. Her lids fell heavily down, the harsh gleam of blue. "I'm tired, I guess I'll sleep. I've got enough for a night in a motel and supper. One way or another, I'll sleep. I need to sleep a long time. I didn't let the bitches whip me down, did I? But I'm very tired, you see." She seemed to have been made made more tired by her long speech.

"Don't you know *any*one in Cincinnati? Anyone at all?"

"No," she said.

"I was thinking you'd go back to California, where you know some people."

"Whatever happens to me, I know *you'll* understand. That's a comfort to me."

"You could stay in the house for a couple of days."

She closed her eyes, let her head fall back against the seat, and she laughed without sound, her throat working. "Shit," she said. The farmer moved to another seat.

"Just stay two days. Trade your ticket in. Get some rest before you go someplace strange."

"No place is as strange as that house," she said. "It's over. I wish you would say, 'I understand.' Just those two words. Because I need someone to believe in me."

"I do understand," I said. "I wish I didn't, but I do— Wait! Your painting. It's still in my car."

"You keep it for me, honey. I don't need it anymore."

The bus began backing out and she smiled a little smile, quick and sad, and leaned against the back of the seat as she let the window down. I could see her dry lips mouth the word *good-bye*. She waved, lifted one finger from the hand curled around the pill bottle. The bus stopped and then moved forward onto the street. I watched it as it rumbled up the street in the sleet and mist. Then it made a slow turn onto another street; I saw her face go by and then, like Poppy into his shell and Irene into her grave, like all of them, she was gone.